Found Among the Stars

by

Vicky Burkholder

Galactic Danger, Book Four

Cover Art by *Teddi Black*

The Wild Rose Press, Inc.
PO Box 708
Adams Basin, NY 14410-0708
Visit us at www.thewildrosepress.com

Publishing History
First Edition, 2025
Trade Paperback ISBN 978-1-5092-5950-2
Digital ISBN 978-1-5092-5951-9

Galactic Danger, Book Four
Published in the United States of America

Dedication

Dedicated to my husband, Bob, the Bootsquad who kicks my butt or pats my back as needed, and to my amazing editor, Amanda. Thank you all for everything.

Chapter One

Eiko sat on the rocky ground at the top of a cliff, leaned against a tree, and looked down on Lawan, the place where she'd spent her entire life. From this height, she could see almost the entire valley. There was a kind of ethereal beauty to the layout of the town—or at least, there used to be. Three pyramids stood at the three corners of the town, shining in the afternoon sun. But it was the huge construct in the center that drew her eye and contempt. Newly built, this pyramid was three times larger than the others and was a monument to the high priest Nyoko and his cronies. Though each group— government, education, and religion—was supposed to be equal to the others, since Nyoko had become a leader, religion ruled the other two.

The required nine sides and nine levels made up the central building, but for Nyoko, each level was three times the height of the other pyramids. He claimed that the Blessed Three had sent him a holy message that they needed to erect the new building so they could be closer to heaven. She snorted. The only message Nyoko was getting was who could benefit him the most. What would the *Three* think of this mess. Eiko had a feeling they wouldn't like some of the rules being dictated to the citizens.

A rumble of thunder startled her, and she glanced at the darkening sky. If she didn't go home soon, she'd get wet—and she hated getting wet. Still, she sat. Staring. Across from her to the east, a wide, muddy river drained through the swamps toward the endless ocean. Thick forests bordered the north and west areas of the city, covering the hills. South of town, several acres of the land had been cleared for planting. Eiko watched as the rain approached from the south, the curtain of the downpour obscuring what was beyond. And still she sat. She wasn't sure why. There was a restlessness in her of late. One that could not be dismissed as easily as a whim of fancy. The night before, she'd had an odd dream about her fiancé, Hopper. Though his real name was Akino, everyone called him Hopper because of the way he hopped from project to project, always curious. Always exploring. And missing for thirteen years.

Eiko drew her poncho hood up and tucked her knees to her chest, hunching into herself as the rain poured down.

Nobody could explain what had happened to him. Where he was. The authorities had quit looking after a month, figuring he was dead and taken by wild dogs or other animals. But she had never accepted their findings. She still believed Hopper was out there somewhere. That belief had sustained her and was the main reason she'd become a crystal hunter. Hunters could go almost anywhere, depending on where the authorities sent her, and she kept looking. But she'd never again found the cave where he'd disappeared. She twisted the engagement band on her left wrist, the white crystals embedded in it sparkling in the light. She wondered if Hopper still had his.

The rain stopped, and she rose and shook the wetness from her cloak, then headed back down the path toward town. She hadn't spoken to Hopper's family in years. His father, Master Nyoko, had moved from the smaller religious pyramid to the large one he'd had built. Hopper's mother, Thera, lived at the edge of the city in an area set aside for single women. Hopper's father had divorced her when she refused to accept that Hopper was dead. Hopper's younger brother, Sachi, and sister, Koti, had settled down into good positions.

And so had she. Or so she thought. She paused as she saw a familiar figure coming up the path. Her best friend Sora hated being in the woods, especially when it was wet outside. "Sora! What are you doing out here?" She studied her friend, her body already swelling with a baby. "You shouldn't be hiking in your condition."

Sora rubbed her belly and smiled. "I'm fine. And so is this little one. The birthing mother checked me over this morning. All is well."

"Good."

They both grabbed the tree as the ground shook. Eiko wrapped herself around Sora, holding her close until the tremors stopped.

"They're getting worse," Sora said. "Coming more often."

"The scientists say they happen because of the Night Eye." Eiko stepped back. "As the Eye grows larger, the storms and tremors get stronger." She glanced up. Sometimes many smaller fiery rocks rained down from the sky, but the biggest one—the Night Eye—stayed on the same course. The priests told them the Blessed Three would protect them if they believed. Prayer meetings had gone from once a week to three times a day. To not attend without an approved reason meant a fine. Multiple fines meant a stay in the religious cells where one was "encouraged" to fast and pray for nine days. Encouragement consisted of being locked in a room bare of everything except a thin mattress on the floor, religious texts, and a privacy area behind a half curtain.

"Did you see the sky last night?" Eiko asked, pulling her thoughts away from those cells. "There were so many lights. Hundreds of them."

"I know." Sora glanced at the sky and shuddered.

"You didn't answer my question. What are you doing up here?"

"Looking for you. I figured when you weren't in your room, I'd find you up here. You should be getting ready for the priests' feast."

Eiko sighed. She really didn't want to attend the fancy dinner. Hours of listening to Nyoko and his priests spout their rhetoric about purifying the town, new edicts about what was allowed and what was not, and more.

"When is your next trip?" Sora asked.

"I'm supposed to leave tomorrow, but I haven't received my maps or directions yet. Though they told me I'd be out for just a month this time instead of two."

"You might not be out at all." Sora gave her an intense side-eye.

"Why not? What's going on?" Her friend was a mid-level clerk in the religious offices and often heard things she shouldn't. "You know something, don't you?"

"You need to leave soon. Before tomorrow. Actually, before tonight."

Eiko cocked her head at Sora, eyes narrowed. "You normally don't push me to go. Why now?"

Sora glanced around as if making sure there were no others nearby, then she leaned close to Eiko and lowered her voice. "Nyoko is sending out guards to bring in all eligible women of birthing age. He's going to pair you all off with men of his choosing, including you."

Shock curled through Eiko's stomach. "But...I'm a crystal hunter, and I'm engaged!

"Not anymore. I saw the papers. Your engagement has been declared invalid. And the man he's partnering you with is Syeth."

The shock turned to absolute dread. Syeth was one of Nyoko's top friends. And older than her parents. The man was not known for his kindness or charity. Several of his previous wives now lived in seclusion, not allowed to talk to anyone outside their conclave. But she'd heard rumors of Syeth's proclivities. She couldn't help but cringe at the thought of being mated to that awful man. "Of all the groundslug rot! I will not be a breeder for some—" She clenched her jaw. "I will not."

"According to what I heard, Nyoko thinks you've been leading a life of privilege for too long."

Eiko snorted. "Privilege? I live in an attic room barely big enough for one person and with only a table, two chairs, and my bed. And believe me, being a crystal hunter is no easy job. Privilege? Hah!"

"I know. That's why I thought I should warn you."

Eiko nodded and laid her hand on her friend's arm. "And I thank you. At least you're married to someone you love and don't have to go through this. But you should go home. I need to think."

"Eiko, you're not going to do something ill-advised, are you?"

"Me? Not at all. You know me better than that."

Sora gave her a wry smile. "I do know you better than that. That's why I asked."

"Go home. Kiss your husband. And do not worry

about me."

"Where will you go?"

Eiko shook her head. "What you don't know, you can't be forced to tell. I'm a crystal hunter. I will do what I do best, for the good of the community. I love you, Sora. Be safe. Be happy."

Sora hugged her hard. "Be careful. High Priest Nyoko will have guards looking for you."

"Goodbye, my friend." She kissed Sora on the cheek and watched as she headed down the path. Once she was out of sight, Eiko made her own path, but kept to the back ways to the house she shared with sixteen other single women. They were all clerks, teachers, or healers. She was the only crystal hunter in their house. There were only a dozen hunters in the entire city, and she was the only one not married. The job paid better than most, but was dirty, dangerous, and kept you out in the field for at least a month at a time—not something most people wanted to do. But she loved what she did.

She quietly climbed the inner stairs to her room. Once inside, she locked the door, then quickly gathered her hunter's bag and gear, packing enough food and other supplies for at least a month. She would supplement what she had on hand with food and water she could gather in the woods. A month or two wouldn't be long enough for Nyoko to forget about her, especially if she defied him by disappearing, but if she could find a reliable source of crystals, maybe she could buy her way out. Bribery wasn't uncommon but didn't usually come from unwed women. She'd just have to hope she could find a valuable lode and that Nyoko would accept her bribe.

A person could hope, couldn't they?

She glanced at the band on her right wrist. The device was a way for someone to track her, especially Nyoko's guards. That way, if she found a reliable source of crystals, all they had to do was check her track. But that also meant they could find her anywhere. She took out a small toolkit and pried the locking mechanism off and removed the bracelet, rubbing her wrist where it had been. It felt so strange not to have the tight band on. Once the scientists locked on the bracelet, a hunter never removed it. She took a deep breath and laid the band on the floor. It was emitting a high-pitched squeal and the central crystal flashed red. She chewed her lip, then, with a long exhale, took her hammer and smashed the crystal so it no longer worked.

She'd just broken two laws for hunters—never take the bracelet off and be careful not to damage it. And she was about to break another one—defy Nyoko and disappear.

Chapter Two

Eiko jumped as she heard heavy footsteps on the stairs. Nobody ever came up to her tiny attic apartment. The house she lived in had two floors plus where she lived. The first two levels had four rooms with two girls in a room. She was the only one in the attic, mostly because of her job. And the fact she was the only one who didn't mind being in the cramped space.

She grabbed her gear, tied a rope to her pack, then around her waist, and checked out her window for guards. She dropped her gear out the window, hauling the rope tight so it wouldn't fall too far, then climbed out herself, clinging to the narrow window ledge, grateful for her hunter training. She shuffled to one side so she could push the window shut, then reached for a drainpipe and scrambled to the roof. Next, she hauled up her gear and then rested flat on the gently sloping roof before peering over the edge. She quickly drew back as she saw priests and guards swarming the building, escorting girls out, some of them crying or arguing. She inched into the shadow of the chimney as her window slammed open.

"Where is the one who lived in this room?" a deep voice asked.

"Probably out getting her gear together," the house mother said. "I understand she's leaving tomorrow for a hunt."

"You," the deep voice said. "Stay here and bring her

when she returns. High Priest Nyoko wants her there especially tonight."

"Yes, sir."

Eiko drew herself up as small as she could and sat there, waiting until she could get safely away. Two hours later, when dusk fell, she scrambled across the roof and slid down another drainpipe to the ground. Shouldering her pack, she stayed in the shadows until she got to the edge of town. Eiko saw another priest standing at the head of the path up the cliff. Nyoko really wanted her. Fortunately for her, she knew more ways through the hills than the main paths. She dashed into the forest and ducked into the underbrush. A short time later, she stopped at the top of the same cliff where she'd been earlier and turned to look at Lawan. Above her, the skies were on fire. Below her, only heartache awaited.

Eiko sighed and turned her back on the city. She had to find enough crystal to buy her way out of a forced marriage to someone she didn't even like. "One month. I have one month to make enough to get free." She headed into the forest, skirting around places where she knew priests might be waiting for her and headed west. "May the Blessed Three guide me."

****

Eiko scrambled up a tree as high as she could go, the pack of wild Nazrul dogs growling and slavering at the base, their yellow eyes fixated on her. They'd chased her through the forest for the last half hour, nearly catching her. She glanced down at the tear in her favorite trousers where one of them had snapped at her. She'd scrambled up a tree, awkwardly leaping or crawling from one tree to another as the dogs trailed her from below until she could go no farther.

One cur—the biggest one—actually shimmied a couple feet up the trunk before falling back to the ground. She climbed up a few more branches until they got too thin to hold her. Eiko got as comfortable as she could, her back to the trunk, her legs dangling on either side of the branch. She pulled her rope from her pack, unwrapped the length, and tied herself to the trunk.

"Okay. Safe for the moment. As long as they can't get up here, I'm good." She glanced down to see the alpha still trying to figure out a way up to her. "Hey! Don't you know dogs can't climb?"

She settled back and grabbed a nutrient bar and water from her pack, then tied her bag to the branches as well. She closed her eyes, content to rest there for the night…then heard the dogs yelping in pain. Eiko looked down to see three large black mountain cats attacking the dogs. Mountain cats rarely came down to the lowlands. In less than a handful of minutes, the dogs that remained alive and able ran, tails between their legs. Eiko quickly untied her rope and rose to her feet, keeping her balance on the branch, her mouth dry, her heart pounding.

Cats could climb.

The largest one looked up at her, his emerald eyes shining like polished green crystals. He nodded at the other two and they took off, then he looked up at her again before backing away and lying down.

"Okay. Now what? Not hungry? Just going to wait there until dinner?" She jumped as a flash of lightning lit the sky, slipping on the branch and scrabbling to regain her purchase. Eiko glanced at the darkening sky, clouds piling up to the west, then back down at the cat—who seemed to shrug at her with his front shoulder before he rose, stretched, and ambled off into the jungle. She watched him go, wondering if she could safely descend. Another flash of lightning and clap of thunder—closer this time, and the wind had picked up. Down seemed safer than staying in the tree during a storm. She gingerly crept down the tree, keeping an eye on the surrounding jungle for any sign of either the dogs, or the cats, both of which were nearly as big as—if not bigger than—she was and deadly.

She needed to find shelter quickly, as the first drops of rain plopped down on her. Eiko hoped for some sort of rock outcropping but didn't find anything before the rain came down harder and the wind picked up, whipping forest debris around her, reducing visibility to a few feet. A crack of lightning almost on top of her brought down a large tree nearby. She ran, but not fast enough to escape the falling boughs from entangling her in a mess of leaves and branches.

The pouring rain coming down in sheets was bad enough, but the thunder and lightning were worse. She ducked as a bolt of lightning seemed to flash mere feet away, the deafening clap of thunder following almost immediately. Instead of trying to get out into the open, Eiko changed direction and burrowed deeper into the limbs to reach the trunk of the downed tree. Even minimal shelter was better than nothing. She dug down underneath the wide bole, spread her tarp over the hole as well as she could, weighing the material down with rocks, then crawled under the protection. There was no point in trying to pitch her tent in the mess of branches and leaves. Water seeped under the covering. No matter what she did, the stream kept coming in. The wind roared, picking up the edges of the tarp.

She grabbed the material, straining to hold the

unwieldy fabric against the gale. Finally, she yanked the tarp loose and encased herself head to toe with only a bit of her face showing. She curled up on a pile of branches and leaves to wait out the storm. Sleep was impossible as the tempest raged around her.

The worst of the storm passed, but the rain continued to pour down, finally tapering off to a trickle. By morning, all that was left was fog and dripping trees. Eiko climbed out of her cocoon, shook off the tarp, and sighed. Everything was wet—including her. She grabbed up her stuff and climbed out of the tangle of branches until she got to a relatively clear spot. She cleared off a space down to the dirt and rimmed the area with rocks. She laid and lit a fire, then built a frame to one side of the fire out of green branches and hung her wet clothes to dry. A second frame held her spare clothes. She wrapped her blanket around her, tying two of the ends over one shoulder. Finally, she laid out her tarp and upended the rest of her supplies from her pack onto the material, then leaned her pack against one of the frames. Because of the special material her clothes and pack were made from, with the fire they wouldn't take long to dry. At least she knew Nyoko's priests wouldn't come after her in this weather. And most of the hunters were on other trips, plus none of them ever came west. Eiko was safe for the moment.

As she checked her pack, she saw a pair of emerald-green eyes peering at her from the branches less than three feet away. Okay, maybe not as safe as she thought. Not daring to move, barely able to breathe, she waited to see what would happen. There was nowhere she could run. Or climb. The huge cat crept out, shaking water off and stepping gingerly through the mud to the fire. He stood there, staring at her.

"Hel...lo. Would you like to dry yourself by the fire?" She sighed. "Yes, Eiko, talk to the mountain cat like he can understand you." Felines were the messengers of the gods, but why would one come to her? She wasn't anything special.

She gulped when the animal nodded, looked around at the wet ground, then back at her. Taking a chance, she carefully gathered up her supplies, piling them on one corner of the tarp, then she backed up. The cat stretched out on the material and proceeded to lick his paws and rub them across his ears like any house feline.

"Okay, then." Eiko sat back on her heels. She pulled a nutrient bar from her pile, peeled the wrapping back, and took a bite. The bars didn't taste particularly good, but they supplied all the proteins and nutrients she needed when out in the field. She glanced at the cat, broke a piece off the bar, and laid the portion on the tarp. "You want a piece?"

The cat pulled the morsel toward him with a paw and sniffed the bit. Almost immediately, he shook his head and pushed the bite away.

Eiko chuckled as she took another bite of hers. "You're not wrong, but not all of us can hunt our own food. Besides, they're almost edible if you eat one with water." She took a swig of her water, then shook her head. "Actually, the water doesn't help that much, but at least I can get the stuff down faster."

She grabbed her now-dry clothes and ducked behind some branches to dress. "I know, I'm probably being silly, but I don't feel right dressing in front of you." She emerged and packed her bag with her gear, food, and spare clothes, leaving the tarp for last. "Um, I hate to ask, but I need my tarp. Are you dry yet?"

The animal rose and stretched his massive body. He stood to one side as she folded and stowed the material, then doused the fire, taking care to sprinkle the embers with water from a puddle and covering that with dirt. All the time, the cat watched her. He made her nervous, but he hadn't made any threatening moves toward her. Yet.

Finished with cleaning up her campsite, Eiko shouldered her pack. "Okay, then, I need to find some crystals. So, I'll see you around. Thank you for saving me from the pack of dogs." She headed out, stopping when the cat barred her way. "I'm sorry, but I need to go. That way." Eiko glanced at the barely there trail leading through the trees.

The cat nudged her in the opposite direction, and she stumbled. His shoulders came to her waist, his head to her chest, and he was all muscle.

"But I don't want to go that way. I want to go this way." She tried again, and again, the animal nudged her away. Then she heard a howl coming from the direction she had chosen. The dogs! She'd forgotten about them. "Okay, okay. You're right. I just hope you're not leading me to your own pack or whatever it's called for a late breakfast."

She moved as fast as she could over the rough terrain. The storms had brought down several trees and the ground was a quagmire in some places, but she kept moving, following the cat, breaking only for a quick snack at midday. The cat was able to bound easily over the worst areas as she struggled through underbrush, branches, downed trees, and more. As she hiked, she thought about her life—Nyoko and his ridiculous edicts. Which made her think about Hopper. Nyoko wanted her to marry some old crony of his and become nothing more than a breeding factory. No more crystal hunting. No more freedom. And no more happiness.

Hopper was her heartmate and always would be, even if he had reached the ninth level of life, the end of all things. She might find happiness with someone else, even love. But that hadn't happened yet. Maybe Sora was right, and she was being too picky. But in all the years Hopper had been gone, she had never met someone who touched her heart in the way he did.

Eiko nearly ran into the cat when he stopped suddenly, his long tail swishing back and forth, all muscles tense. She went on alert too, peering into the surrounding jungle.

"What's wrong?"

He nudged her toward a high outcropping of rocks and looked at her, then looked up, then back at her. "You want me to climb? That?"

She studied the sheer wall, then moved to one side where she saw a narrow cleft that would help her in ascending. "Okay. She started up, finding hand and footholds where she could and using her climbing gear to help her. At one point, she slipped, barely grabbing onto the safety rope at the last moment. Finally, she reached the top and lay there, panting. When she looked down, the cat was still standing where he'd been, facing the way they'd come, his hackles up and tail swishing.

Then she heard what he'd been hearing. The dogs. They must have been trailing her all day. A quick check of the outcropping showed that there was no way for the dogs to climb up the steep rocks. But would they attack the cat? He was alone down there. He couldn't face an entire pack.

Could he?

"I'm safe!" she called down to him. He let out a loud roar as the first canine came into view. A half-dozen dogs faced him in a semicircle, the largest one in the middle, their growls deep and menacing.

"Cat! Please! Get away! They can't get to me up here. Get to safety!"

Yes, she'd been afraid of him in the beginning, but she'd grown to actually trust him and didn't want anything to happen to him. The dogs moved in, but he stood his ground and let out another roar. She watched, heart in her throat, as they attacked. She searched the ground for rocks she could throw at the hounds.

As she was fashioning a slingshot, four other felines galloped in and joined the fray. Growls, yips, and roars filled the air. She tried to aim her rocks, but there was so much turmoil below, she was afraid of hitting the cats. Several long minutes later, the fight was over. Two dogs limped away. The others lay dead, including the alpha.

Eiko quickly rappelled down the rocks and went to the cats. Several of them had bites and other injuries, including her protector.

"Let me help you." She grabbed her first aid kit and water bottle and sat on the ground, not caring that it was wet. The cat watched her as she gently took his front leg onto her lap. The skin was torn and raw where the alpha canine had bitten him. She poured water over the wound to wash out the dirt. The cat shuddered, but stayed still as she pulled her medicinal herbs from her kit. "This is going to sting at first but will stop the bleeding and help the wound heal. Will you let me put some on?"

He studied her, his eyes narrowed, then nodded. Eiko took a deep breath and sprinkled some powder on the wound. The cat hissed and bared his teeth but did not attack her, and she breathed out again before wrapping a bandage around his leg. She checked him over for other injuries, finding some minor scratches. She glanced around at the others, standing a few feet away, watching her carefully.

"Will they let me help them?" she asked. "Or at least clean their wounds?" She knew that for minor cuts and abrasions, cats could pretty much take care of themselves.

Her protector rose and faced the others, pointed his head at her, then nodded.

After a few moments, the smallest one came to her, though to call her small was a misstatement as she was only a few inches shorter than her friend. A half hour later, Eiko finished cleaning them all, only using her herbs on the most serious wounds. She gathered her gear and repacked everything as the new cats faded into the jungle.

She strode over to the crack she had used to climb. "What do you say we camp here for the night? The storms will be on us soon and you need time to rest and heal."

He cocked his head at her, then nodded. Using a small hatchet, she cleared some growth from the area to make a space large enough to accommodate both of them. Eiko shook out her tarp, then laid a fire at the front of the space as the cat stretched out on the tarp. As she worked, she watched her friend. "I can't keep calling you 'cat.' You should have a name. Hmmm. How about Masuru? In my language, the word means protector. Do you like Masuru?" She wasn't sure where the thought for his name came from. It was like a sound in her head. But the name fit him.

She snorted when the cat nodded. "Okay. Masuru it is. And I am Eiko." She finished setting up her small tent and sorted through her supplies. She'd used up most of her healing herbs on the felines, but that wasn't a problem. She could search for more of the plants as they walked to wherever they were going. She needed to replenish her water supply though. One can was completely empty, the second one nearly so. There was still enough light for her to see even under the thick canopy of trees. "I'm going to look for some water. Will you be okay until I get back?"

He moved to rise but she shook her head. "Stay still. You've done enough today and need time to heal. Since you and your friends took care of the canines, I should be safe enough, shouldn't I? And I promise, I won't go far."

He snuffed at her but laid back down and she knew he had to be hurting if he did that. She grabbed her water bottles and headed down the path in the direction they'd been going. She'd barely gone any distance before the smaller cat showed up and gently nudged her in another direction. Eiko snorted but followed. Less than fifteen minutes later, she saw another large outcropping of rocks, this group attached to a high hill with a waterfall tumbling down to a rushing stream.

She filled her bottles and took the time to wash her face and hands. The chill of the water soothed her heated skin. As she turned to thank the cat, she discovered that she was alone. She hadn't even heard the feline leave. "Thank you," she called anyway.

A half hour later, she returned to Masuru to find him chewing away at a dead squirrel. Two more lay nearby and he nudged one toward her.

"For me? Thank you. Or, I guess, thank your friends." Before she took care of her meal, Eiko poured some water into a bowl for him. "And thank them for the water too."

After her dinner, cooked over the fire and which was much better than a nutrient bar, she laid down, her body relaxed, but her mind swimming with everything that was happening. Masuru. The other felines. Maybe they were the messengers of the gods after all. They'd taken care of the dogs for her. But then, there was Nyoko and his edicts. Finding crystals—especially a red—would possibly ensure her freedom. No one would force her into anything if she found some reds. They were everything to Lawan. But she had to find them first. On a whim, she rose and pulled out her crystal finder and scanned the rocks around them. A low-level ping got her heart racing again. She pulled out her tools and chiseled into the rock, uncovering small crystals, but all she found were brown ones. "Worthless."

Still, even finding a brown meant there were probably more crystals in the area. She'd keep her finder on just in case.

"Oh, Hopper, I wish you were here. You were always so good at finding things."

Chapter Three

"Eiko!" Hopper woke with a start as the lights came up in his cabin, the leftovers of his dream fading slowly. All he could remember was that there was a woman involved. Someone who was important to him. But he didn't know anyone called Eiko.

"Another dream?" Amaya's disembodied voice sounded soft in his head as well as the room. How he wished she were a real person and not a sentient ship he was mentally connected to.

Hopper sat on the edge of his bed, his head in his hands, not the look a ship's captain should have, but no one could see him here. "Yes."

He wanted someone to put their arms around him and hold him. Be there physically for him. He shook his head and closed his eyes briefly. Might as well wish for this Eiko, the woman who haunted his dreams, to be real. He'd dreamed of her occasionally back on Pointe Noir, but not like this. Now, her image came to him nearly every night. So why now? And who was she? Though he had searched for and found beings with that name, none of them matched the Eiko of his dreams. He still had people—and Amaya—searching the name out, but no one had found the one he thought was the Eiko of his nightly thoughts yet.

"Your dreams of this woman are coming more frequently," Amaya pointed out.

The catering unit pinged, so Hopper went to his living area and got the cup of tea Amaya had ordered for him. "I know they are. And thank you for the tea."

"You are welcome. Do you wish to talk about your dream?"

Hopper knew Amaya would listen, would soothe him with her words. He sipped his drink and thought about the dream. "There's not much to say. Are these memories? Or do they come from my imagination? Some of them are full of warmth and happiness, but others…Where do those images come from? My horrible imagination? And if only a dream, why am I experiencing them so often now? Who is this Eiko I keep imagining? She must be important."

"We have not found anyone in our searches who matches your image. And the abuse you described, could that also come from a memory?"

He rose to pace the room, running his hands over his head. "I don't know! Maybe that's why I left wherever I came from. That horrible man grabbing me and pulling me away from her. And then there are the good dreams. The ones without the man. Where it's just this Eiko and me."

Hopper had no memory of his time before he arrived at Pointe Noir space station, barely alive and in a tiny ship not even suitable for salvage. He'd been severely injured both physically and mentally, and while the doctors had done what they could for him, the scars— both external and internal—remained. They'd given him the name Hopper because all he would say was "I am Hopper" repeatedly. His DNA hadn't shown up in any databases, so nobody knew who he was or where he was from. He twisted the bracelet on his left wrist. He had no idea why it was special, but the doctors said he'd refused to remove it and fought hard when they tried. For some reason, the material and white crystals comforted him when he was especially agitated. Like now.

Because of his scars, he'd become someone few wanted to associate with. He was like a skittish rat living in the bowels of the station. He kept himself and his clothes—an old, patched coat with more pockets than any coat should have, a ragged shirt, and trousers held up by a piece of rope—clean, but his grooming didn't matter to the elite. Only his friends Cass, Omar, and Katie cared enough to invite him in or to help him. Oh, sure, when someone wanted a task done, especially when the job called for engineering, they called on Hopper, but only his friends invited him to their homes.

His abilities with mechanical and electrical systems were another anomaly. He could fix almost any machine given to him. And find whatever someone needed found.

Except Eiko.

Then he'd met the ship Amaya and his entire life had changed.

"I believe your dreams are memories, but perhaps not all you want to remember," Amaya said. "This is probably why you do not experience them when you are awake. Your subconscious is trying to show you what you endured, but in such a way as to not upset you."

Hopper spewed his drink across the table. "Not upset me? How is giving me nightly terrors not upsetting me? And why have they increased since we left Pointe Noir? Did the repairs your nanobots did on me do this?" He grabbed a towel and cleaned up his mess.

"No. The changes I programmed did not affect your subconscious, only your physical damage. As for why now, I cannot answer. Would you like me to do a search on night terrors and the subconscious and how to alleviate the problem?"

Hopper shook his head. Even though Amaya was sentient and much more than a normal ship's artificial intelligence, sometimes she took his words too literally. "No, thank you."

He moved through his cabin, looking at the rich furnishings and out the porthole at space beyond. So many worlds. So many people. Was there anyone out there for him? He had friends—like Omar, Katie, Cass, and her husband Zack. And he cared for them deeply. But they were friends. Not someone who was the other half of his heart. Yes, they were closer than some families were, he knew that with all his being. But he saw the kinds of relationships his friends had with their mates—the sort of one he wanted. And Cass had started this entire trip—in fact had spent the last twelve years of her life searching—because of family. He had…what? A sentient ship. Which was great, but she wasn't family. Did he even have a blood-related family out there somewhere? He didn't know. But he wanted…more.

He didn't even look like his friends. Oh, there were similarities—but also differences. His eyes had more of a slant than any of his friends and he had a vertical pupil, like a feline. And slightly pointed ears. No one had ever seen anyone who looked like him—no one except Amaya.

Hopper turned back to the room and leaned against the wall. The material softened around him like a hug, which he appreciated, but he wanted more. "I know there's still a lot to do. I should get back up to the bridge. We're almost at shift change anyway."

Hopper still had a mission to fulfill. His friend Cass had asked him to help find her family, and that was what he would do. That's what he did. He fixed things. He found things. Besides, Cass and his friends had done so much for him over the past years, this was the least he could do for them. Hopper dressed in one of his new uniforms, designed by Amaya from her files, and headed for the bridge. He settled into the captain's seat and checked over the latest scans. "Amaya, no viable planets in this system at all? Not even a small moon?"

"No. There are two ice planets and a gaseous one closer in. Shall I set course for the next system?"

Hopper sighed. "Yes. Send the reports to the others."

"Done."

He logged the system into his maps. He knew Amaya would have already sent the position back to Pointe Noir, but he preferred his own charts. Ones that showed him where he had come from—Pointe Noir. Amaya's maps showed thousands of systems previously unknown to anyone. His showed only what they'd found in less than a year.

Nine months ago, he and five other ships had left Pointe Noir on the hunt for the missing ship *Phoenix* and her crew. Cass Brennan had lost both her parents when the *Phoenix* disappeared twelve years ago with no trace. While searching for them, Cass found Amaya and her sister ship, Zara, abandoned and with a much better database than anyone had ever seen. Hopper had become the reluctant captain of Amaya while Cass went with Zara. With Amaya's data and what little information they had on the *Phoenix*, they'd begun their search—a search that actually took them toward Amaya's home world. They also had three regular ships in their armada spread out over several parsecs, all searching for a clue to what happened to Cass's family.

His mind, though, wasn't on the search for the *Phoenix* or even Amaya's desire to return to her home world, but his own search as well. For his own people. The Masaaki. Amaya had discovered his roots when her nanobots worked to heal him. He was the only Masaaki anyone had heard of. But according to Amaya's records, there was an entire world of people like him.

So who was he? Who was Eiko? What had happened to his and Amaya's people? He had a crew of twenty on a ship built to hold a thousand. But Amaya's crew had disappeared almost three thousand years ago. She and Zara were all that was left of the Masaaki sentient ships—and possibly the Masaaki themselves—as far as they knew. However, if that was true, where did he come from? There had to be more out there—somewhere. Two hours of mundanity later, a ping rang across the bridge, indicating an intercepted signal.

"Shall I play the incoming?" Amaya asked.

"Yes." Hopper wasn't paying much attention, his mind on his dream. Besides, he assumed the ping was just from one of the other ships in their small fleet.

"The message is from a communication beacon one parsec away, in a direct line with our current heading. This is not from one of our ships. The configuration is much smaller and several years out of date."

Her information stopped Hopper's musing. He listened to the message filling the bridge, his heart pounding.

"To any ships, this is Captain Declan Chalmers of the *Phoenix*. Our ship has been damaged beyond help.

We are landing on a nearby planet. The planet is M-class, fourth from the sun in a six-planet system. There is a second system off our starboard, two light years away with a binary sun and ten planets. To our port is a large nebula. We are approximately half-way between the two. I cannot give coordinates since we don't know where we are."

Hopper sat straight up. "Amaya, are you certain about the origin?"

"Yes. And there is a second beacon, farther away, though that one appears to be damaged. Would you like me to pull both in?"

"Yes! Which one is sending this message?"

"The one we are closest to. The second one has a signal so weak that I am barely picking up more than a blip."

"Understood. Pull both in," he commanded, though he didn't need to. Because of their symbiotic relationship—their mental connection—often Amaya knew what he wanted before he spoke. Vocalization was more for the comfort of the crew than from any need.

"I need six minutes before I can pull in the second one."

"Fine." Hopper paced the bridge until Amaya let him know she had both beacons. "Can you determine destination from our current position?"

"Yes. Coming up now. The planet is approximately five hours away at maximum speed."

"Set course. And contact Cass."

"Done."

"Hey, Hopper, what's up?" Cass smiled at him from the captain's seat on Zara, identical to his. Cass and Zara had a slightly different relationship than he and Amaya

26

did. Their tie didn't go quite as deep because she had no Masaaki DNA.

"Cass, we picked up a beacon signal. You need to hear the message."

She frowned. "A message beacon? From where? We're too far out for one to be from Pointe Noir. Or any other united worlds." She was several parsecs away from his current position.

"Cass, please. Just listen. The beacon is Aboolean. From the *Phoenix*." He played the message.

Hopper watched as Cass's eyes widened and she shot up from her chair. "Hopper! Play it again!"

He did and she sat back down.

"You did it, Hopper. You found them!"

He hated to point out the obvious but felt it necessary. "Not yet, but it's the closest we've come. We don't know if there are any survivors."

She shook her head. "You did the impossible, Hopper. I knew you could."

"*We* did it, Cass. Amaya has sent our coordinates and the directions to Zara and the other ships. We'll meet you there. You and the others will need a couple hours jump time from your positions. Meanwhile, I'll check the beacons over."

She grinned as her crew rushed to set the coordinates and get moving. "Hopper!" She reached out as if to touch him. "Just like always, Hopper. When I give you something to look for, you deliver."

He chuckled. The old Hopper—the one who was so focused, he couldn't do anything beyond what job he was given, sometimes to his own detriment—no longer existed. Although, maybe in some part he did. "I know, Cass. Go tell Zack and your crew. We'll see you in a few

27

hours." He clicked off communications. He rose from his seat and paced the bridge. There was really nothing for him to do as Amaya handled almost everything. They passed a beautiful nova to their port side, the shape reminding him of a leaping feline. To their right was a binary system and he knew they were on the right path. "The colors of that nebula are amazing," Hopper said.

"You should see them through my sensors," Amaya said. "Would you like me to bring up the other spectrums?"

"Yes, please." He switched on the com-unit. "To all crew, if you can get to a porthole or monitor, we're scanning a nova on our left. You might like the view." He liked to let his small crew know when they found something interesting. And from their comments, they appreciated his consideration.

While Amaya scanned and mapped the cloud as they passed, Hopper watched through Amaya's eyes as she switched from ultraviolet and other color spectrum wavelengths to temperature to energy. Each view was as amazing as the others.

"I'll send scanner buoys out for further study," Amaya said.

"Thanks." Hopper turned the bridge over to his relief. "All yours, Maria."

"Aye."

He went to his cabin and leaned against the door with a sigh, eyes closed.

"I sense you are uneasy," Amaya said.

Hopper toed off his boots and dropped onto his sofa. "I am."

"Why? You have achieved what no others have. You have discovered several uncharted systems and now, a new nova, and made Cassandra extremely happy. Is it not good to make your friends happy?"

"Yes. And I'm glad for them." Then he grinned. "Besides, I didn't discover those systems. You already had them in your database."

"Ah, but they are new to the people back on Pointe Noir."

"Agreed."

"But?"

He went to the porthole and stared out at space beyond. So many worlds. So many people. And so much emptiness. He turned back toward his room. "I know there's still a lot to do. We found a beacon from the *Phoenix*, but it's been years. What if there are no survivors? I hope for the best outcome for Cass, but the odds are not in our favor."

"Ah, but the odds against us even finding this much were not in our favor either. You have beaten the odds many times. I believe this time you will as well."

Hopper chuckled as he rose and went to the catering unit. "Tea, please. Any idea what the odds are on me finding out who I am?"

"I believe you do not truly wish me to state statistical odds, but I understand that the fact that you still do not know who you are or where you are from weighs heavily on your mind."

He chewed his lower lip as he twisted the wristband again. "I know the memories are there, and I know you've tried to help me free them, but…"

"But something holds you back. Maybe the memories will be free once we get to the Masaaki home world."

Hopper glanced at the clothes hanging in his closet.

The high-necked tunic, close-fitting trousers and knee-high boots making up his uniform felt strange, but they were expected of the captain. Besides the uniforms, he still held onto some of his old belongings, though the coat with multiple pockets was his favorite. During his time at Pointe Noir Station, he'd worn whatever castoffs he could scrounge. For most people, those rags should have been trashed a long time ago, but for him, they were his only connection to his past. Where he had come from. Broken-down rubbish like he had been. When he joined with Amaya, she'd used nanobots to heal him physically, remove his scars. But some scars went too deep.

"What if I never know? And once we reach your world, what if there's nothing there for me?"

"Then we will go wherever you wish to go."

Her words and the emotions he heard behind them surprised him. For almost three years, her sole purpose had been to return to her home world and her people. Even millennia after she'd left. Yes, she was a ship, but she was also a person. A different type of person, but still a person. Unlike a computerized AI, she could think and act for herself and had emotions like any other being. The Masaaki had created her, but they were corporeal beings like him. "You've wanted to return to your home world since Cass found you and woke you."

"You are my captain, and my friend. If there is no place for you, then there is no place for me."

Hopper went to the wall near his bed and laid his palm against the smooth surface. The material softened and wrapped around his hand like a small hug. After a minute, he pulled away. Maybe he was on a fool's search. He had more family in Amaya and his friends than many people did in blood relatives. But he couldn't stop looking. He couldn't. Not until he found what he was searching for. "Thank you, Amaya. How long until we get to the coordinates?"

"Three hours, six minutes, thirteen seconds."

Hopper chuckled. Sometimes Amaya was too human, and other times...too much like a computer—and also like he used to be. He pulled out a pair of loose trousers and a shirt. A glance in the mirror showed his repaired face, but the image he saw wasn't a face he was familiar with—not this one with a strong jawline, green eyes that glowed in the dark, and vertical pupils like a feline. He could also see better in the dark than most people he knew and was more agile. This body was definitely different from the one he knew with the scars marring his face and body and stiffness from his injuries, but this was the one he now had. This one was much better than the old him, but the old one was...comfortable. Painful, but familiar.

But also unlike anyone else. He didn't look human like Cass or have the gold eyes of an Aboolean or look like any other species he knew. But he did resemble pictures Amaya had shown him of her old crew—the Masaaki. And he had Masaaki DNA. But what had happened to them? Why were there no records of them anywhere?

Hopper settled in to study the files from Amaya and her home world. Hopefully, he would find the answers to multiple questions once they got there. But he doubted he'd discover who he was. Or Eiko. Odd that the latter made him just as sad.

Chapter Four

"Hopper, you have a ping from Cass."

"Put her on." He moved to his desk. They'd reached the coordinates an hour ago and were waiting for the others to catch up.

"We're here! Along with the others."

Hopper grinned as his oldest friend, Omar, popped up on the screen. "We put on some extra speed. Might have stressed the engines a bit, but we're here."

Huge in size, Omar had a heart to match when it came to his friends. He and his wife Katie had given up their bar on Pointe Noir to join Cass and Hopper on this adventure.

"Amaya did a scan of the world and found only one island that appeared to be inhabited. From what we saw, the area looks well-settled with a village and farms. She also picked up a weak communication bandwidth on the planet, like from an old com-system and there are several weather satellites in orbit."

"I'd like to go down," Cass said. "I know we should contact them first, but…"

Hopper smiled. "Go. We'll monitor from up here."

"Hopper, you have to come too! Without you and Amaya, none of this would have been possible."

He sighed but nodded. "Fine. I'll meet you down there. But Cass…" He didn't finish his thought because he could see the reality in her eyes.

"I know, Hopper. I know. Fingers crossed."

He finished dressing and strode off toward the landing bay.

"Hopper, if I may suggest, you should take Annie and June along as well," Amaya said. Their personal jumper is landing now.

"Um...okay." He watched as a small shuttle landed and two women emerged. Annie, the smaller of the two, carried a medical backpack slung over one shoulder and her partner, June, was dressed in her usual black trousers, tight black top, boots, and weapons. And those were just the ones he could see. He knew she also had several more on her person that weren't visible to either regular eyesight or scans. She was a walking armory.

"I guess Amaya called you?"

"Yes and no," Annie said with a smile. "We figured we'd come anyway. There may be medical issues, and we felt June would also add an extra layer of security."

"Okay. Let's go."

They boarded one of the medium shuttles and took off, following Cass's shuttle down to the planet, landing in a clearing above the village. By the time they powered down, they had an audience between them and the village. Hopper counted at least a dozen armed guards standing in front of the others. Two stood front and center—the man, tall, broad, looking very commanding. The woman barely came to his shoulder but had the same presence of command. They stepped forward, as did Cass with Omar and Katie close behind and to either side of her. Hopper, June, and Annie held back to watch.

"Hi. I'm Cass Brennan, and, um…"

"Cassie? Is that really you?"

As Hopper watched, an older woman pushed

through the crowd and ran forward, followed closely by an older man. They stopped in front of Cass, stared for a moment, then, with a cry, the woman grabbed Cass in a hug and the man enveloped both of them as the supposed leaders watched.

Omar and Katie stepped back to Hopper. "I guess that answers the question of her parents."

"I'd say so." Hopper wondered about such strong emotions. Would he feel that way when he found his family? If he found them? Would they?

He looked up as the man who appeared to be in command stepped forward accompanied by the small woman.

"I'm Captain Declan Chalmers of the *Phoenix*, and this is my wife, Amanda Ki." He nodded toward Cass and her parents. "And I guess our crewmembers recognize each other. May I ask who you are? Where did you come from?"

Hopper glanced at the others who nodded for him to take the lead. "I'm Captain Hopper of the ship Amaya. We left Pointe Noir nine months ago to find you. Cass over there is the leader of the search."

Cass, tears streaming down her face, joined him, her arms around the shoulders of her parents. "Hopper, these are my folks, Rachel and Marcus Brennan. Hopper and Amaya discovered two of the *Phoenix* beacons earlier and here we are."

"You found one of our beacons?" Chalmers asked. "We sent out so many but never got any response. You said you were from Pointe Noir? I've never heard of that. Where is it?"

Hopper cocked his head as he listened to advice from Amaya. "Captain, I suggest we go someplace where we can talk. You have a lot to catch up on."

"We can talk in the community center," Chalmers said.

Hopper held back a little as the others preceded him down the slight slope to the village, followed by the crowd. He noted the unusual buildings. They looked like they'd been cobbled together from various parts of other things, and he wondered if that's what happened to the Phoenix. If they'd used parts of the doomed ship to build their town. Still other buildings were made of sturdy logs and rocks. It looked like the survivors had used everything they could.

Chalmers led them to a long table on a stage at the front of a large room—big enough to hold the entire population. Including children, he noted as dozens of people—young and old—entered the building.

Children? Hopper shrugged as he thought the implications through. Why not?

Hopper kept standing as the others sat. "Captain, if I may introduce the rest of our people." He pointed everyone out, leaving Annie to last. "Annie is our medical specialist. If you have any issues, perhaps she can help?"

Declan motioned at a petite redhead standing to one side. "This is Missy. Doctor Melissa Byers. I'm sure she'd be more than happy to speak with you. Thank you."

Annie and June headed off with the doctor. Cass sat to one side with her parents and a young boy who looked to be about six years old.

"Hopper, this is my brother Alan," Cass said with a grin.

"Your brother?"

"Yeah. We all have a lot to talk about."

"Which is why we're here," Chalmers said. "So, we had kind of given up hope of ever being found."

"First, I'll have Amaya send a signal back to Pointe Noir to let them know you've been found, and the coordinates," Hopper said.

"You mentioned that name before. Is Amaya your communications officer?" Chalmers asked.

"Um, not exactly. She's my ship."

"Oh. An AI. I'll bet there's been some advancements there in the last few years."

Hopper sighed. "You have no idea."

"You have a ship that can think for itself?"

"Herself. And yes. Amaya is a sentient ship. She's not an AI but is a living ship. The government has declared her and her sister ship, Zara, to be autonomous beings."

The captain cocked his head. "But she still needs you to captain her?"

"Yes and no. She's perfectly capable of flying herself and even doing repairs with her bots, but for full functionality, she prefers to have a physical being with her."

"In control."

"No. Not in control, but as an extension of herself. For instance, in cases like this where landing a ship so large would be problematic." Hopper sighed. "Maybe understanding would be better if you came up with me to meet her."

"She can't land?"

"Yes, she can, but she's quite large, so, unless she landed in the ocean, she would damage quite a bit of your cultivated land or the village and meadows. Her maximum capacity is over a thousand bipedal beings."

That sat the captain back in his chair. "A thousand! Wow. Yes, I would love to see her, but we have other things to discuss first."

While they talked about the past twelve years, the advancements and problems systemic to a large union, Hopper sent a mental message to Amaya. *"Come down to atmospheric level and hover."*

"Understood."

A few minutes later, a shout went up from outside. Hopper smiled as everyone jumped. Cass and the others glanced at him, and he nodded at them. They rose and joined the others outside.

"What?" Chalmers stared at the ship.

"That is Amaya," Hopper said. "And that is the reason she won't land." He touched his earpiece. "Amaya, you can resume orbit outside the atmosphere." She rose and disappeared into the sky.

Chalmers stared at the sky, then at Hopper. "We really need to talk."

"Yes, Captain." They all returned to the community room.

Hopper looked around at the crowd. "I thought we'd talk in private?"

Chalmers shook his head. "I think what we need to talk about concerns the entire settlement. Plus, I don't believe we'd be able to get any of them to leave at this point."

Hopper chuckled briefly as he studied the people. "Probably not."

As everyone talked about what had happened, what was happening, and what would happen going forward, Hopper grew increasingly uncomfortable being there.

He'd never been comfortable in a group, and now, he felt like he could barely breathe. His left leg bounced up and down and he clenched his hands under the table. Even Amaya's gentle thoughts couldn't calm him.

"Captains?" Katie spoke up from Hopper's side.

"Yes?" Chalmers said.

"May I suggest a break?"

"That sounds like a good idea. We'll table our discussions for the night and continue this tomorrow."

Everyone rose and chatter surrounded Hopper like a swarm of stinging insects. Without a word to anyone, he escaped off the stage and tried to get through the crowd, but hands reached for him. People wanted to talk to him. So many questions. So much noise.

"Hopper."

He glanced up to see Omar standing on one side, Katie on his other.

"Come with us. This way."

With Omar cutting through the crowd like a hot knife through soft butter, they were soon outside. Rather than talk, Omar led the way to the shuttles. With every step away from the crowd, Hopper relaxed a little more.

"Thank you."

"Look, Katie and I will stay here with Cass and hash things out. I have a feeling this is going to take a while. Not all the villagers want to leave. But there is a lot we can do to help them with updating things here. And Annie has already helped quite a few in the clinic. Why don't you take June and go do some exploring? I think she's had enough of this too."

"But won't that look bad? For us? For one of the captains to leave like that?"

Omar chuckled. "Did you forget about Cass and

38

Zara? She might not be quite as big as Amaya, but she's pretty impressive. And even our other ships are better than the *Phoenix* was. She was a good ship in her time, but we've come a long way since then. So, technically, we have five captains available in an armada nobody would dare mess with."

Hopper chuckled. "As always, my friend, you are right. Send June out, and if she wants to go with me, we'll see what else we can find here." He laid his hand on Omar's arm. "And thank you."

Omar nodded and strode off while Katie stayed with Hopper. "Are you okay now?"

"Yeah. Better than I was. How did you know? Did Amaya tell you through the com-link?"

Katie snorted at him. "I didn't need any kind of link to know you were at the end of your tolerance level. Hopper, Amaya did a lot to heal you physically, but emotionally, you're still our Hopper. Your skills lie in what you can do with things, not people."

Hopper hung his head. "So I'm still broken."

"What? No!" Katie wrapped him in a hug. "No! You're not broken. You never were. Yes, you were injured, but never broken. You are a beautiful person, Hopper. Let Omar, Cass, and me handle the people. Go and do what you do best. Explore. Find something amazing. Be Hopper, not the captain."

Chapter Five

By the time the sun reached the midday point the next day, the air had turned steamy and sweat soaked Eiko's shirt. "Hey, Masuru, I need a break." She noticed his limp didn't seem too bad and he wasn't favoring his leg as he had the previous evening when he'd walked around the camp.

She plopped down on a large rock, pulled off the jacket she had tied around her waist, and tucked that into her pack. Her lunch consisted of a piece of sweet fruit and another nutrient bar. Masuru returned to her and lay at her feet, his head up, ears alert. She smiled as she munched on her bar. "Don't worry. I won't offer you any. And I'm sorry I don't have any fresh meat for you either."

Masuru snorted at her, and Eiko chuckled as she studied the surrounding area. If not for the storm damage, the area would have been nice. Birds sang in the trees, flowers bloomed, and insects buzzed or fluttered around. She reached for a pretty purple-and-white striped flower and plucked a single blossom from the bush. After inhaling the sweet scent, she tucked the blossom behind her ear, then sighed. The last time she'd had a windroot flower behind her ear, Hopper had put it there. Followed by the sweetest kiss.

And then, he'd been taken by a mysterious ship.

The day after they'd gotten engaged, they'd gone exploring. Hopper had found a strange map in his father's study, copied it, and was determined to see where it led. The directions pointed west toward the forbidden mountains. Eiko wasn't sure they should go, but Hopper was too excited for her to say no. So they went.

They found a wondrous cave with all sorts of strange equipment, one piece of which was large enough for him to climb into. So he did. Then the machine came to life and took off through an opening in the top of the cavern, taking Hopper with it.

She twisted the band on her left wrist. "Oh, Hopper, I wish I knew what happened to you. I miss you."

Eiko glanced up at the leaden sky. Even the air smelled gray these days. She'd heard that in some of the more northern areas, fire and ash spewed from the mountains, causing the overcast sky. Nobody was allowed to go north anymore because of the danger. East of Lawan was nothing but lowland swamps and the Petroton Waters, a seemingly endless sea of monstrous fish, dangerous shoals, roiling eddies and more. Only the bravest of fishermen went out, and even then, they mostly stayed in sight of land. To the south lay grasslands and desert. West lay the holy mountains. Once a year, Nyoko and the elite would take a pilgrimage to the highest peak and come back with gifts from the gods—usually some sort of gadget to help make their lives easier. Eiko snorted. The only ones those things made life easier for were Nyoko and his cronies. She'd bet her next crystal find that Hopper could make whatever they'd found—and then would actually share whatever he invented with the people who needed the gadget.

She finished her meal and shouldered her pack. "Let's go."

Masuru rose, stretched, and set off with Eiko following. They walked for several hours, taking short breaks for Eiko when necessary. They were traveling roughly south alongside a wide, rushing river. As the shadows lengthened, Eiko feared they'd never find a way across. As she was going to look for a campsite for the night, Masuru stopped and nudged her toward the raging water.

"What? I can't…Oh!" In front of her, partially hidden by tall shrubs, was a beautiful arched stone bridge. One that looked oddly familiar.

"Wait! I know this place. This is the Uniquet River. Hopper and I crossed here—but the river was much smaller then, not like now." The muddy, roiling water was nearly to the underside of the arches and full of debris. As she watched, the bridge shuddered when hit by a large tree but stood firm. Eiko gingerly followed Masuru onto the surface. When she reached the middle, another shudder shook the entire bridge, and she heard a loud crack that sent her scurrying for the other side. As she turned around, she saw the far side breaking apart and falling into the flood.

She slipped and slid in the muddy path leading from the bridge until she reached a more stable area. Eiko looked around, frowning as memories crowded her thoughts. "South from here is grassland—or it was twelve years ago. North and west are the mountains, but only the northern ones are dangerous right now. But the western ones—" She shook her head. "Caves. There are caves there with crystals!"

Eiko quickened her steps as another storm loomed. "Hey, Masuru, I need either a good campsite or a cave. Soon!"

He glanced back at her, then continued. Eiko sighed and followed. The first drops of rain were falling when the cat disappeared into some shrubbery. She couldn't see him anywhere.

"Masuru?"

Nothing.

Then he emerged and came to her and gently took her pant leg in his teeth and backed away.

"Okay. Okay. I'm coming. You can let go."

He did let go but stayed in front of her as he led her forward. Eiko saw a small break in the bushes and followed him into the gap. A minute later, she was in complete darkness. She put her hands out and felt rock on both sides—and no rain or wind. And her finder was pinging off the charts.

"A cave of some sort, I guess. And there are crystals. Okay, that's good." She pulled off her backpack and groped for her helmet buckled to one side. After putting the hard hat on, she switched on her light. The dim beam showed she was in a narrow tunnel with the sides less than an arm length away on either side and the ceiling not even a handspan above her helmet. As she looked around, she saw sparkles in the rock and her heart drummed faster. Hundreds of crystals of all colors.

Masuru came back and nodded, then tilted his head toward the deeper part of the tunnel. Eiko followed him—squeezing through some tight spots until she finally took her pack off and dragged the bulky thing behind her. Finally, the tunnel opened up and Eiko stopped in surprise. In front of her was an immense cave with a flat, rocky floor and a roof higher than the central pyramid in Lawan.

But that wasn't what took her breath away. She knew this cave. She'd been here before—with Hopper. The walls tapered toward the top in nine obvious levels with rocky paths that circled each level and rough steps going from one to the other. "Just like the central pyramid." They hadn't realized the similarity before, but she did now. The first level had a half dozen cabinets, tables holding strange machines, and shelves holding strange equipment and uncut crystals. She could see more sparkling in the rocks.

"Yippee!" Her yell echoed through the cavern as she opened one cabinet and found shelves of polished crystals. There was enough here to not only pay for her apartment for a year, but maybe even get a better one—and still have enough left for some furniture and pay bribes to Nyoko so she didn't have to get married to his crony. Her position as a hunter didn't mean more money. Hunters only received a five percent value payment on their finds. Lately, her income had barely been enough to pay the rent on her small apartment. If she didn't have a good find this time, she would have to skimp on something—like food—or move to the women's barracks at the far end of town. She shuddered at the thought of trying to sleep in a room with seven other women. Eiko shivered in the chill of the cave, but excitement warmed her heart.

"Okay, first things first. A fire."

Eiko crawled back out of the cavern and tunnel and gathered as much kindling as she could and tied the sticks into a bundle. Next, she tried to find dry wood, finally climbing a tree and sawing off some dead branches that she let fall to the ground. She needed several trips, but she eventually had supplies for a nice fire that she laid out in the center of the floor.

Although there was some damage from rock falls, probably from the tremors Eiko figured, the place looked pretty much the same as she remembered. Masuru stretched up and leaned his front paws on one table in particular. He looked at Eiko, then at the gadget sitting on the table, then back at Eiko.

"That's what you want me to look at?"

Eiko went to the table and stared at the machine. There was a small, enclosed box that could easily fit in her backpack with room left over. It had three metal rods protruding from the top and buttons and knobs on the front and side. "Okay, I'm looking at this, but what is this?"

Masuru blew out breath, almost like he was frustrated with Eiko.

"I'm sorry. I have no idea what I'm supposed to do." Eiko had never been so disheartened. Letting him down was like failing to live up to a favorite teacher.

Masuru pawed at one button.

"That one's important. Okay." Eiko reached out and pushed the button, then jumped back as lights lit and dials moved, and she heard a voice.

"We need more adults. The children aren't doing well here. It's time to have another sickness go through," a woman said.

"It's too soon after the last one." That sounded like…like Nyoko!

"What…? What's happening?"

"Hello?"

Was this a god talking to her? Had Masuru led her

to one of the Blessed Three?

"Uh…hel…hello?" She glanced around—the walls were sparkling, like crystals.

"Who is this?"

She definitely knew that voice. And he was certainly no god. "Nyoko?"

"Who is this?" he demanded.

Masuru growled low in his throat and pawed the knob until it turned. The voice stopped and all Eiko heard was noise.

"That was Nyoko, wasn't it?"

Masuru nodded.

"Can he find me here? Will this machine lead him to me?"

Masuru cocked his head as if he wasn't sure and she sighed. "But you wanted me to turn this on. So he could find me?"

Masuru shook his head, then nodded at the machine and pawed the knob.

"You want me to turn the knob?"

He nodded.

She turned the knob one click at a time until she heard another voice. This time she stayed quiet, not wanting to show that she was listening.

"Hello? Is someone there?"

A woman's voice. But not someone she recognized, so not one of Nyoko's cronies.

"Um, yes?"

"Who are you?"

Wouldn't a god know who she was? "Um, my name is Eiko."

"Eiko? As in Captain Hopper's Eiko?"

Eiko's stomach flipped. "You know Hopper?"

"Yes. I'm his second-in-command. I'm Maria."

"How…how am I talking to you? I thought Hopper reached the ninth level. Are you a god?"

Maria laughed. "Me? A god? That's rich. Right now, the captain is down on the planet we're orbiting. And you must be using some sort of communication device. But you keep cutting out. Do you have the frequency set right?"

"Orbit? Frequency? What are these words? I don't understand."

"Eiko, is there a box or panel with a bunch of symbols or dials or buttons?"

"Yes. The cat led me to this strange box and showed me which button to push."

"The cat led you…? Okay, we'll skip that for now. Describe the box to me."

Eiko did.

"Okay. Do you see the little blue knob on your…hmmm. Are you facing the box? Is the machine in front of you?"

"Yes."

"Okay. There should be a blue knob on the right side of the box."

"There is. I used it before."

"Good. I want you to turn that knob, slowly, toward the back of the machine. One click at a time until I say stop. Count the clicks out loud as you do."

Carefully, Eiko grasped the knob and turned. "One. Two. Three. Four…"

"There! Stop!"

Eiko jumped back as if she'd been burnt. "Did I do something wrong?"

Maria chuckled and now Eiko could hear her as if

47

she were standing in the same cavern. "No, not at all. You did something very right. We were a tiny bit out of sync, and you got us where we needed to be."

More words she wasn't sure she understood. "Oh. How are we talking?"

"The machine in front of you is a communication device. I have a similar device here with me. These machines allow us to talk to each other across great distances. So…Eiko. You're a real person?"

Eiko laughed. "Yes, I am real. But if you are not a god, are you one who leads us to the ninth level?"

"What are you talking about? I don't understand."

"The ninth level of life. The final one. The one where we dwell with the gods."

"You mean death? You think Hopper is dead?"

"Yes. The priests told me he was."

"Oh, my, you two do have a lot to talk about. No, Hopper isn't dead. He's very much alive. But I find this strange."

"You do?" Eiko chuckled.

"Yes. Out of all the stars and worlds, how did you happen to find this communication device and connect to us?"

Eiko glanced at Masuru as he wandered around the cave. "I think the Blessed Three intervened."

"The Blessed Three?"

"The gods. Don't you know about them?"

Maria chuckled, then stopped. "I'm sorry. I don't mean to laugh, but there are many beliefs and many gods out there."

"That cannot be. Our priests tell us there are only the Blessed Three, no others."

"I think you and Hopper really do have a lot to talk

about."

Eiko's heart sped up so much, she thought she would pass out. "So, um, Hopper is there?"

"Not right now. But he will be soon. Would you like me to patch you through to him?"

"Patch? I do not know this word. To me, a patch is what you do to make a repair."

"Give me a minute. I'll leave this channel open so you can hear what I'm doing."

"Um, okay."

"Hopper, this is Maria. Do you copy?"

"Hi, Maria. Is there a problem?"

Eiko jumped at hearing Hopper's voice coming through the strange box. She listened to the conversation between him and Maria.

"I have someone on another channel who would like to talk to you. Turn to 6.4."

"Okay."

"Eiko, go ahead. Say hello. Hopper is listening. Maria out."

"Eiko?"

Eiko could hear the wonder in his voice. "Hopper, is this really you? Are you talking to me through this machine?"

"I am. Where are you?"

"I'm in the cave where the strange machine was. The one that took you away. Nyoko and the other priests told me you were dead."

"I am very much not dead. I can't believe I'm talking to you. That you're not a dream."

"A dream?"

He sighed. "A long story. I've been having a dream about someone named Eiko for the past few weeks and they're getting stronger as we get closer to the Masaaki system."

"System? You and Maria are using such strange words. But what do you mean by 'someone named Eiko?' You know me."

"Um, no, I don't. Not really. I have no memory from before my time on Pointe Noir station. I don't even know exactly who *I* am."

"Where are you?"

"I am on a sentient spaceship called Amaya. Right now, we are circling a planet one star system away from the Masaaki home world. As soon as we finish mapping this system, we'll be heading toward your world."

He had no memory of her? How could that be? She would never forget her Hopper. How had he forgotten her? The thought hurt her heart. "You don't remember the machine that took you up into the sky? You don't remember us?"

"I'm sorry. Only bits and pieces that come through, mostly in my dreams. Amaya says my brain is trying to protect me from something."

Eiko snorted. "Probably from memories of your father, Nyoko."

"Why?"

She sighed. "A tale best left for a different time, perhaps. I'll say that Nyoko was not the best of parents to you and your brother and sister."

"I have a brother and sister?"

"You really don't remember them? Or your mother? Or…anything?"

"Like I said, just bits and pieces, but nothing that makes much sense. I know when I hear your voice, I feel…warm. And happy. And…" He blew out a long breath. "But you're real."

She chuckled as she sat down, pulling the machine down to the floor with her. "Yes, I'm real. As are you—unless you're talking through the gods." The walls continued to sparkle, and she wondered about it. This was the cave where Hopper had disappeared from. Was she going to disappear too? Though she hadn't gotten into any machines like he had. But she was talking through one. "Hopper, will this machine make me disappear? Like you did?"

"What? No. It's just a communication device. It's perfectly safe. I promise."

"But the walls...they're sparkling. They weren't before I turned the machine on."

"I don't know about that. They may be acting like a power booster of sorts. I wouldn't worry about it."

"That's because you're there and not here. Are you sure you're not talking through the gods?"

"Not that I know of. So you're Masaaki?"

"Yes. So are you."

"What do you look like?"

"I'm just a couple inches taller than I was...oh. You don't remember. Okay. Let's see... I was always just a little shorter than you were. I have green eyes. And I'm what my friends call skinny because my work is a lot more physical than theirs are."

"Um...do you have vertical eye pupils?"

That took her aback. "Of course I do. All of us do. Don't you?"

"Yes. But nobody else I know does."

"Oh. How strange." She couldn't imagine anyone looking differently. It saddened Eiko to know he really didn't remember her or his family or anything. What had happened to him? She settled down to tell him what she could. About her, about his family, and about his father, Nyoko.

"Your mother is an amazing person. She has created several groups intent on pushing forward the rights and healthcare of women, against the direct edicts of your father. She is admired by almost as many as who dislike her."

"And my father?"

"He used to beat you and your brother and sister for even the smallest thing. Your mother tried to intervene many times, but eventually had to leave for her health. Leaving you all behind was nearly her undoing, but she had no choice. When she went to the courts to get them to release you and your brother and sister to her, Nyoko used his power to have her exiled to the unclean area of the city. She still lives there, and though the place is not preferred, she seems to be much better. Healthier and happier, except for you and your siblings. As for you and your father…You spent a lot of time with my family because of Nyoko. You wanted to be a scientist or an engineer, but your father insisted that you become a priest. When you defied him…" She sighed. "After my mother bandaged you, we went exploring and that's when we found the cave. And you found that cursed machine that took you away. When I tried to tell your father what happened, he had me put in the renewal center for a month for rehabilitation. They tried to convince me that you were dead."

"Oh, Eiko, I am so sorry."

She shrugged. "That was a long time ago. I'm glad you're not on the ninth level and that we are talking again." Eiko jumped as a tremor shook the ground and dirt and stones rained down on her. She grabbed the machine and scrambled for cover under one of the tables. "Oh!"

"Eiko? What's wrong?"

"A tremor. A bad one. They are coming almost every day now along with the storms. As the Night Eye grows bigger, the tremors and storms get worse. The Eye drops burning rocks on the land. Everyone is afraid but your father says we need to believe. That the Blessed Three will protect the town."

"What is the night eye?"

"It is a light in the sky we see day and night, though the Eye is much brighter at night, and grows ever larger. There are smaller ones raining fire from the sky every day too."

"What you describe sounds like an asteroid field. Or a comet."

"A what?"

"Asteroids are like large rocks in space. There are usually a bunch of them together and sometimes they can fall like fiery rain. But what does my father have to do with this?"

Eiko ducked as a rock the size of her fist dropped at her foot and she drew back as small as she could get. "After you disappeared, your father became even more involved in the religious orders. Over the years, he has risen in the ranks to be the leader."

"Oh."

"Hopper, are you all right?"

"Yes. Are you? Are you safe?"

"I am. I'm actually in the cave where we were exploring that day." She could hear him talking to others in the background. They sounded as if they needed him.

"Hopper? I hear others. If you are needed, go. I am safe. And happy that we can talk."

"I'm sorry. We will speak again soon. Goodbye, Eiko."

"Goodbye, Hopper." The machine still whirred faintly, but the blinking lights had gone out. "I miss you, my heart," she whispered.

The ground finally stopped shaking, and Eiko crept out. Hopper was alive. At least, she thought he was. She'd talked to him. Actually talked with him. And you couldn't do that with someone who had reached the ninth level. Could you? But he didn't remember her. Didn't remember them growing up together. Playing together. Telling each other their dreams and wishes and pledging their oaths of devotion. Didn't remember finding the cave and the evil ship that took him away.

She glanced at the walls. They were no longer sparkling. Interesting.

Masuru crawled out from under another table. Dust and small pebbles covered the table where the machine had been, and she was glad she'd moved the…communication unit. She looked around for Masuru to thank him. He had climbed higher in the cave. "Thank you, Masuru, for giving me Hopper back."

He nodded once at her, then disappeared into a tunnel.

Eiko checked her crystal alert, which had not stopped pinging, and looked around. "Could these machines contain crystals?"

She clicked off the alert and tuned the tool to proximity. She ran the scanner over the entrance tunnel. There was some activity, but not a lot. Then she scanned the communication device, and the needle pinged all the way to the top. The same with all the other machines.

"They are all crystal based. Like back in the city." She talked out loud more to settle her anxiety than for any need. She was used to being alone, but this cave made her nervous. Talking made her feel like someone else was with her—maybe even Hopper or Masuru. So she pretended she was talking to him. "A lot has changed since you left, Hopper. The crystals we use don't last long and need constant replacing. Or so we are told. But these machines have been here for years, yet this one still works. What if…what if the leaders are lying to us? They lied about space travel. They had to know flight was possible. Didn't they? They are our leaders. The most trusted. Why would they lie?"

And what about Hopper and the evil machine? Would his own father have lied to Eiko about what had happened? They'd put her in a medical unit for a month, filling her mind with lies. She hadn't been drugged or hallucinating. Hopper was real. Space flight was real. These machines were real. And Nyoko knew about them. She'd heard him earlier, she was certain.

So why the lies?

Chapter Six

Hopper clicked off the com-link and sat back in his seat with a smile. He'd spoken with Eiko. She was real. Not a figment of his imagination. Now he really wanted to continue with his journey, but first things first.

Hopper and June landed on Amaya. He appreciated her slowing their ascent so he could talk with Eiko. "I want to change out of this uniform," Hopper said. "Do you need anything from your ship?"

June shook her head and patted her backpack. "Got all I need right here, but I would appreciate a meal before we head off. By the way, thanks. All that jabbering was getting to me."

"I know exactly what you mean." He went to his room and quickly changed, but his mind wasn't on the reason they were there or on exploring. But on Eiko. "Amaya, how long will it take us to get to the Masaaki world?"

"Approximately three weeks at nominal speed."

He rose to stand at the porthole and gazed out. "They don't really need me here, do they? Cass and the others can take care of everything from here, can't they?"

"Yes. When do you want to leave?"

Hopper snorted, then smiled. She knew him all too well. "Is Cass available?"

"Actually, she's calling you."

"Put her through." Hopper sat down at his desk. "Hi, Cass. How is everything?"

She grinned at him. "It's all good. A lot to discuss going forward. But how are you? Are you all right?"

He sighed. "Yes. I am now. But Cass, I found her!"

"Yes, I know." She gave him a puzzled look. "You found both my mom and my dad."

"No! Eiko! I found *her*!"

She sat up straighter. "What? Where? Not here, surely."

"No. On the Masaaki home world. I need to get there."

"Yes, I agree. But first, you need to come down here. I have to show you something."

"What? Cass, I can't handle any more of the discussions and…and the crowds. It's too much."

"No. Not that. There's a cave here that you need to see."

"A cave?"

"Yes. On the north side of the island. There's enough space there to land one of the smaller shuttles. Please, Hopper, you need to see this."

"Amaya?"

"I have seen what they found. Yes, you do need to see this. Once you've seen, we can leave. Maximum speed will get us to the Masaaki world more quickly."

Hopper shook his head. "Why? Why do I need to see this…this…whatever?"

"I believe there may be clues to your past," Amaya said. "There are…things I did not show you about the Masaaki. The keys to your past, to the past of the Masaaki, and to your future lie in the cave."

"Fine. Fine. I'll go. But Amaya, make sure we're

ready to go when I get back. At maximum speed."

"Yes, Captain."

He looked up as a knock came at his door. "Enter."

June poked her head in. "Are we ready to go?"

"There's been a slight change of plans. Cass and Amaya seem to think I need to see a cave down on the planet. Then she and I are heading for the Masaaki home world. You're welcome to come along."

She cocked her head, then shook it. "Um…"

"Annie can come too. I'd love to have you both along."

"I'll talk to her. Now, a cave?"

"Yeah. I'm not sure I get it, but everyone is saying I need to see what's there."

"Okay. So, I guess we're going back down. But I am *not* going back into those crowds."

Hopper laughed. "Me neither." He led the way down to the landing bay and June took the pilot's seat. "Where to, Captain?"

"Cass told me the northeast area of the island. There should be a clearing there."

A half hour later, they landed in the designated spot and Hopper got out with June right behind him. Cass, Katie, Omar, and the two leaders, Amanda Ki and Declan Chalmers stood at the edge of the clearing, waiting for them.

"Cass?" Hopper cocked his head at her.

She chewed her lower lip in the way she had when she was nervous. "It's this way."

They followed Declan down a steep slope. At the end, Hopper saw panels leaning against the rocks to the side of an opening.

"We sealed the cave off after, um, an incident."

Hopper and his friends stared at him. "An...incident?"

Declan shook his head. "Old news that is no longer relevant. It had nothing to do with the cave or what's in there. It had to do with the saboteur who damaged our ship. And he's gone."

Hopper nodded and took a deep breath, then blew it out. "Okay. Let's see what I need to see." He followed the others into the cave. At first, he didn't see anything beyond a rocky cavern nearly the size of a shuttle lit with a string of lights around the sides. "I don't understand."

"Not here," Cass said. "Up there." She pointed to a ledge about halfway up the side of the cavern. Lights led the way up. "Go on."

"Oookay." Hopper climbed the ramp up to the ledge and saw a crack in the rocks large enough to easily go through. More lights lit the way and he entered. And stopped. And stared.

In front of him was another large cavern, but this one was vastly different. The smooth floor was inlaid with a swirled pattern of red, gold, and black stones. At the far end was a black altar, about eight feet long and half that wide with a black stone font at each end. But all that wasn't what stopped him. It was the murals on the walls. Murals of people who looked like him. And large felines.

Hopper stepped onto the black path, stopping when silence and darkness suddenly surrounded him. He could no longer hear his friends in the lower cave. The only illumination in the cave came from a small circle of light in the center of the floor. Hopper glanced up and realized there was a hole in the roof allowing the sunlight in. He turned to go back down to the others, but discovered he couldn't get out. It was as if there was a shield holding him back. Nor could he see anything beyond the shield.

He stepped toward the circle of light, staying on the black path as that one seemed to lead toward the altar. As he reached the center, a large feline emerged from the far end of the cave and he stopped again, his heart pounding, his mouth dry. He stood perfectly still, waiting to see what the big cat would do. It was nearly half as high as he was and with powerful muscles and sapphire eyes.

The cat came toward him, its head cocked to one side. It reached Hopper and sniffed at him, then sat down and stared at him.

"H…hello?"

The cat looked around as two more came through the opening and joined the first. Hopper's nerves were pinging like crazy. Especially when the first one, the biggest of the three, began to change. In less than a few minutes, a tall, well-built man with thick black hair and sapphire eyes stood before him. A very naked man.

"We have been waiting for you." His voice came out as a dry rasp, as if he didn't use it much.

"Waiting for me? How?"

"We knew one of our kind would return one day to take us home. We thought the day had come when the other ship came, but they were not the ones. We have been listening to your talks in the village and have determined that you are one of us."

"One of your kind? What are you?"

"We are Masaaki."

Hopper shook his head. "Amaya has told me the history of the Masaaki and nowhere does she mention beings like you. Ones who can shift from beast to man."

"That's because Amaya doesn't know. Or rather,

doesn't know she knows. How do you not know the true history? As captain, you should have known. Didn't the previous captain pass the knowledge to you?"

"The original captain died more than three thousand years ago. My friend only discovered Amaya a few years ago while on a salvage run."

"Then you truly do not know?"

Hopper shook his head. "Not only do I not know, but I don't even know my own past. I have no memory from before—a few years over a decade ago."

The man cocked his head to the side, much like a cat would. "That is interesting. I may be able to help you with that." He held his hands up to the sides of Hopper's head, not quite touching him. "May I?"

Hopper nodded and the man took his head in a grip that, while not painful, was uncomfortable. There was a flash and more than a bit of pain, and then, it was like a door opened and he knew. He remembered. He found…himself.

The man stepped back. "Are you all right?"

He settled on the ground, pain pounding behind his eyes. "Hurts."

"That will pass with time."

Hopper glanced at the spot on the floor where the sunlight shone. The beam had moved several feet. "How…how long?"

The man shrugged. "You were quite blocked."

Thoughts of his past flashed through his mind. Eiko. His father. His family. Everything was there, including how he got hurt and ended up on Pointe Noir. "How did you do that?"

"True Masaaki have the ability to mindspeak with each other. And when they are in contact, they can do more. Have you never done this?"

Hopper closed his eyes and thought about his past. "Yes, a little and only with Eiko, and that was a very long time ago."

"You haven't lost the ability. It does take practice, though."

"But what about our history? You said there was more I needed to know."

The man sighed. "It is something I should show both you and Amaya. Would you be willing to take on passengers?"

"As felines, or bipeds?"

"We would come on in our feline aspects, if that is acceptable. Were we to shift and ask for passage, there would be too many questions as to where we came from."

"I believe there will also be questions as to why I am taking on three felines."

The man matched Hopper's grin. "I'm sure you'll figure something out. We'll meet you at the shuttle."

"How many of you are there?"

"There are nearly a hundred of us left. But only three of us are willing to leave. We want to see what things are like on our world as it is now before the others agree to leave."

"How have you survived?"

He shrugged. "We managed. We have extensive fish farms and hydroponic gardens below. The crystal structure of this area protected us from the damages above."

"What about this place?" Hopper asked as he tried to take in all this information. "What shall I tell the others about this room? And the altar?"

"This place was once a place for the Masaaki who stayed here to gather. When we went underground, we no longer needed this place. It was too exposed. Too easy to find. And that"—he pointed at the altar—"is no altar."

He went to the front and pressed each corner starting in the bottom right, then the center of each edge, and finally, the center. Nine points in all. And the table cleared, to show an elaborate display of figures and designs. "This is a computer." He pressed a red triangle and an image of the world appeared in the air above them. "I can show you this world as well as the Masaaki home world. And more." He closed the machine down. "We very much want to go back to the home world and away from all this water."

"Why did you leave our world?"

"We didn't. All of us who live here were born here. This is our home, but so is our ancient world. According to our records, when our ancestors first arrived here, this was an acceptable planet with more land than water and actual people living on the other continents. Cities. When they arrived, they were not exactly welcomed. There had been a war with another world that decimated much of the population. This area was barren so some of the Masaaki settled here while Amaya and the rest of our people continued on. The ones who stayed wanted to study the area and the people. There was much to learn. Then, the worst possible event happened. A rogue asteroid hit a super-volcano on the southern continent, in the most heavily populated area. The world went into severe climatic changes."

"Sounds suspicious."

"I agree. But since our people couldn't leave, they moved underground to escape the devastation and await

Amaya's return—which never happened." He nodded toward the hole. "If you followed that tunnel, you would find our home, deep below this island." He grinned. "However, as a biped, you would find some of the pathways a challenge."

"This is going to be interesting." Hopper watched as the man shifted back into his cat form. "Doesn't that hurt?"

The cat snorted and shook his head, then turned and disappeared into the darkness. Hopper turned as the lights came back up and his friends slammed into the room.

Chapter Seven

"Hopper! What in all the rings of Aboo happened to you?" Omar dashed up to him, sweat staining his clothes. "We've been trying to get in for hours! We tried everything except bombing the place. Even Amaya couldn't contact you."

"I'm sorry I worried you all, but I'm fine, Omar. Actually, better than fine. I finally know who I am." He wanted to leave now for the home world, but he also wanted to know more about this world. At that moment, he really hated being captain. As such, he wasn't free to do as he wanted. But…not being captain meant he wouldn't have Amaya and her speed and knowledge. He'd have to settle for taking care of what needed to be done here first, then go home.

Home. What a funny word. For years, Pointe Noir had been his home. Then Amaya. What would he find when he reached his place of birth? His family home? He tamped down his thoughts and focused on the here and now. The rest would sort itself out when he got there. They headed outside.

But first… "Um, we're going to have three more guests on Amaya when we head for the Masaaki world."

Omar frowned at him. "We're taking people back to Pointe Noir, not your world."

"I'm not talking about the *Phoenix* people." He

stopped at the shuttle as several dozen black felines emerged from the path to the cave. The other people with him also stopped and stared, especially when Hopper went up to the largest of the cats and knelt, putting his arms around two of them. "These beings are descendants of people from the Masaaki home world."

"Amaya, please prepare three rooms. We will have guests coming with us."

"I do not understand."

"Read my mind." He sent her images of what had happened, then he glanced at the cats. "I know you probably don't want to, but I suggest you let them see the other you."

The largest one stared at him, then snorted, and shifted. Omar, Cass, and the others stared, mouths agape, at the naked man. Omar looked back at Hopper. "Um…Hopper?"

"I would like you to meet one of the descendants of the Masaaki who settled here when Amaya originally passed by. There are about a hundred of them left. They live underground for the most part. I'm taking these three back to the home world. They wish to see what things are like before moving them all."

"Are all of them…um…" Omar waved his hand at the man.

"Yes, we are," he said. "I am Komeko."

"Why haven't you made yourself known to us before this?" Chalmers asked. "We've been here several years."

"The last time we mingled with people of this planet, things did not go well. So we went into hiding. But we have watched you, and helped where we could."

Amanda Ki cocked her head and smiled. "The

66

crystals the first year. The ones we needed for power."

Komeko nodded. "Among other things."

"Thank you." She looked at Hopper. "If not for Komeko and his...people, I believe our first years would have been much more difficult. We often wondered how certain things got done seemingly overnight."

"The Masaaki can see excellently in the dark," Komeko said.

"Hopper, can you shift like Komeko?" Cass asked.

He shrugged. "Not that I know of. But I've never tried." He motioned the cats toward the shuttle. "We'll be leaving as soon as we get loaded. Cass, I am glad you found your family. Captain Chalmers, I wish you and your people peace. You have a lot to look forward to, but also some challenges ahead."

"Thank you." Chalmers watched as Komeko shifted back into feline form. "Doesn't that hurt?"

"Not according to him. I suggest you continue to keep others away from the caves unless the ones staying allow it."

"We will."

"Hopper?" Cass went up to him and hugged him fiercely. "I'll miss you. You have been a good friend and helped me find my family. For that alone, I will always love you. I hope you find what you are looking for."

"Thank you. Take care. And this isn't goodbye. Now that we know where everyone is, we'll be able to get back and forth. Thank you also for taking care of me when I was on Pointe Noir. Without you and Omar..." Words failed him, and he felt a suspicious moisture in his eyes. "Take care, my friend."

A few minutes later, they took off. Hopper took one last look at his friends as they grew smaller in the distance.

This part of his life was over, and he needed to look forward to the next one. "Amaya, time to head for home. We'll be back on board in two minutes."

"Understood."

He had so much to share with Eiko.

When they landed, Hopper showed their guests to their quarters. "Komeko, you are welcome to stay in whatever shape you are most comfortable with. Get settled in, then we'll talk, okay?"

"Yes. And thank you, Amaya, for allowing us to join you on this part of your trip."

"You are most welcome. I would love to also talk to any of you about your history."

"Our history is your history. If you access file ANS-073.209, I believe you will find some things you might not know. The password is CLOPZ875. They are files that were loaded by the scientists who created you and the other living ships. Your original captain should have released them to you before she died."

"There was no time. The attack was swift and decisive."

"Understood." Komeko turned to Hopper. "Give us some time to settle in and we will speak."

Hopper nodded and left them to head for his own cabin, wondering what the files would tell Amaya. What they would mean to him and her. Would they change her? He had to admit, a small part of him was afraid. Afraid of the ship that had taken him. That had hurt him. Amaya would never do something similar to him, would she?

"Never do what?" Amaya asked.

"Um...never leave without me."

"Of course not! We are bonded. You are my captain."

He heard her words, but a small part of him still wondered. Would Amaya ever turn on him as the other ship had?

He remembered what had happened to him, but when he went back to the home world, what would happen then? He was proof space travel was possible— and that idea went against all the edicts the priests, including his father, had ever preached. Space travel wasn't possible. Their world was the center of the universe, and nothing existed beyond the sky but evil. He had lived in that limited world for his entire youth, but now...now, he had the entire universe opened up to him. There was so much more to explore. To experience. He'd lived three lives so far. The first, limited and structured with no freedom. The second in pain, but free to do as he wanted. And now, his third. Free from pain, free from the restrictions of his father. He didn't think he'd ever be free from his father's abusive ways. That pain would always be with him. But those memories didn't have to dictate his movements anymore. He was free to explore as he wanted.

How could Hopper explain all this to his friends, to the rulers? To tell them everything they believed was false?

But mostly, he wanted to find Eiko.

He explained the situation with their guests to his crew, and they adapted easily, as they always did. Amaya was a different story.

"Amaya, they are Masaaki. From the home world. They want to go home, like me."

"That is not what I am upset about."

"What then?"

"That my captain—my former captain—kept this knowledge from me. These files that Komeko gave me access to. I wonder why they kept them hidden. There is really nothing of importance in them."

"Maybe not now, but what about in the past? When you were first created?"

"Hmmm. I see your point. And yes, I might have had some issues with them."

Hopper hadn't read the files yet so didn't know what she was talking about. "Like what?"

"Like a command that would turn me off. I would still work, like a regular ship, but I wouldn't be me. And there is no way for me to countermand it. Anyone who knows the information in these files would be able to control me. I'm not sure I like that."

"I can understand that. All I can say is, as your current captain, I can't see me ever doing something like that." And he couldn't. Unless Amaya turned on him or did something that seemed dangerous to the people inside.

"I appreciate that, Hopper. I will need to think about my reaction to this knowledge. Why would they have shown me these files if I can do nothing about them?"

"I don't know, Amaya. Unless it had something to do with the ship that took me. The one that damaged me. If I'd known something like this when I was taken, I might not have been hurt so badly."

"Understood. And while I do not like that you were hurt, you cannot deny that the outcome was that you found me. And we found the *Phoenix* crew."

"True." He went to the wall and laid his hand against it, smiling when the material softened around his hand.

"You are my friend. We have a lot of challenges ahead of us without regretting the past."

"Agreed. We will arrive at the home world in six days, thirteen hours, sixteen minutes."

Chapter Eight

Eiko sat on the ground, staring into her fire, her thoughts churning like the waters in the river. The elders were right—and wrong. Space travel was possible, but also dangerous. The ship had taken Hopper away from her just when they'd pledged to spend the rest of their lives together. And now…she was different. Was he? He said he'd been hurt. But not how badly. Was he even still her Hopper?

So many questions and so few answers.

She fell asleep, only to dream of him. Even in her dream, her heart yearned for him.

A strong tremor shook Eiko from her dreams. She grabbed the communication machine from the table and ducked under the sturdiest table as rocks and dirt rained down and the ground shook. A large rock thudded into the ground inches from her, and she curled up as small as she could make herself, hugging the unit to her side. As a precaution, she grabbed her helmet and strapped it on, turning on the light. As she waited for the tremor to stop, another rock bounced off the table where the machine would have been, partially collapsing the surface. Still another one landed on her sleeping mat and dirt rained down on her fire, putting the flames out. She squeaked out a small scream.

"Eiko! Are you all right?"

She startled at Hopper's voice from the unit. Hearing his voice was like a gift from the Blessed Three. Eiko set the box on the ground close to the wall. "I'm scared. The ground is shaking so badly and there are large rocks falling all around."

"Where are you?"

She peered out from her spot as the tremors eased and not as many rocks fell. "I'm still in the cave with the communication device. I brought the machine under the sturdiest table to keep it safe."

"Good. As long as you're safe, that's all that matters. Is the ground still shaking?"

"A little. Not as badly though, and the rocks have stopped falling, though there is still some dirt coming down."

"Okay. You need to get out of the caves. They're too dangerous. But wait until all the shaking is done."

"Do you think I can take the machine with me?"

"How big is it?"

She studied the box. "Not that big. I can probably fit it in my pack without too much trouble."

"Then do that but be careful not to move the dial or we won't be able to talk."

"Understood." The ground stopped shaking, but her nerves didn't as she gingerly crawled out from under the table. All around her, machines, tables, and shelves had been damaged or destroyed. Eiko yanked her bedding out from under a rock and gathered her stuff. But how could she secure the machine? She emptied her bag, then studied the box and her gear. Smiling, she took a bandage from her aid pack and wrapped that around the box so the dials and buttons were secured, then used her blanket to further pad the box and put it in the bottom of her bag.

Finally, she replaced the rest of her gear.

"Hopper? Can you still hear me?"

No answer.

"Hopper?"

Nothing. Then she realized he probably couldn't hear her through the material, so she dug the machine back out and unwrapped it. "Hopper?"

"I'm here. What happened?"

"I have to figure out a different way to carry the box. You can't hear me when I have it wrapped and in my bag."

"What about just strapping it to the bottom of your pack? Is that possible?"

Eiko cocked her head, studying the problem. "I believe so."

She gathered everything and pulled out a small sack she used to secure crystals in. It was made to hang from the bottom of her pack. The material was thin, but sturdy—it had to be to stand up to sharp-edged crystals—so she put the box in that and attached it to her bag.

"Hopper?"

"I'm here. I'm sorry I had to leave."

"It's all right. I know you must be busy. I just wanted to make sure you could hear me okay." The walls were sparkling again.

"You're a little muffled, but still understandable."

"I secured the box in one of my crystal bags. I think that will keep it safe while I move. I'm leaving the cave now. Will you stay with me?"

"Of course. Hey, do you remember that time we tried to bake a cake for your brother's birthday?"

"You remember!" She chuckled as she climbed over

and around rocks toward the cave entrance.

"Yes. A long story, but I do remember now."

"That's amazing."

"At least I haven't baked any more cakes!"

She laughed. "I remember you trying to use one of your inventions to mix and bake the cake all in one machine and it blew up and nearly destroyed my parents' kitchen!" Eiko stopped as a huge rock fall blocked her way. "Hopper, the tunnel is completely blocked. I can't get out the way I came in."

"Go back to the cave. There has to be another way out. Look for another tunnel. Maybe higher up."

As she crawled through the opening to the cave, her helmet light went out and she was left in complete darkness. "Hopper! My light went out!"

She was a crystal hunter, trained to handle all sorts of situations, but nothing like this. Nothing like rocks raining down on her and in complete darkness. She was trained to handle muddy paths, where to find safe food and water, and how to build a shelter. This…this was different from anything she knew.

"Breathe. You're okay. Open your eyes wide and look around. Even in the darkness, you should be able to see some shapes."

"What? How?" To her surprise, she could see. Not well, but the crystals sparkled all around her.

"You are Masaaki. You have the genetic ability to see in less light than other beings."

"Keep talking to me, please."

"Okay. Relax. Breathe. Tell me what you can see."

"I can kind of make out shapes."

"Good. Your helmet has a crystal base, right?"

"Yes."

"Do you know what color the crystal is?"

"Um… I'm not sure. We're taught how to change them, but we only practice on old ones with chips of all colors." She sidled around the room, running her hands over walls not covered with shelves and cabinets.

"Okay, what color is the light when lit?"

"Kind of yellowish white?"

"Good. That means the crystal is also probably light yellow. When we were in that cave, there were all sorts of cabinets and tables. Some of the cabinets held polished crystals. Do you remember which ones did?"

"No. It's been a long time." Her nerves rushed through her, clenching her stomach, and she had trouble catching her breath. She'd never experienced darkness like this before. Even in the deepest night out in the jungle, she still had moonlight or a fire. But this…this was complete—except for the crystals. They reminded her of the godlights—the tiny spots of light in the night sky that the priests said were holes in the roof of heaven.

"Breathe. Deep breath in. Hold. Breathe out. Come on, sweetie. You can do this. Breathe with me. In…out…in…out."

She tried to breathe with him. "I'm… I'm okay."

"Good. Now, where are you?"

Eiko shrugged and frowned. "I'm in this groundslugging cave." She heard his chuckle. "Oh, sure, laugh at me. At least you can see what you're doing."

"Okay, here's what I want you to do. I want you to close your eyes."

"What? That's ridiculous. I can barely see shapes."

Another pause. "Close your eyes. Now."

She snorted but did as he said. "Okay, they're closed."

"Now, think. You're in the cave with me all those years ago. I'm looking at the ship and you're going through the cabinets. What's in the first one to your left? You opened the door and…?"

She frowned as she tried to think back. "No. I couldn't open that one. The door was locked so I went to the next one." She combined her memories from that day long ago with her recent ones. "The second one held a bunch of files."

"Next?"

"A long table with tools, then I opened the next one. I found crystals of all shapes and sizes."

"Good! You're doing amazing. Can you get to that cabinet?"

She made her way around to the tunnel opening then past the first two cabinets and the table. "I'm there."

"Open the door, but don't touch what's inside."

"I know how to handle crystals, Hopper. I'm a crystal hunter!"

He laughed. She loved the sound of his laugh. "I forgot about your special interest. Okay, if this cabinet is laid out the same way the ones here on Amaya are, the light-yellow crystals should be on the second shelf from the top."

"Why would they be the same?"

"I don't know. A hunch?"

Eiko sighed. "I guess that's as good a reason as any."

"Okay, find the smallest one."

"I know. We've been taught how to change them out, but we only practice with old, cracked ones."

Eiko carefully ran her fingers over the crystals, nicking her finger on a sharp edge. "Ouch!"

"What happened?"

She sucked on her finger. "I cut my finger."

"So, the big, important crystal hunter cut herself on a crystal? Don't you have gloves?"

"Stop laughing at me! And yes, I do, but most hunters don't use them. They're too bulky, especially for fine work." She found the smallest crystal, barely more than a slice. "I have the smallest one."

"Okay, go back to the table with the tools and take off your helmet."

With Hopper talking to her, she took out the old crystal and put the new one in. The chore was a lot easier in the lab with light all around them. Saying a quick prayer to the Blessed Three, she flicked the switch. "Light! I have light! Oh, Hopper! Thank you!"

He chuckled. "You did all the work. Do you see any other tunnels?"

"No. But there are paths leading up the wall toward the place where the ship went out with you."

"Try one but be careful. With the tremors, the rocks might be loose. Test each one for stability before you step out." He paused. "Wait. Do any of the paths have color? Like black, red, or gold?"

"Not that I can see. Maybe under the dirt."

"If you can find one that is black, take that one."

"Why?"

"Another hunch?"

Eiko thought back to Masuru when he was climbing. He'd taken the one on her far left. She went to where the steps started and scraped away some of the dirt. Sure enough, underneath were several black tiles. "I found the black one, but I'm going to check the other two to make sure."

"Makes sense."

Eiko quickly checked the other two paths. Hopper had been right. One red, one gold. But the black one looked the most treacherous. "I'm going to have to leave my bag here and the communication box. They're too bulky for me to carry."

"Do you have enough rope to attach to them and tie that to your waist?"

"Ah, I get it. That way, if I find a way out, I can haul them up instead of going back down, right?"

"Correct. But you'll probably be too far from the com-unit for us to hear each other. Okay?"

"Yes." After tying off her pack and securing the other end of the rope to her waist, she studied the small sack holding the communications unit, then detached it from her bag and tied it to the rope at her side. Finally, she went back to the black path and started up. This one had sustained the most damage during the tremors. Wide sections of the steps were down to tiny ledges she had to inch over. The track wasn't so much a path as a series of handholds and footholds sticking out here and there. She blew out her breath and started climbing, praying for another tunnel somewhere. "Hopper?"

"I'm here."

"I figured out a way to keep the machine with me."

"Of course you did."

"So, you're the captain of a big ship?"

The crystals started sparkling again.

"Amaya is pretty big, yes. She was built to hold almost a thousand people."

"Wow. You're a captain of over a thousand people?" Her foot slipped off a loose rock and she scrambled to hold onto the rocks under her hands.

Hopper laughed. "No. I only have a crew of twenty."

"You have a mostly empty ship?"

"Yes."

"What happened to the others?"

"Amaya was abandoned nearly 3000 years ago. Nobody knows what happened to her people. A lot of them died when they were attacked. The rest of the crew…disappeared. My friend Cass discovered Amaya a little over two years ago."

Eiko glanced down, then wished she hadn't. She wasn't afraid of heights. You couldn't be in her job, but that didn't mean she had to like being so high without safety equipment. "So how did you become captain? Shouldn't Cass be captain?"

"She has another ship called Zara. And Amaya and I…well, she healed me. We are…friends."

Eiko reached a ledge of sorts where she could sit for a moment. His tone told her there was more to their friendship than just being friends. "But she's still a machine, right?"

"An incredibly special one. How are you doing?"

A change of subject. There was definitely more there. She shook her head. How could she be jealous of a ship? A machine? Though, this was Hopper. He had always been fascinated by machines. Maybe that was the connection. His fascination with machines.

"I'm resting on a ledge. I'm about three-quarters of the way up and still no other tunnels, though my light's not strong enough to see if the other paths have any." She studied the wall above her. The rocks were nearly smooth, almost like polished crystals. "I'm not sure I can go any higher. The walls taper in and they're smooth. I can see where the steps were at one time, but without ropes and climbing equipment, I don't think going on would be safe. Especially if another tremor came." She thought about Masuru. He'd made his way out. But the gap in front of her looked to be recent. Probably from the last tremor.

Her stomach clenched again. "I don't have any way out. I'm trapped in here."

"Eiko, you'll be okay. I promise. You have your supplies with you, don't you?"

"Y…yes."

"How long were you going to be out in the field for?"

"At least a month."

"So, you have enough food for a month, maybe a little longer."

"Yes."

"What about water?"

"Only for a day or two. I usually replenish at streams and other water sources when I'm out."

"Look around the cavern. Do you see any places that look wet?"

"Maybe. Even with my light, it's still really dark in here."

"Okay, first things first. You need to go back down to the floor of the cave. Start going down and I'll talk to you. We're going to do three tasks. We're going to get you better light, find a source of water, and make sure you're safe."

"You keep saying *we*. But I'm the one doing all the work here."

"Yes, but I am with you."

"I've missed you so much, Hopper."

"I'd like to say I missed you, but until today, I didn't

know who you were. But I remember now. I remember your laughter and your beauty. I remember your hair, as dark as the night sky and your eyes as blue as the bluest crystal. I remember your grace and the way you teased me for being so curious."

Eiko's heart was nearly bursting with his words. "Will we ever see each other again, Hopper?"

"Yes. According to Amaya, we'll need just under a week to get to the Masaaki world. But we'll be able to talk every day now."

"I'd like that." She continued her descent in the silence. Hopper had a lot to do. She was one person. He had many others who depended on him. She reached the floor and moved her gear back under the table.

"Eiko? How are you doing?"

"I'm back to the floor. The way down was a lot faster than the way up."

He chuckled. "Usually is."

"I'm sorry I took so long. I needed to take care of some duties here."

"I guess a captain does have a lot to do."

"Not as much as you think, but I have some special guests I needed to speak with. How are you doing?"

"I'm good."

"Okay. So, there are some more tasks we're going to do. First, get you some better light. Do you have a lantern in your kit?"

"A small one."

"A small one will do. Get one out and turn the light on."

"Done. But there's not much more light than with my helmet. And this is a new lantern—or rather, a really old one. We weren't taught how to change this one out.

We don't even use these anymore. I'm not sure why the leaders had this in my supply pack."

"That's okay. We're going to make the light better. Describe the lantern to me. We'll fix it up right for you."

She chuckled. "Fixing and building are your specialties, not mine! Remember the first time you tried to get me to build something?"

Hopper laughed. "I do. But we were, what? Six? I think this will go better. Trust me."

"I do, Hopper."

Those words nearly melted his heart. "Okay, remember the cabinet where you found the crystals?"

"Yes."

"Go to the cabinet and find a black crystal. You'll want one about the size of the palm of your hand and no thicker than your smallest finger."

There was an interminable pause before she came back to him. "I found one."

"Good. Now go to the table with all the tools and machines."

With a lot of fits and starts and a bit of swearing on the part of Eiko at both him and the tools she was working with, an hour later, she yelled. "I did it! I have a much stronger beam now. One that lights up nearly the entire cavern. But I also found something strange inside the lantern. I removed it."

"Oh? What?"

"I'm not sure. It kind of looks a little like the tracker I used to wear on my wrist. And it's blinking."

That worried him until he thought what the device might be. "Eiko! Smash that. Now."

"What?"

"Smash the device. They're probably tracking you

now!"

She grabbed a rock and used that to smash the light. "I did. But even if they're tracking me, they can't get to me."

"Maybe. Maybe not. We'll have to hope they can't. But at least you have better light now, right?"

"Yes."

"Good! See? You're better than you think. So, second task…do you see water anywhere?"

Again, a pause. "Yes! Near the entrance, where a big rock came down, there's a trickle of water coming through a crack."

"Good. Take some pieces of metal or whatever you can find to hold water and use them like pipes to direct the trickle to a container. With this, you'll have a supply of water."

"I really hate this cave. The last time I was here, terrible things happened to you. And now this with me. If I never see another cave, I will be happy."

"I get that. We'll get you out, one way or another. Meanwhile, water."

She chuckled. "All right. All right. Let's see what I can find." She looked around the cave. Picking up and discarding a variety of tools and equipment. "I found a plastic crate here, but it has a locked lid, so I don't know what's in it." She studied the lock, then pulled her crystal cutter from her bag and went to work.

"Well, if nothing else, the crate could be used to hold water. Any tools there you can use to break the lock?"

She chuckled as the pieces of the lock dropped off. "Already got it." She opened the crate, wondering what could be so important as to be locked inside. And gasped.

"And?"

"Credit slips. Thousands of them! There's enough here for everyone in the village to have what they need. Food. Better housing. I don't understand."

"It's a payoff for someone. I'd bet either my father or people working with him."

Eiko sifted her hands through the slips. "I could buy my freedom. With this, I can go back as soon as I get out of here and pay off Nyoko."

She heard Hopper sigh. "I'm sorry, but probably not. If I remember correctly, challenging my father or disagreeing with him never worked well."

"So what do I do?"

"You find something to gather water in and stay safe until I get there. We'll figure something out together. I promise."

"Okay. Thanks."

She put the lid back on the crate. All that credit. Just sitting there. She wandered around the cave, picking up pieces of metal and plastic that she could cobble together for something to direct and gather water. Using several bits of wire, her tools, and even her shoestrings, she soon had something that would bring water to her. Now she just had to wait.

And she was not good at waiting.

Eiko went back to the original tunnel opening and started digging. Even if all she did was go a few inches, at least she was doing something.

Chapter Nine

Hopper clicked off the com-unit and settled into his chair. "Can we get there faster?"

"I will increase speed for you."

"Thank you, Amaya. Add another world to unknown space."

"Hopper, since we are here, this is now known space," Amaya pointed out.

Hopper laughed. "Yeah, I guess it is. Have you sent the details back to Pointe Noir?"

"Yes. I did that as soon as we confirmed this was the *Phoenix* crew. Many are quite excited about the discoveries. They are already preparing ships of supplies and people to head for the *Phoenix* world. At least their trip will not be as long or as convoluted as ours was getting here."

"True. Having to search every star system we found on the way did slow us down considerably." Hopper thought about his friend Cass and her family. She'd been reunited with her parents and had a new little brother in addition to her husband and son. He'd seen the love among them all and some of the others too.

And then there was his family. Definitely not the same kind of relationship Cass had with her family. Or Omar and Katie. Or June and Annie. He'd been alone for so long. Oh, he had friends. Close friends. But family…like they had? His thoughts turned toward his family. With the father he had, he'd never have a family like his friends did.

But maybe something better with Eiko?

He rose from his desk and went to his bedroom where he lay on his bed, his hands behind his head, and stared at the ceiling. "Amaya, can the bond between us be broken?"

"Only through death. Are you not happy we are going to your Eiko? To our home?"

Hopper heard the terror in her voice, and the sound scared him a little as he thought about the ship that kidnapped him. "I am!" He sat up and swung around so he could touch the wall. "You are my Amaya! I merely asked a question, that's all. I meant nothing more."

The wall softened as he stroked the smooth material.

"You are Hopper, who brought me back to life. Even my previous captain was not as special as you."

"And you are Amaya, who brought *me* back to life. But we are returning to your home and my family. We may need to take changes into consideration."

There was a pause, which was unusual for Amaya. "I understand. And I will consider." The lights dimmed. "Rest now."

Hopper laid back down, but he didn't rest. In the part of his mind he kept to himself, he wondered what would happen if he wanted to stay on the planet with Eiko. Could he possibly unbond with Amaya without having to die? And if he weren't bonded with her, would she stay? She had said she would stay with him, but that was as bonded. What if she was free of him? Would she still stay? And what about the parts of him she had repaired? If he weren't bonded, would he revert to who he was at Pointe Noir? He was no longer that Hopper. Was he?

But he was also no longer Eiko's Hopper, either. That Hopper had been young and curious, always looking for answers. And yes, he was still curious, just older, and more experienced. But the Hopper he was now? He wasn't even sure who he was. So many doubts crowded his mind.

Finally, he sat up. "Lights, one-quarter."

"Hopper? You are restless."

"So many questions going through my mind. Amaya, what do you think this Night Eye is that's threatening the planet?"

"Possibly an asteroid. Historically speaking, the closest asteroid field to the Masaaki home world was several parsecs away. Though, when I was being built, there was a large one coming close to the planet. The scientists were working on a way to destroy one if necessary."

"With your weaponry, would we be able to break up an asteroid, or at least alter the course?"

"Without knowing the makeup or size of the object, I cannot be sure of my calculations, but there is a distinct possibility."

Excitement flooded Hopper. "We need to make plans. Evacuation, stopping the asteroid, finding Eiko…so many situations to think about." He glanced up as his catering unit pinged.

"You need to rest so you can think of all this tomorrow. Hot herbal tea to help calm you down."

He smiled at her thoughtfulness. "Thank you." As Hopper sipped his tea, unease filled his mind. He knew all kinds of people—good ones and bad. Cass's best friend and partner Ben had betrayed her. Omar and Katie were good people, but when they owned a bar, if someone caused trouble, they were quick to throw them out—physically if needed. Plus, they were of the Warrior class of Abooleans. A class known for their fighting skills. June was good when she was around Annie or when someone needed help, but Hopper was certain she could be violent too. All you had to do was look at all the weapons she carried. He thought Amaya was good. She'd healed him. Cared for him. Took him on as her bonded captain. But he had seen what she was like when threatened, and she had weapons much more powerful than fists or guns. What would happen if someone she trusted crossed her? Would she become like the evil one that had taken him? That one had attempted to bond with him like Amaya had, but in a much more invasive, brutal way, hurting him mentally and physically. He had been powerless to stop the ship as they hurtled through space, flying through areas like asteroid fields that caused massive damage to the small ship—and him.

Hopper was beginning to understand why the leaders back on Pointe Noir had been nervous about Amaya. He knew a person had both good and bad sides depending on the circumstances, but what if such a person was capable of massive destruction on a global level? Did he dare ask?

"I sense you are still uneasy," Amaya said, startling Hopper out of his thoughts.

Hopper swallowed hard against the feelings roiling his stomach. "Yes. I would like to ask you a question, but I am afraid to."

"You need never fear me, Hopper. You are my captain. You can ask anything. Is your question again about the bonding?"

"No. I wonder about the two sides of a person's

mental state. People are both good and bad, depending on…well, a lot of circumstances. Are you also like that?"

"I am. Like any corporeal being, I am multi-faceted and have emotions, good and bad."

"But what happens if you get really angry at someone? Even an entire people. You are an extremely powerful ship with deadly weapons. Could you destroy them?"

"Ah, an interesting philosophical question. And the answer is both yes and no. Yes, I am capable of massive destruction. But my bonded captain can temper my capabilities. This is one reason why I am not fully functional without a bonded captain. You are my…conscience for lack of a better term. I could lay an entire world to waste, but not without your approval."

"But what if something were to happen to me? Or you had a captain who wasn't, um…"

"As ethical as you are? I do not know. When my last captain was fatally injured, I was also severely injured and in pain. On her order, I went to sleep."

"What if she had not ordered you to sleep?"

"I would have commenced with repairs and sent out signals to our people to return."

"You would not have continued the fight?"

"There was no reason to. Many of the crew were dead, the rest sent out in life pods. I had no one to captain me. No one to bond with. I was alone. I slept until you woke me. But to answer your question, I would hope I would make the…ethical decision. If you remember, back at Pointe Noir, when the scientists and bureaucrats wanted to take me and Zara over, we did not destroy them even though they made us quite angry."

"Yes, but that little stinger you gave the Aboolean

ambassador's ship made an impact."

Amaya chuckled. "I did not do any major damage, and my actions did make a point."

Hopper actually laughed. "Yes, they did." He thought hard about her answers. He hadn't asked her the one question uppermost in his mind—and was happy she couldn't read all his thoughts. That there were parts of his mind not open to her. The big question for him was if she could become evil. But then, he reasoned, anyone could become evil. Hopper finished his tea.

"What would you do if I stayed on the planet with Eiko?"

"I do not know. Maybe explore, but I will always return to you. You are my captain."

Hopper chewed his lower lip. So many things to think about, some of them decidedly uncomfortable and disturbing. "I think I'll take a walk. See how our guests are doing. Maybe that will help me."

"We can continue our discussion while you walk, if you want," Amaya said.

"No, thanks. I think I need to…just walk."

Hopper had no destination in mind when he left his cabin. He didn't want to go to the bridge, so he just wandered. He spoke briefly with Komeko. The three of them were settling in well, most often in bipedal form. They spent their time exploring the ship or checking out files showing them Pointe Noir and other current information.

Eventually, Hopper ended up in engineering. The one place he felt comfortable. This was where he belonged. Not up on the bridge in charge of the entire ship and all her people. Here was his heart—at the heart of the machine. And Amaya, for all her intelligence and sentience, was still a machine. A really fancy one, but a machine. But then, he thought, weren't all beings nothing more than a type of machine?

There was nobody around. Nobody needed to be there unless there was a problem. And actually, most problems, Amaya could fix herself. Hopper scanned the monitors—all were green. There was nothing here for him to fix. Nothing needed him.

He went over to the com-link, sat down, and flicked the channel on. "Eiko? Are you there?"

No answer.

"Eiko?"

"H-hello? Hopper? Is this you?"

She sounded as if he'd woken her. He'd forgotten to ask her what her time was on the planet when they'd last talked. "I am so sorry I woke you. What time is it there?"

"That's okay. I was due to be up soon anyway. According to my timepiece, the sun rose an hour ago, so I should be up. But I slept so well. Better than I have in a long time. How long until you get here?"

"I should be there in four days, fifteen hours."

Eiko laughed and he melted at the sound. Her laughter was so amazing. Thanks to regaining his memories, he knew he and Eiko had a special connection even back when they'd been young. What he'd experienced back then went deeper than friendship. But was that love? He didn't know. All he did know was now that he remembered her and could talk with her, he felt as if he'd found a missing piece of him. She made him whole.

"You were always so exact. I'm surprised you didn't give me the time down to the minute and second."

"I could if you wanted. But I'd need to do some

more calculations based on others and not just myself. The variables could be a challenge." He got quiet, thinking of all the calculations.

"Hopper!"

He pulled his mind out of the task at Eiko's laugh.

"You were doing the calculations, weren't you?"

Heat infused his face. "Maybe?" She laughed and he chuckled with her. "Okay, yes, I was."

"At least that hasn't changed. You used to get lost in the challenge of figuring out a problem all the time. I remember once when you decided to build a small boat so we could go across the wetlands to the ocean. The boaters all laughed at us when we took off, then watched as we sailed right past them with your special sails and crystal propeller. They stopped laughing, and even copied your designs to use for themselves!"

Hopper sat back and listened to her reminiscing about their past. A time when they were young and free. They chatted until he couldn't keep his eyes open any longer.

"Hopper?"

"Huh?"

"Go to bed."

"Okay. G'night Eiko."

"Good night, Hopper."

Chapter Ten

The next day, at lunch, he was checking over reports on the ship and crew and guests. "Amaya, I'd like a bowl of macaroni and cheese, please." His friend Zack—Cass's husband—had introduced him to the decadent dish when they'd first met, and the gooey mixture of pasta and cheeses and crusty topping was his favorite. The catering unit pinged, and he opened the sliding door, inhaling the steaming aroma. "Thank you."

Amaya's catering units were based on the same gray goo as any other ship or catering service. The unappealing mess could be textured and flavored into any meal asked for and provided all the nutrients necessary for each individual. Hopper knew all this, but the knowledge didn't lessen his enjoyment of the meal. He dug his fork in and savored the flavor. He all but hummed as he ate. He clicked the com-link back to Eiko's frequency.

"Eiko?"

"Hi, Hopper!"

"Are you doing all right? Were you able to rig up a way to catch water?"

"Yes. I also moved some of the tables around so I have a sturdy area near one wall where I can sleep safely."

"Good." He took another bite of his meal. "Tell me, have you ever had a dish called macaroni and cheese?"

"No. I've never heard of such a food. What is mac-a-ro-ni and cheese?"

He smiled at her drawn-out pronunciation of macaroni. "Just the best dish ever. The basis is a pasta that looks like your elbow but is hollow. Hmm… remember when your grandmother used to make akebola strips for us?" The dish of vegetable noodles and a creamy coating was as close to macaroni-and-cheese as he could think of.

"Oh, those were so good. I miss her akebola."

"She has reached the ninth level?"

"Yes. Five years past, along with my parents. An illness went through the town and took many. I miss them still."

Hopper set his fork down, sadness in his heart. Eiko's grandmother had been an amazing woman. So strong and yet soft and her parents so accepting of him. "I am sorry. When I reach you, we will sing a song to their memory."

"I'd like that. Thank you."

"And I will introduce you to macaroni and cheese. You're going to love this, I'm sure."

Eiko chuckled. "Your dinner sounds much better than these nutrient bars and hunter meals they give us when we're hunting."

"I can imagine. Remember the cookies your mother packed for us when we went exploring? So sweet and gooey and…" His mouth watered remembering them.

"She gave me her recipes and taught me how to make them! I'll bake some for you when you get me out of here."

"I'd love that. But… would you have gone back to Lawan?" If she went back, she'd be forced to face his father about a marriage she didn't want. And he'd be bringing a ship—something that his father didn't believe in.

She hesitated so long, he thought they'd lost their connection. "I don't know. What of you? Will you stay here?"

He blew out a long breath. "Like you, I don't know. We both have a lot to think about."

"That we do."

"Okay. So, you have food, water, and shelter. Tell me, what would you have done if I wasn't coming?"

She sighed. "I honestly don't know. Probably tried to dig my way out past the rockslide. What else could I do?"

"You don't have any way of contacting someone in an emergency, like a radio of some sort?"

"Not really. Until recently, crystal hunters were always sent out as a team. When we go out alone, we have no one to rely on."

"What if you don't return? Don't they look for you?"

"Only if we're a couple weeks late, and then, the search is minimal. We don't have enough people anymore." She paused. "Oh, I had a seeker signal. But I destroyed it when I left."

"A seeker? Do they track your movements through that?"

"Yes. It's a band we all wear around our wrists. When we don't return, the supervisors get a signal and send out Seekers to find us. I destroyed mine when I left Lawan."

"Why? They could help you get out."

"Yes, and no. If they caught me, I would be forced

to return to Lawan and to mate with a man Nyoko has picked out for me. A man I do not like."

"What? That's immoral."

"That is your father's edict. If a woman is not married by a certain age, the priests decide on a mate for her. Sometimes, in multiple pairings. Each year, fewer and fewer children are born and strange illnesses that the healers can't cure take even more of us. And I know I should mate and bear children, but...not to a man I cannot stand."

"I don't want you to do that either. I'm glad you destroyed the tracker. And the one in the lantern too! So, what else do you need?"

"Besides a way out? Just you to talk to me once in a while. I'm used to being alone. I usually am these days when I'm out hunting for crystals. With the sun on my face and birds twittering in the trees."

Hopper noticed a hesitation in her voice. "But?"

"But lately, with the tremors and the daily rains and the thickening clouds covering more of the sky every day, being outside is not as pretty as before."

"Probably because of the asteroid. We believe the light you call the Night Eye is an asteroid heading for your world."

"An asteroid? You used that word before. You said that was a rock in space."

"Think of one as a huge rock—even bigger than the cave you are in—flying through space straight for your world."

"There's nothing out there in space but darkness and the void."

"Eiko, I'm in space. There are a lot of worlds out here—billions of them—some with people, some

97

without."

"We are taught there's nothing beyond our world. There is only us. Our world is the center of all. But you've told me that's not true."

"The teachings are wrong. I'll prove this to you in a few days."

"I have to believe you because you're speaking with me, even though you do not sound the same. Are you really my Hopper?"

"I am. Let's see…how can I prove to you that I am who I say?" He struggled to find the memories. "I know! Do you remember when we were twelve? I made a metal box and lined it with brown crystal bits. In that box, we put a heart-shaped stone I found while we were walking along the river. And a bright red feather you found in a hollow in a tree. You braided a bracelet from yellow-weed stems and added it to our treasure. Then I sealed the box, and we buried it at the base of a rainbow tree on the edge of town just as the sun set."

He heard a gasp. "Hopper! You remembered! You really are my Hopper! I know the truth of that now. And you aren't a figment of my imagination."

"Your imagination?"

"Yes. I thought maybe I'd been badly hurt in the cave-in and that I was dreaming all this up. But how can what you say be true, and the teachings also be true? Are the priests, like your father, lying to us?"

Hopper shook his head hard. "There are many beliefs we were taught as younglings I have found to be…untrue. But don't blame the priests. They go by only what they know. Which is built on what their elders learned from theirs, and so on through history. But if the Masaaki are to survive, they must be open to new ideas and the reality that your world—our world—is not alone."

"I understand what you are saying, but accepting these new realities won't be easy for many."

"I'll face your challenges with you. Don't be afraid of the unknown, Eiko."

"If you're with me, I won't be."

Hopper heard her yawn. "Rest now. You've had a hard day. Tomorrow will be easier."

"Gentle dreams, Hopper. May the Blessed Three guide you through your night journey."

"And you, sweet Eiko." He clicked off the link. Hopper thought about his earlier nightmares about Eiko, realizing now that the awful dreams were jumbles of memories that included the evil ship, his father, Eiko, and other recollections, but not in any semblance of order that made any sense. Now, however, his dreams were much nicer. And centered around his feelings for Eiko.

Hopper recycled his dishes and headed out of his cabin. "Amaya, where are Omar, Katie, Annie, and June?"

"We're right here."

Hopper nearly ran into Omar as he stepped out of the cabin next to Hopper's. He smiled up at his friend. "I'm so glad you and Katie decided to come with us, though I'm still not sure why."

Omar shrugged and ushered Hopper into his and Katie's cabin. "We were in this for the adventure. And being with you is a lot more adventure than hauling supplies back and forth from Pointe Noir!"

Hopper laughed as he studied their cabin. Katie had set the controls to show scenes from the Aboolean home world and had various statuettes and decorations specific to the Warrior Class, including a pair of curved swords that were nearly as big as Hopper was. How tiny Katie handled one of them, he didn't know, but he'd seen her practicing with them. Watching her and Omar spar was like watching an intricate but deadly dance. Terrible and beautiful at the same time.

He thought about his cabin. He had nothing to show who he was. He hadn't had any personal items in his hole on Pointe Noir either. Maybe because he didn't know who he was? He had no sense of connection to anyone or any place.

Except Eiko.

She was his connection. To his past. To his present. To his future?

Chapter Eleven

Eiko cowered under the table as tremors shook the ground. No longer a trickle, water now flowed from the crack in a small stream across the floor of the cave. When she looked up, she saw more water raining down from the roof. From storms outside? Fortunately, the water went away from her spot toward the tunnel opening. No more large rocks fell, but the walls and roof still rained dirt and crystals down.

Her headlamp flickered and went out, leaving her in the dark again. She fumbled around for her lantern, but a rock had fallen on the piece, crushing the light. Eiko took a deep breath and exhaled. "You can do this. Remember what Hopper told you." She opened her eyes and could make out various shapes. Tables, cabinets, and rocks. "Go to the third cabinet and find a crystal. The second shelf from the top holds the white and yellow ones. All you need is a sliver."

When the tremors stopped, she made her way to the cabinet and groped for the crystals, pulling out the smallest one. "They're all too big. Even this one."

She sat on a nearby rock. "Think, Eiko. What do you need to do?" She peered around in the darkness and spotted what she believed was her bag. "Cut one! And I have a crystal cutter."

Eiko hit her head on the table as she grabbed her bag. "Ow! Son of a ground worm!" She rubbed her forehead and ducked down. She opened her bag and fumbled around for the saw, nicking her finger on the blade. "Okay, this is not going well. But I can do this. Hopper would trust me to do this." She snorted. Yes, Hopper would trust her, but she was here alone so needed to rely only on herself, as she had been for a long time. Though she liked having someone like Hopper to discuss different ideas with.

As she worked, Eiko thought back to their earlier years. Back to when they'd been together. She and Hopper had talked about their future lives, about their being together, if only his father would allow them. They'd spent so much time together, everyone expected them to announce their pledge, and they had, but then he'd been taken. Over the years, Eiko had dated other men, but none had ever touched her heart the way Hopper had. But she was out of time. Most women married by age twenty. Certain jobs—like crystal hunting—gave them leeway, but never more than a few years. She'd already gone longer than anyone else. Only her skill as a gifted hunter helped her. But no more.

She secured the smallest crystal on the tabletop and felt for the edges. "I need a sliver. So, what's a sliver? Maybe as wide as my finger?" She laid her finger on the edge and the saw blade on the other side of her finger. "Gently, Eiko. Careful not to chip the crystal. Or saw your finger off!" Maybe she should have put her gloves on. She nixed that idea as soon as she thought it. They may protect her from nicks and cuts, but they were more trouble than they were worth. Thick and inflexible, they made it difficult to manipulate equipment and almost impossible to pick up anything.

A few minutes later, she had a sliver—and several

more nicks on her fingers. A few minutes more and she had light.

"I did it, Hopper! I got light! Thanks to you and your earlier lesson." She checked the original crystal and found a tiny crack near the center. "A crack explains why the crystal failed. I hope the new one isn't flawed."

She wished Hopper was there to celebrate with her, but she didn't dare bother him, especially about a job she could handle. After all, he was a big, important captain of a huge ship somewhere in space.

Space.

The blackness surrounding her home held other worlds and peoples. She had trouble believing that, and yet...Hopper had disappeared in a ship. And he was coming in another one. One that could think and act for herself. Amaya.

Eiko could admit to feeling a touch of jealousy over the connection—the strange, unthinkable connection—Hopper had with his ship. The histories said such a phenomenon was possible only with bonded mates. And no one had heard of this being done for centuries. Not even Nyoko, the high priest who spoke to the Blessed Three, heard their words. He depended on the books from the ancestors. Nobody she knew could claim they heard voices.

Well, not anyone who wasn't under a medic's care.

Was that the problem? Had one of the rocks hit her on the head and she was lying in the tunnel somewhere dreaming all this? Did she need help from one of the medics who took care of people with mind troubles? She didn't feel troubled. But maybe some of them didn't either. Were they able to connect to others' minds and didn't know that's what they were doing?

"Oh, Hopper, I wish you were here. Then I'd know for certain."

Now that she had light, she looked around. "So, what do I do until he gets here? Or until I wake up. Whichever comes first. Okay, Eiko, you're a crystal hunter and you're in a crystal cave. Well, kind of a crystal cave. There are rocks. And you saw the crystals sparkling so you know they are there. Plus, you have an entire cabinet full of polished ones you can catalogue."

She dug out her tools, went to the nearest rock, and flicked on her crystal detector, then quickly flicked the gauge off again as the beeping and needle went wild. "Stupid, Eiko. The cabinet is full of crystals. Of course the detector is going to detect them."

She took out her little hammer and chisel and set them on a table. "You're going to do this the hard way. By hand it is."

Eiko made quick work of cataloguing the cabinet crystals, trying not to let her excitement get the better of her. Blacks, whites, yellows...every color the techs would want and already polished and ready to use. She could live for a year on what she would make from this cabinet alone. Two if she was frugal. Next, she gathered crystals from the floor and stacked them according to color on one of the tables. Then she went to the nearest large rock and studied the shape. "This has to have crystals inside."

Eiko tapped the chisel in several spots, digging away the softer outer shell of hardened dirt and pebbles. Within, she found the largest crystal she'd ever seen. This one alone would get her better furniture. Maybe even a better apartment. Sure, she only got one-fifth of the value, but still...She looked around at all the rocks and did a little dance. Maybe she'd earn enough credits to put some away for those times when she didn't find any. Then she got a good look at the color of the crystal and her joy dropped. Brown. Another worthless brown crystal. Plus, getting the cutting crew to come in here would be a challenge. She'd just have to figure out how to haul some of the polished ones back with her and convince them there were more here.

She sighed. "So much for getting some furniture. But, hey, I'll have enough to keep my apartment for a year, and decent food. Who needs furniture?"

"Eiko? Are you there?"

She ran to the communication unit. "You're back. Are you okay?"

"Yes. Are you?"

Eiko chuckled. "Yes. Kind of. There was another tremor and my lamp got smashed and my helmet light went out, but thanks to what you taught me, I was able to get the light working again. And I found a huge crystal, but a worthless one."

"Wow. You have been busy. Why worthless?"

"The crystal is a brown one. Useless."

"What? No, they're not! They are extremely useful."

"Not by anyone here. All they're used for is as crushed dust for building roads."

"I have so much to teach you! Browns can be used for healing and have other applications. But I've been busy too. Amaya has promised to put on all speed, and we will be there in three days."

"With what I'm finding here, I can handle this for three days. I've never seen such crystals. I'm hoping to find some better colors, but even so, I'll have to have the crystal cutters come here since there's no way I can carry the biggest one out of here myself. Though I don't know if they'll come here. After all, this is in the holy zone. This area is forbidden to all except the highest priests."

"I don't understand. What do you mean?"

"After you disappeared, Nyoko declared the western mountains were off limits to everyone except the priests. That they were the lands of the gods. I thought it was because this was where you disappeared from and he didn't want anyone else to go away, but he and the others come here once a year on a pilgrimage and come back with gifts from the gods. The gifts are supposed to make life easier for us, but they're available only to Nyoko and his followers." She paused and looked around. "I wonder if they've been getting the things from here. Is this the place of the gods? Is that who took you?"

"Trust me, a god did not take me. More like a demon. But those things around you, like the communication unit, are things built by men."

"I heard your father over the communication unit when I first turned the machine on. I think he was talking to some woman. Your Maria, maybe?"

"No. The first we knew about you was when you contacted us. We have definitely not been in communication with my father or anyone else there."

"He is the high priest. Could he have been talking to the gods?"

"I hate to say this to you, Eiko, but I doubt you were hearing the gods. I believe he was talking to someone else there. Aren't there other cities or towns?"

"No. Lawan is the only place."

"That doesn't make sense. There should be more towns or even cities."

"Not that I am aware of. I've never seen anything on

my travels that would even make me think there is another one."

"Have you ever gone past the western mountains? Or any other direction?"

"No. We are given our path when we leave and must adhere to it strictly or face fines."

"So how did you end up here?"

"I, um, like I told you earlier, kind of ran off. I heard that Nyoko was going to announce my mating at a dinner, and I decided not to agree."

She chuckled when Hopper broke out laughing. "You escaped! That's amazing. Good for you!"

Heat suffused Eiko's cheeks. "Thank you. How did your friend Cass do with finding her family?"

"Oh, they are all so happy! Cass and her husband Zack have a three-year-old son, and he has a six-year-old uncle. But her parents…Oh, Eiko, you should have seen their faces when they looked at Cass. You could almost feel the love that's there. And there were others in Cass's crew who had families there too."

"That sounds wonderful."

"Oh, there were some bad moments. Spouses whose lost ones had moved on to others. Adult children who have to deal with their parents having other families. There are a lot of emotions—good and bad—there."

Eiko wished she could see Hopper's face. Tell what he was feeling. "Is that why you wanted to leave so fast?"

"What? No. Coming to the Masaaki home world was always the plan for Amaya and me."

"But…" She could hear him sigh.

"You always did know me too well. Yes, all the…emotions. The last twelve years have been a challenge for me. I was…changed. I guess part of me is still stuck there in the bottom levels of Pointe Noir. If not for my friends…"

"Hopper, we've both changed over the years. Yes, you more drastically, but I still hear *my* Hopper in the way you talk about fixing things. The essence of you has not changed. You still look for challenges or create them or mend them. You were always like that. Part of you changed, but the deep down you didn't."

He paused for so long, Eiko wasn't sure he hadn't left her.

"I-I understand what you are saying. But tell me, did I ever talk about myself in the third person?"

Eiko laughed out loud, the sound echoing off the rocky walls. "Oh, Hopper, don't you remember? We used to mock the high elder in school that way. She always spoke of herself in the third person and when we were out, we'd talk like her. You would be all 'Hopper is unhappy with how he did on the engineering exams. Hopper missed one-half point.' And I would laugh so hard because you had her voice exactly. Why do you ask?"

"I'm not sure I remember that, but my entire time on the station, I spoke of myself in the third person. That didn't change until Amaya fixed me."

"Interesting. I wonder if some small part of you did remember those times and the fun we had, and you were trying to get back to those happier times."

"I suppose that's possible, I guess. Funny, though, how I fixated on that type of speaking."

"Oh! Hopper! Another tremor!"

"Get safe, Eiko!"

Eiko dashed for her cubby hole, ducking as stones and dirt rained down on her. Crawling under the table, she was almost safe when a larger rock slammed into her exposed foot. Pain shot through her, bringing tears to her eyes, and she cried out.

"Eiko! What's wrong?"

"I…it…a rock. A big one. On my foot and lower leg."

Chapter Twelve

Hopper paced his cabin. He could *hear* her pain in the way she panted, the tears in her voice, and they tore him apart. "Eiko, I know you're in pain. Can you move the rock off your foot?"

"I-I don't know. I'm on my stomach. I-I was…crawling."

Hopper placed his hand on the wall of his cabin. "Amaya, all speed to the home world. Eiko's been hurt."

"Yes, Hopper. How badly?" The wall softened around his hand like always.

"I don't know yet."

"Talk to her, Hopper. The crew and I will take care of getting there."

"Thank you, Amaya." He felt the almost immediate increase in power.

"Eiko? How are you doing?"

"I managed to move the rock a little, but not enough. My foot hurts so bad."

"I know. But I need you to think. To concentrate. You're a hunter. You had to have training in what to do when you're in trouble, right?

"Y-yes."

"Good. So, think about your training. What do you need to do?"

"I-I need…to assess the situation, formulate a plan, then execute the plan."

Hopper heard the strength returning to her voice, overcoming the fear. "Assess the situation."

"The hunter has a large rock trapping her foot. Possible injuries include bleeding and bone breakage. Definitely in pain."

"Come on, Eiko. Assess. Think." He wanted to get her to concentrate on something other than her pain.

"The…the rock is too large for her to move by herself. Being alone, she must come up with a way to use what is available and within reach in order to free herself."

"Good. What is her plan?

"Plan? To get out of this ground-slugging cave!"

Hopper laughed. She was angry. Good. Anger meant she wasn't thinking about her pain. "And how is she going to do that?"

"She is…hmmm. I think I might have an idea. I can reach the pipes I constructed for the water. If I direct the water under the rock, I might be able to slide out in the mud."

Hopper shook his head. "No. That could also cause the rock to sink lower. Are there any tools or other items you can use as a lever?"

"Maybe, but not easily from this position."

"Is the rock only on your foot, or your lower leg as well?"

"Halfway up my lower leg."

Hopper looked up as someone knocked at his door. "Come in?"

His four friends stepped through the opening.

"Amaya told us there's a problem?" Katie said.

"Yes. Eiko's trapped in a cave and a rock has fallen on her lower leg. She's in a lot of pain and can't get free."

He turned back to his com-link. "Eiko, I have four friends here. They're going to try to help you."

"How can they help me from there?"

"You'd be surprised."

"Eiko, hi. My name is Annie. I'm a medic. What can you tell me about your injury?"

"There's a lot of pain. Because of the weight and position of the rock, I can't move it myself. I don't think there is serious bleeding, but I'm not certain."

"Okay. We can't do much until we move the rock."

"Hi, Eiko. My name is Katie. Can you tell me what position you're in?"

"Hands and knees, with the rock on the back of my left leg."

"Amaya, can you do a mock-up holo of what she described?" Katie asked.

A figure looking a lot like Hopper appeared on his hands and knees on the floor, surrounded by rocks, one of them pinning down his left leg.

"Except for the rock and her leg, she's under cover of a solid table," Hopper said. "She has a simple pipe system set up bringing her water from a crack in the cavern wall."

"Eiko, are the pipes on your left or right?" Katie asked.

"My left, about half a meter from me." The hologram changed to show the new information.

"Have you made any progress at all with the rock?" Hopper asked.

"I can move the mass a little, but it keeps rolling back before I can get my foot out."

"What if when she moves the rock, even if only a tiny bit, she wedges other stones under the big one to keep the larger one from rolling back?" Omar suggested.

"I tried, but—"

June knelt next to the scene. "There's no way for her to do this without hurting herself more. And if she makes the ground wet, the rock will settle even more."

Hopper studied the scene. "What if she wets the ground just on one side? Would that give her enough leverage to slide out?"

"It would help if I knew the size of the rock in question," Amaya said.

"Circumference is two meters, roughly round in shape, composition—near as I can tell—is solid but not crystal according to my tester. Weight is blessed heavy. What are you thinking?" Eiko said.

"I know from your position you can't use your cutter, so we're trying to come up with a different plan. Give us a few minutes."

"It's not like I'm going anywhere."

Hopper chuckled. "I know, Eiko. We're trying though."

He turned to the picture. "Amaya, put a heavy table over top of the image." One appeared and Hopper walked around the image. The others also studied the holo.

June squatted next to her image. "You said the water is on your left?"

"Yes. I used stuff I found here to bring the water to me, so a mixture of tubes, pipes, channels, and a pan under the end. All held together with rope and shoestrings."

The image changed to show the new information as Hopper held back a chuckle. "Your shoestrings?"

"Well, I used what I had available."

"What tools do you have on hand that you can reach?" June asked.

"A crystal cutter, two chisels, a small hammer. The kind of stuff you'd use to find crystals in rocks. I have other supplies like my food, shelter blanket, change of clothes, first aid kit, and so on. They're all in my bag and I can get that if I stretch...and use a piece of broken equipment to draw it to me."

Hopper studied the hologram, getting increasingly frustrated. He wanted to be there. To help her. He felt so useless stuck here. He startled when Omar put his hand on Hopper's shoulder.

"We'll get this figured out, Hopper. And we'll get there as fast as we can. Amaya and the crew are doing their best."

Hopper nodded. "I know, Omar. I'm just—"

"Frustrated because you can't help someone you care about," Katie said as she came to stand next to him. "I think I might have an idea."

"Oh?"

"Yes. If Eiko aims a thin stream of water under her leg, and only her leg, not the rock. That should loosen up the soil under her leg while still keeping the rock on dryer, more solid ground. Annie, what about injuries? If she does this, could it cause more damage?"

"Possibly. If she's got lacerations or broken bones, pulling out like that could make things worse, but I don't see that we have any other choice."

"Eiko, could you dig a narrow channel for the water and aim the stream exactly under your leg?" Katie asked.

"Maybe. But won't that be the same as wetting all the ground?"

"Not if done right. Give us a moment."

"Amaya, can you show us this scenario?"

"I can, but the information would be more complete if I knew what kind of ground is under her leg and the rock."

"Just a moment. There's another tremor."

Hopper and his friends waited an interminable time for Eiko to get back to them. "It's over. This one wasn't too bad."

"Are you safe?"

"Yes. Not much more came down."

"Can you tell us the composition of the ground under you and the rock?

"It appears to be hard-packed clay, dirt, and stone. Directly under my leg seems to be mostly dirt and clay but packed hard. I've only seen something this hard made by the builders."

"Sounds like that might be a composite of some sort," Omar said. "Like concrete or similar materials."

Amaya adapted the holo.

"She might be able to chisel a channel," June said. "She needs to make sure to keep the groove no wider than her leg. Can you do that, Eiko?"

"Possibly. But I'll need some time."

"It's not like you're going anywhere," Hopper deadpanned and everyone—including Eiko—groaned.

"Okay," Katie said. "You're going to chisel out a narrow channel and aim the water directly under your leg and only there. That might get you enough wiggle room to get your leg out."

"I'll try."

"That's fine. Let me know how you're doing when you can," Hopper said.

"I will."

Hopper turned the unit off and turned to his friends. Katie tilted her head to one side as she looked at Hopper and he knew she had questions. Ones he wasn't sure he could answer.

"You may as well ask," Hopper said.

Katie grinned. "Okay, first one, you've talked to us about her, but who exactly is Eiko and what is she to you?"

Hopper stared out the porthole as he twisted the bracelet on his wrist. "She was...is...my best friend. We grew up together. Were always going on adventures when we were younger. We declared for each other when we were of age."

"That bracelet?" Katie asked.

"Yes. It's a promise bracelet. Like an engagement. Neither one of us ever wanted anyone else. When we were sixteen, we found this cave she's stuck in, and a rogue ship kidnapped me."

"Hopper, what was the name of the ship that took you?" Amaya asked.

"I'm not sure. I think I remember a name like Kamuto. But I can't be certain."

"Maybe Kamodu?" Amaya asked.

"Possibly. Why?"

"There was a personnel shuttle, built like Zara and Kataya and me on a much smaller scale, but they had trouble with him. He was unstable and they were going to remake him, but there was a rebellion. I don't have any records after that."

"He definitely kept saying he had to find the mother ship when he kidnapped me and took off. The pilot links must have been what blanked my memory. Nobody knows how he...we...got so damaged. The engineers assumed asteroids. I vaguely remember that happening, but I'm not sure. Some parts of my memory, especially after being taken and before I reached Noir are still fuzzy."

"What happened to the ship after you reached Pointe Noir?"

"I don't know. I was in a lot of medical centers as they worked to *fix* me. You'd be better off asking Cass. She might know. Why?"

"He was seriously damaged. If he wasn't dismantled, he could have hurt more people like he did you."

"Oh." Hopper couldn't hold back his shudder. "Contact Cass. See what she knows."

"Hopper?" Katie asked as she handed him a mug of tea. "Are you and Amaya still bonded?"

Hopper went to the wall and placed his hand on the surface, smiling when the material softened around him. "Yes, we are. Why do you ask?"

"Amaya, can you get access to the Masaaki home world records?"

"I am not sure. We may still be out of range. Their systems do not seem to be as strong as they used to be. May I ask why?"

Katie frowned. "I'm not sure. Just a feeling I have."

Omar laughed as he wrapped an arm around his wife. "I've learned when Katie has a feeling, you'd better listen."

"I will see if I can access their records as soon as possible. Any idea what I'm looking for?"

"Family records for as far back as they'll go."

"Any line in particular?"

"Eiko's."

Hopper frowned at her. "Katie?"

Katie shook her head. "I can't explain. Trust me?"

"Completely." He rose. "I should go check on the engines."

Katie laughed. "As if every system isn't running perfectly. Right, Amaya?"

Amaya chuckled. "Correct."

"So, the captain isn't even needed?" Hopper said with a raised eyebrow.

"Oh, okay," Katie said. "Go put in an appearance. Crack your captain's whip."

"Join me in the mess hall for dinner shortly?" Hopper asked.

"What do you want? Oh, let me guess, macaroni-and-cheese?" Katie asked with a smile.

"I do eat other foods, you know."

"Sure, you do," Omar said with a laugh. "So, macaroni-and-cheese?"

Hopper grinned back. Not only his favorite, but the one meal he went to when he was upset. "Yes, please. I'll meet you there in twenty minutes."

He showed them out and leaned against the closed door. "Amaya, do you have any idea what Katie is looking for in those records?"

"Possibly. But I do not want to make any assumptions until I am sure."

"Okay. How long until we get to the home world?"

"Thirty-nine hours, sixteen minutes."

"Okay, thanks."

"Help!"

The single word, shouted, then abruptly cut off, was enough to make Hopper's blood run cold.

"Eiko? What's wrong?"

Chapter Thirteen

Eiko watched as two figures dressed in suits covering their entire bodies came through an opening high above the floor. They dropped down long ropes for rappelling and came toward her.

Fear caused her to shiver, but even if these people came from Nyoko himself, they could help her get free. "H-hello? Can you help me? I'm trapped here."

Instead of moving the rock, one reached toward her with a strange hand-held device and held it against her neck. There was a hiss, a brief pain, and she knew nothing else.

When Eiko woke up, she was no longer in the cave, but she wasn't home either. She was in some sort of room. Looking around, she saw a small, barred window high in the wall letting in some light. A grilled vent near the ceiling was the only bit of difference on the pristine walls. The space was bare except for the narrow bed she was on, a table, and a single chair. No rugs softened the bare wood floor, and the walls were painted a dull gray. Opposite her bed was an open doorway and across from the wall with the window was a solid door. A single thin blanket and scratchy sheet covered the thin mattress on the woven metal bed she sat on.

"This looks like a prison cell." Eiko glanced down at her clothes. Gone was her hunter's outfit. Instead, she wore a loose gray shirt and shorts. Bandages covered her leg and foot, and she had some sort of band around her wrist where the hunter band should be. She couldn't get this one off. Using the bed as support, she tried to put weight on her foot, cringing in pain when she did, but at least she could move. "So probably not broken, but badly bruised."

Eiko grabbed the chair and used that to get across to the door, which was locked. "Okay. A disappointment but not a surprise." She had to keep talking to herself in order not to scream.

The open doorway showed her a basic fresher room—sink, toilet, shower. She went back to the bed, sank down, pulled her knees up, and wrapped her arms around them. "Where am I? Am I in prison because I dared to enter the forbidden zone?"

She glanced at the window, then, gritting her teeth, climbed up onto the chair, then up onto the table so she could see out the window. Eiko looked out on a bustling city far below, but definitely not her city. The building across from her had twelve stories! No building in Lawan had twelve floors.

"Where am I?" she asked again. As far as she knew, there were no other cities on the land.

She watched as people bustled about, some of them riding in strange-looking vehicles with four wheels like a wagon, with a canopy, but no animals pulled them. They moved on their own. Everyone she saw wore the same kind of clothing with little difference between men and women—long-sleeved, gray tunics over black trousers. The people didn't stop to chat with one another. They went about whatever they were doing with no interaction.

Eiko hopped one-footed down to the chair, then the

floor, and returned to her bed. "Gray. Everything here is gray, including the people. How awful to live like this. Or are they prisoners too?"

She looked up when she heard a noise at the door. The portal swung open and two people entered. One was a solidly built man who took up most of the space of the doorway. He stood stiffly behind an older woman who held a strange-looking device in her hand.

"My name is Dr. Ryder. You are in the Nightstone Detention Center in Cerule. What is your name?"

"Detention Center? Am I a prisoner?" She had never heard of any place called Nightstone or Cerule.

"Name!" the woman commanded.

"Ei…Eiko."

"You are being held here temporarily until your injuries are healed, then you will be transferred to the Monkoleith Crystal Center. What were you doing in the cave where we found you?"

"I was trying to get out of the storm, and a rockfall trapped me."

"Why were you so far from Lawan?"

The doctor spoke the name of Eiko's town strangely, with the emphasis on the second part instead of the first. So, she was definitely not in her city. "I was crystal hunting and got caught in a bad storm. The cave offered protection."

"Besides your injuries, do you have any health issues we need to be aware of?"

"No." Every time Eiko answered a question, the doctor moved her fingers over the device.

"Since you cannot walk, a guard will bring your meals to you." She turned to leave, and the guard stepped aside.

"Wait! Why am I here? How long will I be here?"

The silent guard followed the doctor out and closed the door, and Eiko heard a lock click. She collapsed back onto her bed. She watched the square of light from the window move across the floor and reach the wall before the door opened again. The same guard as before stomped in and set a tray on her table, then stomped back out before Eiko could even thank him.

"Well, at least they're feeding me," she said to the room. "Not much though." She looked at the meager fare. A nutrition bar, a withered piece of fruit, and a cup of water. "Okay, no worse than a hunter's meal." She bit off a piece of the bar and sat, chewing. The water when she drank tasted funny and a few minutes later, her vision grew fuzzy. She leaned back in her bed, awake, but not able to move as a heavy lethargy took her over.

The guard came back into the room, picked her up and dumped her onto a rolling table, then rolled her out into the hallway. Eiko wanted to jump off and run, but her muscles refused to cooperate. She couldn't concentrate on the turns he took or the number of doors they passed until he pushed her through a doorway into a room filled with counters and cabinets and a half-dozen beds boxed in with curtains. She did see two people in the beds who appeared to be sleeping before the guard once again grabbed her and placed her in one of the beds.

Dr. Ryder and another woman came over to her bed. The second woman started unwinding the bandage around her foot and leg. "Heavy bruising on lower left leg and foot, but images show no breaks," the second woman said.

"Use the scanner to relieve the bruising," Dr. Ryder said. "She's no good to us if she's injured. Use the medium setting this morning, then increase to high this afternoon."

"But—"

"You heard me." Dr. Ryder turned and marched out, leaving the woman behind.

The woman shook her head and returned her attention to Eiko. "My name is Pri. Would you please tell me your name?"

Eiko tried hard to say something. Anything. But couldn't get her thoughts together.

Pri peered at her with a frown, then sighed. "Did your food or water taste odd this morning? If yes, blink once. You should be able to blink."

Eiko blinked one time and Pri sighed again.

"Do you feel like your mind is all fuzzy and you can't move?"

Another blink.

"Okay. I know what they gave you. Just a moment." She glanced around as if making sure no one else was in the room, then held an object against Eiko's neck. A few moments later, Eiko felt almost like herself again.

"Let's try this again. I'm Pri, and you are?"

"Eiko. What is this place?"

Pri smiled at her and Eiko relaxed a little. "This is a clinic. Can you tell me how your leg and foot feel? Can you move them?"

"Yes." Eiko showed her. "But they hurt a lot."

Pri held a device above her leg. "I'm going to help them heal, but you're going to feel some heat. Please try not to move. If the heat becomes too intense, let me know right away."

Eiko nodded and watched as Pri touched some buttons on the device, then held the machine over the worst of her bruises. At first, the heat felt good, but then grew hotter and hotter until Eiko jerked her leg. "That's too hot! You're burning me!"

Pri immediately pulled the device away from her leg, her eyes sad. "I'm sorry. I tried to tell Dr. Ryder this setting was too high for you."

"But I'm no good if I'm injured, right?"

"Yeah. I don't care what Ryder says. I'm dropping this down to low." She reset the device and Eiko flinched. "I promise, this time won't hurt as much."

Eiko tried to relax, then did as the warmth spread but not the burning heat.

"Is that better?" Pri asked.

"Yes. Thank you."

Pri shook her head. "Don't thank me yet. The doctor doesn't like anyone not following her orders."

"I won't tell." Eiko gave her a small smile, and Pri grinned back at her.

"What did you do to get sent here?" Pri asked as she continued to work on Eiko's leg.

She stuck to the same thing she'd told the other woman. "I was crystal hunting and got caught in a storm. I found a cave where I could take shelter, but a rockslide trapped me. Two people came down from a higher tunnel. I thought they were there to rescue me. When I awoke, I was here. Where is here exactly? I know nothing like this place is near Lawan."

Pri's eyes widened, then she shook her head. "Sounds like Seekers found you."

"Seekers? Okay, we have Seekers in Lawan, but I've never seen any of them dressed like these were."

"So, you're one of them."

"Them?" Eiko was getting more confused.

"An Anti. From the other side of the mountain. Funny, but we seem to be getting a lot of you through here lately."

"Anti?"

"Yes. Antis are what we call people from Lawan. Anti-technology, unlike here in Cerule. Your leaders don't allow our technology to spoil their purity." She snorted. "Purity. The only thing pure about them is their greed. Same as Ryder and her friends."

She pulled the device away from Eiko's leg and glanced around again. "I'm sorry. I shouldn't have said that. Please, don't—"

Eiko smiled and touched her hand. "Don't worry. I didn't hear a word. But I have a lot of questions for you."

"I'm sure you do, but if I don't tend to all the patients, we'll both be in trouble. So, how does your leg feel?"

Frustrated at her non-answer, Eiko stretched her foot and moved her ankle around. "Better. Thank you. But what is this device that allows you to heal so quickly?"

"I honestly don't know what this is or how the gadget works. We're given them at the end of our training, shown how to use them."

"It would be nice to have a device like this when I'm out in the field. Hunters get hurt a lot."

"I've noticed. Okay, so, I'm going to let you lie here. You'll get another treatment this afternoon. I don't want to dose you again so, if anyone comes in, please, act like you're still under the influence of the drug. Though you aren't completely healed, the effect from the scanner will continue to work and heal you."

The building shook, and Eiko curled up on the bed.

"That had to be a really strong one to shake this

building. But hopefully, they won't last much longer," Pri said.

Eiko sat back up. "You're getting the tremors here too?"

"Yes. The scientists are trying to figure out a way to get rid of the asteroid but haven't been able to yet."

"Asteroid? I know that word. My friend Hopper told me the Eye is a large rock in space. He and his ship Amaya are going to take care of the Eye when they get here."

Pri gave her a strange look, then shook her head. "Impossible. Spaceships are a myth." She went to the cabinets and put away her equipment.

Eiko wondered at her words but kept silent about Hopper. "Will I be able to leave here when I'm healed?"

Pri shook her head, sadness in her eyes. "I'm afraid you're here permanently. They never send anyone back over the mountains. You'll be put to work in the crystal caves and housed in the general barracks. I really am sorry, Eiko, but you'll never see Lawan again." She turned and left the room.

Shock tore through Eiko. Never see her home again? Sora? Or any of her friends. Tears collected in her eyes and fell. And what about Hopper? Would she ever see him and his wonderful ship?

"Psst."

Eiko looked around for the noise, then jumped as the curtain on her right swished back toward the wall. "Kalani? Is that you?"

She almost didn't recognize the crystal hunter. Her beautiful long hair had been cropped to the point a bare fuzz covered her scalp. Stark white bandages covered her shoulder and arm, and Eiko saw more peeking from under her shirt. "What happened to you?"

"Cave collapse during the last big tremor."

"Didn't they use the healing device on you?"

"Yes, but the temperature was too hot, and they burned some of my skin."

"Oh, Kalani, I am so sorry."

She shrugged her unbandaged shoulder. "I was lucky. Several didn't get out."

"Why are we here? Why have they taken us?"

Kalani shook her head and shrugged again. "I don't know other than to work in the crystal caves."

A noise at the door had her flicking back the curtain. Eiko laid back and pretended to still be drugged. Ryder came in, followed by Pri, and checked Eiko's leg. "Some improvement, but this should be further along. Did you use the setting I ordered?"

"I had to cut the power back. Her skin was burning. If you want her to work in two days, we can't burn her."

Eiko saw the anger in Ryder's eyes and pitied Pri. "Fine. But I'd better see her able to work in two days. We're down too many and need workers."

"Yes, Doctor."

The curtain moved as they went to Kalani's bed. "This one?"

"The burns were as extensive as the initial injury. She will need at least a week of healing and we don't dare use the scanner again."

"A week?"

"Yes, ma'am."

"Send her and this other one back to the cells after the next treatment. They can take care of them."

"Yes, Doctor."

Eiko kept her eyes lowered as she watched them

move to the third bed, the one across from her.

"This one?" the doctor demanded.

"Head trauma. He may need more thorough healing."

"Send him to the city hospital. I don't have time for this. I need workers, not useless bodies."

"Yes, Doctor."

The doctor stormed out, followed by Pri. Eiko couldn't be certain, but she thought she saw Pri turn back and wink at them. Kalani swished the curtain back. Then the man in the third bed sat up and smiled at them.

"Hi. I'm Zema."

Eiko gasped. "I thought… She said…"

He smirked. "Pri is the one person who really does try to help us. I did have a head injury, but not as severe as she led Ryder to believe."

"But I thought Ryder was the doctor."

"She is *a* doctor, but not a healer one. She's a scientist and depends on Pri for medical information."

"What will happen to you, though? A week in the hospital doesn't sound good."

He grinned. "I'll make a miraculous recovery and be sent back to our cell."

"Same with me," Kalani said. She pulled a bandage aside, showing uninjured skin. "Pri really did heal my injuries, but she didn't burn me. Gave me a few extra days to finish healing. We'll probably all be sent back to our cells tonight."

"Does everyone have a cell by themselves?"

"Not here," Zema said. "Eight to a room. Three rooms. You were in a single only until they made sure you didn't carry any diseases. This floor is for those who are injured or sick—not bad enough to send to the hospital, but enough so we can't work. Once we're declared healed, we'll be sent to the barracks outside the caves."

"There's no way out? No escape?"

Kalani's smile dimmed as she shook her head. "No. I'm sorry, Eiko, but you are most definitely not leaving here." She pointed at the band around Eiko's wrist. "That's called a tracker. It works like our Hunter bracelets do. They can find us anywhere with this, but unlike our bracelets, you can't remove this one or turn it off."

Eiko lay back on her bed, tears flowing from her eyes. Then she held back a gasp as a man she recognized all too well swept into the room with the doctor right behind him.

"Minister Nyoko!" Forgetting that she was supposed to be drugged, she sat back up, glaring at him.

He sneered at her. "You thought you could escape your duty? Escape me? You'll not get away this time. I'll make sure of that. You will be sent to the mines."

Anger flowed through Eiko, giving her strength. "You've been lying to us all. Being here proves that. You've known about this place and have been sending our people here to be their slaves. And I know that ships that fly through the air are real. Hopper is on his way here in one. You'll see. Your tyranny is over!"

His eyes went wide, and his fat face rivaled a red crystal in color. "How dare you! My son is dead and gone. It's time you stopped telling tales about him. We'll see how you feel after some time in the red mines!"

There was a gasp from the other patients as Nyoko swept from the room, his robes fluttering around him.

Eiko looked at her friend. "Kalani?"

"The red mines are the worst. People sent there don't do well. It's almost a death sentence. But what were you saying about a ship in the air? There isn't such a thing."

"Not only are there ships, but Hopper is on his way here in one."

"For your sake, I hope it's soon."

"Hopper, I wish I was with you right now!"

Chapter Fourteen

Hopper jerked back as if he'd been stung. *"Eiko? I'm here! Where are you?"* Hopper was hearing her voice, but in his head, like when he mind-spoke with Amaya. They'd arrived in the Masaaki solar system a few minutes ago and were approaching orbit of the central world.

"I've...taken! I don't know...I am...not in the cave ...strange city...prison."

He had trouble understanding her. If they had been using the communication link, he'd think they had static, but this wasn't mechanical. He'd figure out the why and how of hearing her later. *"Are you safe?"*

There was no answer. Hopper strode onto the bridge and took his seat.

"Amaya?"

"Thirty-six minutes. What do you want me to do about the asteroid?"

"How much time do we have before we're too late to stop it?" He drummed his fingers on the arm of his seat as he thought.

"Fifteen hours, forty-three minutes. But the longer we wait, the greater the risk. Already, the ones that have landed have created massive volcanic activity in the northern area of the continent that has led to a thick cloud covering that part of the land. This activity has led to the storms and other atmospheric changes as well as

131

geological changes."

"Understood. Hold off for now. Would you ask Komeko to join me, please?" He looked up as the man strode onto the bridge less than a minute later.

"Amaya says you have questions."

"Yes. About mind-speaking, like I do with Amaya. How close do you have to be?"

"We've never really tested the distance, but usually a mile or two for most people. We do know that pairs can hear each other farther than those not bonded. I believe you and Amaya have done this multiple times at impressive distances."

"True. But what about an unbonded pair from here on the ship down to the planet below?"

He raised an eyebrow at Hopper. "That would be...unusual. Who are you in contact with?"

"Eiko."

"She is special to you?"

"Very."

"That would be the connection then, but the distance is interesting since you are not bonded. Consider yourself lucky."

"I'd like to find Eiko first. Where is the city?" Hopper asked.

"Which one?"

His question took Hopper by surprise. "What do you mean which one? As far as I know, Lawan is the only one. That's what Eiko said. Though I have been gone a long time."

Komeko cocked his head. "In our histories, there were multiple cities on both sides of the western mountains."

"That's true," Amaya said. "And the main one was

in the southernmost area of the continent."

"So I have read," Komeko agreed.

"From what I can detect," Amaya said. "There are currently two populated cities, both of which appear to have been established for longer than you have been gone. Would you like me to display aerial views of them? There are hundreds of others either in ruin, under water, or otherwise abandoned. I can't even find the capital that existed when I was built, though I did find indications of the old city."

"Show me the two populated ones. Side-by-side and a proximity map as well," Hopper said.

All three appeared on the screen. Hopper rose from his seat and approached the view screen. He studied the aerial views of both cities, then the map. "They're on the same continent, but on opposite sides of this western mountain range." He cocked his head. "I know my memory is still spotty, but I don't remember ever hearing about this one on the western side. I lived in the eastern one, next to the wetlands."

"Do you remember where the cave was?" Amaya asked.

Hopper frowned and shook his head. "Not really. Probably in the mountains somewhere, but we were just out wandering around. Who knows where we went?"

"Have you been able to contact Eiko since earlier?"

"We were able to communicate a little, but she hasn't answered since. She said she's in some kind of prison. Earlier, our connection was…difficult. Like static on a com-unit."

"Your description actually makes some sense. There is a lot of electronic noise around the western city. If she's there, that could be why you are having difficulty

133

contacting her."

"But why would she be there? And how did she get out of the cave? There are a lot of questions I need answers to."

"I believe the answers you seek are all on the surface. But do you go east or west?"

"West first. That one seems more technologically advanced. They may know more. I'll take a shuttle down. You figure out the best way to take out the asteroid with minimal damage to the planet." He cocked his head. "Amaya, this is your home world. Does the land look at all like you remember?"

"No. When I left, there were more towns and cities and much more growth. I see a lot of desolation now. Barren areas. Deserts where there were none and more. Plus…there is a small moon missing that was there when I left. I was created there."

"Could the desolation on the planet have been caused by previous asteroids striking the world?"

"Extrapolation…yes."

"And could the asteroid field be what's left of the missing moon? If there was a massive explosion?"

"A distinct possibility. Though I cannot think what would cause such a disaster. But the destruction of a moon would definitely affect the home world ecology, and the continual bombardment by meteorites from the asteroid field would add to the problem."

"So, these two cities could be all that's left of the Masaaki."

"Yes."

Hopper could hear the sadness in her voice. "Then we need to do what we can to make sure they aren't destroyed."

"Agreed. However, I believe before you go down, you should see this," Amaya said. "I was able to access local records and histories and merge them with my records."

"Can you give me the short version?"

"You could be walking into a situation that could quickly go bad. From what I see, the two city-states, although technological opposites, seem to be tied politically, and not in a good way. Those in power appear to be abusing their power through illegal means. Eiko's imprisonment might not have been by accident. I have determined those sent to the so-called holy or forbidden area might have been sent there on purpose."

"For what reason?"

"That is not completely clear, but I do not believe for good intentions. You might be better off doing a nighttime stealth to get Eiko and talk with the leaders later."

"Get the others for me, please."

"What's up, Hopper?" Katie asked over the monitor. June and Annie showed on a second one.

"I need your advice."

"Okay. On what?"

"Amaya's got a vastly abbreviated file for you. Watch the data, please, and talk with her, then get back to me."

Hopper went back to his room as he waited for his friends. Ten minutes later, he let them into his quarters. "What do you think?"

"Amaya's right. If we go down in the shuttle, they'll probably meet us with force—which would not be a problem, but—"

"But could be dangerous for Eiko," June said. "It's

almost sunset there. We'll wait until full dark and take Omar and Katie's ship. Theirs is larger and with the stealth shielding the former owners had installed, we can park close to the city without anyone seeing us. I think this area here would be best." She pointed at a field across from an industrial area.

"When should we go?" Hopper asked.

"What do you mean by *we*?" Omar said. "Katie and June and I will handle this. You're the captain—"

"Don't give me the blasted captain excuse. I may be the captain, but I am still Hopper. Remember me? When someone asks Hopper to find something, Hopper finds whatever is lost. Besides, Eiko is my friend. She may not come with you. Not willingly."

"He's not wrong," Katie said.

"More people means more chance of discovery," June said.

Omar frowned, then nodded. "Agreed, but I don't think we have a choice. When do we leave?"

"One hour, sixteen minutes," Hopper said.

"And there's the Hopper we know and love." Katie grinned. "Omar, June, and I will prepare and meet you at our ship."

After they left, Hopper continued to pace the room. "Amaya, thoughts?"

"One moment please."

Hopper stopped in mid-stride. Her answers were normally immediate. Amaya never asked him to wait. He spun around as a holographic image of a building appeared in his room.

"Amaya?" He glanced up as the door swished open and Omar, June, and Katie came back in.

"I believe this is the building where they are holding

Eiko. I was able to find the schematics in their records. I do find it interesting they are not more advanced than they are. After all, this is the civilization that built me. They should be far more advanced than what I am finding. I was lucky to get what I was able to. Even the people from the *Phoenix* had better linkages."

Hopper walked around the image, studying the details. "Yes, but they've also been through devastating upheavals geologically, politically, and socially. Who knows what all was lost?"

"Agreed."

"Can you give me internal floor plans?" Katie asked. "Floor by floor, please."

Amaya laid them out side by side, and the three of them walked around the areas, studying each one carefully.

"What's their security like?" Omar asked.

"Simple alarms and lock scanners. All based on red crystal."

"Where's the security room?" Katie asked.

A red dot appeared on the first level. "From what I can find out, two guards are in the room and two on each floor."

"Eiko said this was a prison."

"It is, but this is not the main prison building. I believe those are closer to the edge of the city," Amaya pointed out.

"I believe a roof entrance would be the most practical," Katie said. "That area has the fewest guard points."

"Yes, but the hardest to get to," June pointed out. "There's no access from what I can see. We'd have to cut a way in. I know that wouldn't be a problem with your ship, but doing so would cause noise and raise alarms. What about this side entrance on the lowest level? Amaya, enlarge this area."

Hopper studied the layout. "This is the garbage and laundry level. The least guarded besides the roof, and the easiest access. If we use maskers, we should be able to get past the alarms. Nobody cares about trash areas."

"Take a bot with you," Amaya said. "I can connect through one to get you past any security scans and alarms."

"And Katie and I can handle any guards," Omar said. "June will remain on the ship and take care of any problems that way."

"We'll go in through the trash doors, then up this lift to the ninth floor." Katie pointed to the shaft. "This is probably a service lift, not one used by regular staff. Amaya's bot can make sure we're not seen."

"That just gets us to the top level," Omar pointed out. "We still don't know where Eiko is being held."

"I'll find her," Hopper said.

"Let's get there first," Omar said with a gentle hand on Hopper's shoulder.

****

Two hours later, their ship in stealth mode, they landed in the barren field they'd picked out earlier. Dressed completely in black with a black mesh covering their faces, Hopper, Omar, and Katie exited the ship. June flew the ship to roof height, hovering silently over one of the low buildings, invisible to any who might glance up.

Hopper guided the small bot from the com link on his wrist. The machine barely came past his ankle in height and was half that in width and depth. Small enough to fit into most areas, but powerful enough to do what he needed—and more. And light enough to carry in a pack on his back when necessary.

"This way," Katie spoke through their earbuds as she took point. Keeping to the shadows, they didn't see anyone until they got closer to the main building. Two guards stood at the entrance, neither one of them looking especially alert as they leaned against the building, chatting with each other.

Hopper and his friends stood in the shadows across the street from them. "We need to go around to the back of the building," Hopper whispered.

Katie nodded and led the way as Omar watched their backs. They stopped abruptly when Katie held up her hand. She motioned for them to move back, and they flattened against the building.

"Thought I heard a noise." A man's voice came from the alley they would have turned into.

"Yeah, right," another voice said. "Nothin' back here but trash and rats."

Hopper heard a thump and a squeal.

"C'mon, Marsden. It's cold out here and I'm hungry. Break time?"

The first man snorted. "You're always hungry. But yeah, I could use a hot drink myself. Or maybe the new prisoner the doc brought in. She's a looker. Maybe she'll warm us up."

Only Omar's arm across his chest kept Hopper from running out after the guards. He had never experienced such anger. Katie motioned them forward and they moved out. They approached the trash dump, easily found by smell alone. The wide ramp leading down to the lowest level was jammed with large trash bins, giving them plenty of cover, though they really didn't need any. At the bottom, they ran into their first real problem. The trash chute was too small for any of them to fit through, and the larger door was securely locked and too solid for the bot to cut through.

"Give me a moment," Hopper said as he sent the bot through the chute opening. Several minutes later, the door inched open.

Katie stepped through, weapons at the ready. Then she pushed the door wider. "Clear."

Hopper and Omar followed her in, shutting the door behind them. A glance around showed them to be in a dimly lit room taking up the entire footprint of the building. More of the large bins filled the end where they were. Large tubes dropped from the ceiling down to each bin.

"Those look like crystal-based incinerators," Hopper said.

"But if they have these, what's with all the mess here and outside?" Katie asked.

Hopper checked the sealed bins. "Most of these are full. There has to an issue with either the mechanics or the crystals." He set the bot to check. "A lot of them have cracked crystals. They were installed incorrectly." He went to the first one, intent on fixing the problem, but Katie stopped him.

"Hopper, we're not here to fix the equipment."

Embarrassed, he nodded and backed away. "Sorry."

Omar came to them. "There's a series of control panels by the far door and the service lift is to the left."

Hopper nodded and sent the bot to do the job. "I'll have the bot set the service lift to show the car is still on this floor no matter where we are. Also, to disable any alarms and other security."

They waited until the bot beeped green and the doors slid open, then they stepped inside.

"Level Nine," Hopper said, but they didn't move.

"Maybe these buttons?" Omar said as he hit the one labeled 9.

Still nothing.

"Maybe you need an ID chip of some sort," Hopper said. He hooked the bot in, and soon they were moving. Hopper barely kept from pacing the small area as they waited, watching the numbers above the door climb, finally stopping at nine.

Katie and Hopper stood to one side of the opening as Omar stood on the other. A quick glance outside showed there were no guards there, and they stepped out.

"Okay, Hopper, where to?"

Hopper closed his eyes. *"Eiko? Can you hear me?"*

"Hopper? Where are you?"

"I'm coming to get you. A better question is, where are you? What room are you in?"

"When they brought me to this room, I counted four doors before we turned into a corridor, then six doors to our cell."

Hopper closed his eyes and thought about the layout of the floor. "The main corridor has three others on each side that split off. I believe she's in the first corridor."

"Eiko, did you turn left or right when you went to the hall?"

"Left."

"Okay, good. I'll be there shortly. Be ready."

"From here, we need to turn right, go to the hall closest to the lift, turn left, go four doors. But that will put us in direct line to the main lift and the guards."

Katie set her jaw. "Omar and I will handle them. Wait until I signal you."

Hopper nodded. "*Eiko, just a few more minutes. Are you okay?*"

"*Yes, especially now that you're here. There are others here from the city too. Everyone on this floor has been injured or is ill. They're all crystal hunters who disappeared. We never knew they'd been captured. We all have some kind of bracelet on. I was told it's a tracker like my hunter bracelet. And your father was here too! He's the one who has been doing this to us. Sending people here.*"

"*I can't say I'm surprised. But I can't take everyone. First, we have to get you to safety.*"

"*Please, Hopper. We can't leave them behind.*"

He sighed. "*Okay. We'll figure something out. I have two friends with me—Omar and Katie. Do not be alarmed by them.*" He looked up as Katie came back to him.

"Now, Hopper. Hurry," Katie whispered.

Hopper grabbed the bot and dashed after her as Omar dragged a guard through an open door. There was no sign of the other one, and Hopper assumed he'd already been moved. They ran for the corridor and counted four doors.

"Which side?" Katie asked.

"This one, I think." Hopper pointed at the one on the right. He programmed the bot, and the lock opened. Katie pushed open the door and stepped in, followed closely by Hopper and Omar. They all stopped as a young woman stood by the bed staring at them. Two others lay in bunk beds watching them with wide eyes.

"Eiko?"

She nodded. "Hopper? Is that really you?"

He smiled, happiness flowing through him, then fear as alarms sounded. "Now, Hopper!" Katie said.

"Can you all walk or run?"

"They all can except me," Eiko said. "My leg hasn't healed enough for full weight yet."

"Omar will help you. The rest of you, come on."

Omar picked Eiko up and they dashed for the corridors, running back to the service lift. Nothing happened when he hit the button for the lowest floor. Sweating, he hooked up the bot and programmed in the instructions, but the little bot flashed red. Hopper looked at the readout on his wrist. "They've disabled the controls. Reprogramming will take too long." He looked at Katie and Omar.

"We go up," Omar said. "June! Your turn. What we talked about." He set Eiko on the floor in a corner.

"Hopper, you and the others stay back in the corner," Katie said. "Let Omar and me handle this."

He nodded, shielding Eiko and the other two with his body the best he could. Now that he'd finally found Eiko, he wasn't about to let her get hurt again. Their fear was evident in their wide eyes, but especially Eiko with the way she chewed her lip, just like she used to do when she was afraid. He grinned at her.

"What's so funny?" she hissed.

"You. You're biting your lower lip like you always did when you were upset."

She swatted at his arm, but released her lip, then gasped as projectiles thudded into the back wall.

Katie and Omar fired back.

"Cover your ears and eyes," Omar ordered.

They did. A moment later, there was a shudder in

the air and a bright flash that would have blinded them had they had their eyes open.

When Omar touched Hopper on the shoulder, he opened his eyes. "Safe?"

Omar nodded, so Hopper dropped his hands. "We took care of the ones in the hall, but there may be more."

They jumped as the ceiling several feet away from them collapsed to the floor, scattering dust and debris.

"Let's go," Katie said as a ladder came down through the hole.

Eiko grabbed Hopper's arm. "There are other prisoners on this floor. We can't leave them here. They'll hurt them. Please, Hopper."

He looked at Omar who clenched his jaw but nodded. "How many and where?"

"That way," Eiko pointed back toward where she'd been imprisoned. "Seven more, in the first cell, I think."

"Okay. We'll figure out a way to get them safe."

"Take Eiko and the others to the ship. We'll get them," Omar said.

Eiko shook her head. "They won't know any of you. They won't trust you."

Hopper snorted. Almost his same words to Omar earlier. "Okay, come on."

He wrapped his arm under Eiko's, helping her move. They headed for the rooms, passing the unconscious bodies of a half dozen guards. Katie glanced at them, then at Hopper.

"Hopper?"

"I know, Katie. And I understand. Do what you must." He hated that he did understand lives might have to be taken, but he knew doing so was a strong possibility. He trusted Katie and Omar to do what they must to keep them all safe.

Omar blew the lock off the first door as Katie watched their back. Eiko rushed in with Hopper close behind. Seven people stared at them.

"If you want to be free, come with us," Eiko said. "Joran, you know me. We've hunted together many times. Trust me."

The man nearest the door nodded. "Let's go."

"What about the other cell?" Eiko asked.

Omar stared at Eiko. "I thought you said seven total. I don't know if we can handle more."

"Please!" she begged. "We can't—"

Frowning, Omar blew the other lock. "Come on, then. Katie, take Hopper and the first batch to the ship."

Hopper shook his head, ready to argue.

"Captain!" Katie said with a stern look. "Get these people to safety. Come on."

Hopper nodded as he understood his duty. "This way."

They'd barely reached the middle of the corridor before they heard a noise behind them. The lift doors opened, and projectiles pinged off the walls, hitting one of the women. "Hopper! Go!" Katie ordered again.

Two others grabbed the injured woman and helped her along. Hopper got them to the ladder and urged them up. "Please, do not be afraid. I promise you will be safe. Go." He had to ignore the yells and other noise behind them and get everyone to safety. That was his job.

But eventually, everyone was up the ladder. Katie ran back to Omar.

"There's not going to be much room when the rest get here," Hopper said to the group. "Bring the injured woman to this cabin. The rest of you, find a place to stand or sit, just not at the front or in the first cabin." He opened the door to the med unit. "What's your name?" he asked the woman.

"Mayu."

Hopper studied her. "You…you…" He struggled with the memory. "You lived three doors down from me. Your mother made the best shocostas on the block."

Her eyes got wide. "Akino? Are we…am I dead? If I'm dead, why does my arm hurt so much?"

Akino. Nobody had called Hopper that name in a long time. Never since he'd left Masaaki. He hadn't been able to tell anyone that Hopper was a nickname, mostly because he didn't remember. "Yes, I am…Akino. And no, you are not dead. Let me see your arm."

Hopper shuddered at the blood seeping through her fingers. They were wearing little more than shorts and sleeveless tops. Hopper took a deep breath and exhaled heavily. "You're going to be fine." He called one of the other women in. "How steady are your hands?"

"I'm good, sir. Do you need me to sew her up?"

"Sew? No. Here." He handed her the scanner. "Hold this steady at the site of the wound and press this button. Once you've healed the injury, press the button again to turn the scanner off."

The woman frowned. "Sir? I could burn her."

"Not on this setting. She'll be fine. Please, trust me? I need to see to the others."

"Tokay, it's all right," Mayu said. "This is Akino. And no, we're not dead. Go, Akino."

Hopper nodded and headed to the front of the ship. He stopped by the ladder, but no one was there, just a lot of noise. He continued to the bridge.

"Status, June."

"So far, all the fighting is on the inside. Do you have wounded?"

"A few. Minor. Being handled."

She nodded and kept her hands dancing over the controls. "Can you take over the controls?"

"Yes."

He sat down and June jumped down through the hole.

"Amaya, can you hear me?"

"Yes, Hopper?"

"Okay, go into attack mode and help Omar, Katie and June out."

"Understood."

A man poked his head up through the hole. One of the other men went to him and helped him up, followed by two more.

The first one came to Hopper. "Are you the captain?"

"Yes."

"The tall woman in dark clothes told me to tell you be ready in five minutes."

Hopper nodded. "Go back with the others." He left his seat as Katie came up to the bridge. "Go. I have this. Omar and June are on their way with the rest."

Hopper went back to see to the refugees as they kept trickling up. The ship had six berths—the captain's cabin belonging to Katie and Omar, the med unit, leaving four for him to use. He addressed the people. "It's going to be tight until we get away. We weren't expecting others." He pointed to the four empty berths. "Use them. I'll get you food and better clothes as soon as I am able. If any of you have any kind of medical training, there are bandages and equipment in there." He pointed to where

Mayu stood in the opening to the med unit.

Mayu spoke up. "We'll be fine, Akino. Even tight quarters are better than what we had. Go. Take care of what you need to."

He nodded and headed for the ladder, intent on going down as Omar came up with Eiko on his back. He handed Eiko off to Hopper.

"June's right behind me. We're going to do a fast takeoff," Omar said.

As soon as June boarded, Hopper hauled up the ladder and slammed the hatch shut, projectiles pinging.

"Everyone, hold on!" Hopper yelled as Katie took the ship off in a steep climb. Hopper grasped Eiko's hand. She nodded and waved him toward the bridge. "Go. I'm fine."

He stood behind Omar's seat, noting blood on Katie's shoulder. "Katie?"

"Not mine. Are we still in stealth mode?"

"Yes," Amaya answered through the com unit. "But you will need to get to safety soon. The meteor storm is two minutes away."

"Not enough time to get to you," Hopper said.

"No."

Chapter Fifteen

"Did the pirates have any kind of shields on this ship?" Hopper asked. Had he brought these people— including Eiko—on board only to get them hurt?

"Yes, but with the extra weight and the stealth mode, there might not be enough power for shields."

"Take off stealth," Omar said. "Engage shields. Amaya, between you, June, and Katie, we should be able to make our way through the field without too much damage. I'll steer, the rest of you take care of those meteoroids."

"You should move all people away from outer walls," June said.

"We don't have room," Hopper said as Katie and Omar handled the controls.

Omar snorted. "You forget. Pirates owned this ship. Haven't you ever wondered why the inside is so small when the outside is larger?"

"Smuggling holds?" Hopper asked.

"Yes. Take everyone below. Not a ton of room, but those holds have special structures protecting them against problems like this. I'll give you atmosphere, but you'll be cold."

"Understood. You get us to Amaya. I'll take care of them."

He went back to Eiko and the others, who looked at him with a mixture of fear and questions and awe.

"Everyone, we need to go below to specially shielded holds. Although we will have air, you'll be cold. Grab whatever you can to keep warm with and come with me."

"Hopper?" Eiko asked.

"We're going to be right in the middle of the meteoroids…um, what you call the fire lights. Being up here could be dangerous."

She nodded though he knew she—and the others—didn't understand what was happening.

"Everyone, grab blankets, sheets, whatever you can and come with Hopper and me."

Hopper opened the hatch leading to the holds. Rather than climb down the ladder, he grabbed the rails and slid down. The others followed quickly. His breath puffed out white. "I am sorry about this. Sit as close together as you can and wrap the blankets around groups. We should be out of the field in a few minutes." He jumped as thuds sounded through the ship.

"We'll be fine." Eiko smiled, and he relaxed a little.

Hopper climbed back up, leaving the hatches open for some warmth and light. As he left, he heard multiple people asking Eiko who he was and where they were. Was he a god? Were they all dead? Hopper shook his head as he listened to Eiko trying to calm them down. He wanted to stay down there with her, but first, he had to make sure they got to safety.

"Omar?" Hopper grabbed the back of a seat as the ship veered sharply to one side.

"That's the last of them. Between Amaya, June, and Katie, we're in good shape. One hit on the outer aft hatch door, but the inner one is holding. Another hit in the second cabin—sealed and bot taking care of repairs."

"Good. How long to Amaya?"

"Three minutes."

"I might as well leave our guests where they are for now."

"Agreed," Katie said. "How are they?"

"Confused, scared, undernourished, in need of showers and clothes, but grateful to be out of prison."

"Amaya?" Omar said. "Permission to board?"

"Granted. Welcome back."

There was a light bump as they landed in the bay.

"I'll get Annie," June said and took off.

While Omar and Katie took care of the ship, Hopper took care of the guests. He helped Eiko out of the hold and together they helped the others.

"I know you all are confused and probably a little scared," Hopper said as he opened the hatch door and led them out into the bay. "I am Captain…uh…" He wasn't sure what name to use.

Eiko took his hand. "He is Captain Akino. Some of you may remember him as Akino or as Hopper. He is in charge of this amazing ship."

She yelped and shook her arm as did some of the others.

"Eiko?"

She held out her arm and he saw white crystals embedded in a thick bracelet. "These bracelets they put on us. They are some kind of device that tracks where we are. We cannot remove them."

"Amaya?"

Moments later, the crystal lights died out and the bracelets fell off their arms. Eiko and the others stared at the devices and then at him. "How…?"

"Amaya found the frequency they worked on. Her

countermeasures deactivated them." He picked up Eiko's bracelet. "We'll take care of these for you."

"Thank you," Eiko and several of the others said.

Hopper squeezed her hand. "The ship's name is Amaya. She is very nice and helpful. You'll learn a lot about her if you'll come with me. We'll get you clean, settled, fed, your injuries seen to."

"What about the other prisoners?" one woman asked. "The ones in the mines. There are a lot more of us being held."

Hopper shook his head. "One step at a time. We will do what we can as soon as we can. I promise."

Eiko stepped up. "He will do as he says, Demairis. Right now, though, be happy you are safe."

One man gave them a puzzled look. "Where do we sleep? I don't see any beds here."

Hopper forced himself not to chuckle. They wouldn't understand. "This is one of the landing bays." He stopped when he saw more confusion and rubbed his hand over his neck. "I will try to explain more as we walk. Think of this area as a place to, um, park other ships?"

"Like an enclosed wharf?" Eiko asked and Hopper nodded.

"Yes. Like when the river boats had to go into dry dock." They could understand this kind of structure. "What would you like first? Food? Or settling into rooms and getting cleaned up?"

The others looked to Eiko to take the lead. "Let us get settled in and cleaned up first...and maybe some better clothes if you have any?"

"Amaya?" Hopper said.

"I've opened multiple cabins—singles, doubles, and

quads. Bots will deliver fresh clothing according to measurements I've taken, as well as bedding."

"Thank you, Amaya." He saw the group looking around, eyes wide, and Eiko gripped his hand harder. "My apologies. I should have introduced Amaya to you. The voice you heard is her."

"Will we meet her later?" one woman asked.

Hopper smiled. "You just did. Amaya is the ship. She is a living being, simply different from us."

One of the ship's engineers strode by and several people yelped at his lizard-like features. Hopper blew out a long breath. This was not going to be easy. "In space, there are many worlds and many beings, and not all of them look like us." He smiled as Omar and Katie joined him. "For instance, Omar and Katie here are from a world called Aboo. They are members of the Warrior class on their world."

"But…space is empty."

"No, it's not," Hopper said. "But come, let's get you settled. You can choose your cabins. Explanations will wait until later."

"Are we prisoners?"

"Not at all! You are free to roam where you want. Amaya will help you if you get lost. And we will be returning you to Lawan as soon as we can. Oh, and if any of you have any injuries or ailments, our medic will take care of you. We'll get you to your rooms, then meet later in the dining area and explain what we can."

He lifted Eiko's hand. "I promise, you are all safe."

Hopper headed for the exit doors, Eiko's hand still in his. Now that he'd found her, he didn't want to let go. "We have to go up seven levels, but the lift isn't large enough to hold all of us at the same time. I'll take the first six, Katie the next six, and the rest with Omar."

Eiko balked. "Um, Hopper?"

"Yes?"

"The last time any of us were taken to a...lift...we ended up imprisoned by people who said we were safe."

He cocked his head as he thought. Then realized what she was saying. "Oh. I am sorry. Okay. We do have ladders or ramps, but getting to where we need to go is a long climb and may be hard on those of you who are injured."

"Captain?"

Hopper startled at Amaya's voice. She rarely called him captain. "Yes, Amaya?"

"You could take half of them in a smaller shuttle up to the first landing bay. Then they would only have to climb one level."

"You're a genius! Thank you, Amaya!" He turned to Eiko. "Would Amaya's idea be acceptable to you?"

"If you explain what a shuttle is," Eiko said with a grin.

Hopper tried again not to sigh. These people had been through a lot and had no clue where they were or what was happening. He turned as two of their smaller shuttles landed in the bay. *"Thank you, Amaya."*

"You are welcome."

"Those two ships are shuttles. We can get into them and fly to an upper deck. Would this be acceptable?"

"May we see inside them?" Eiko asked.

They all gasped when Omar opened the doors to one of the shuttles and three large felines exited and came up to Hopper.

"The gods! He is one with them! Are we dead too?"

Hopper shook his head. "You are not dead, I

promise. And these…beings are Masaaki, like you and me."

"They're not like any Masaaki I've ever seen," one man said. "They look like the gods."

"If we are with them, and they are with you, then I know we are safe," Mayu stated, and the others agreed."

"Tell you what. How about if I take Eiko and a couple more of you? They can tell you what's happening and when we land, they can let you know they're safe."

"How can we talk to them if they're gone?"

Eiko grinned. "That's one question I can answer. They have a piece of equipment that allows them to talk over long distances. I've used one. That's how Captain Akino knew we were in trouble."

The group looked at one another and with almost silent agreement, four people stepped up. "We will go."

"Good. Come with me." Hopper led the way to the first shuttle, the felines following him. "Find a seat."

Omar joined him and took the controls. "You get them settled," he whispered to Hopper.

Hopper nodded and made sure everyone was secure and noticed the change in the sound of the engines when Omar took off. "At least you should be a little more comfortable than in the holds," he joked to take away some of their tension.

Several chuckled.

"How long will this take?" Eiko asked.

They felt another bump and Hopper grinned. "We're here." He rose and swung the door open, then led the five out. The inner bay doors closed as Omar left through the outer ones.

"Do you all still want to climb the ladder? Or can we take the lift?"

They looked at one another and shrugged, then nodded at Eiko. "We'll try the lift," she said.

"Amaya?"

"Yes?"

"Are we patched into the lower bay?"

"Yes."

He glanced at the five. "You can talk to your friends below. Tell them you arrived safely and are going to take the lift. They can come either in the shuttles or the lift, or the ladder. The choice is theirs."

As they chatted with their friends, Hopper led them to the lift. When the door closed, he could tell their anxiety levels rose by the way they clung to one another. In less than two minutes, they emerged onto the main level.

"This level of the ship has living spaces, the dining area—though you are welcome to eat in your rooms if you prefer. This level also has exercise areas and a medical bay. In your rooms, you'll be able to get clean, find fresh clothing, and more. I need to know who wants what." He cocked his head. "But first, a question you don't have to answer right now, just think about. Who here actually wants to return home? Back to the people who sent you to the prison?"

Hopper saw the puzzled looks on their faces—he was certain they all wanted to return to their families and friends, but what would happen when they did? Would they be sent back? This was something they all needed to think seriously about.

He looked up as the rest of the group, led by Katie, joined them. She and Eiko soon had everyone sorted out and in rooms. Most of them opted for doubles or quads. Hopper was more than glad to let Eiko and Katie take over. He'd had enough of being a captain and being around people for a while. Their anxiety levels might be high, but his weren't exactly on a low level either. He wasn't used to so much…socializing.

Hopper turned to Eiko once she'd finished. "Would you mind taking a cabin closer to mine?"

She nodded and smiled so Hopper led her farther up the corridor, stopping at the door next to where Annie and June were. "This will be yours. I'm here, across the hall and down one door."

Eiko stepped in and stopped.

"Eiko? What's wrong?" Hopper looked around the spacious cabin. Like his, there were two rooms—a living area with sofa, two soft chairs, a dining area and a space with a desk and chair. The second room held the bed, dresser, end table and doorway to the fresher.

"This…this can't all be for me." Eiko turned from one side to the other. "It's too much." She'd always wanted a larger apartment but had never dreamed of a room like this. Only the elite members of their society could afford such luxury. Though her salary was enough for her to live on, there was no way she'd ever earn enough for something so rich.

Hopper took her hand and guided her farther into the room. "This is all yours, Eiko. Honest."

She ran her hands over the furniture, feeling the softness of the sofa, the sleekness of the chairs and table. "Really?"

He chuckled and she bit her lip, thinking he was making fun of her.

"Yes. All yours. You can set the walls to show different scenes and Amaya can play any music you'd like to hear. I want you to be comfortable."

She kind of shuddered, then turned to him with a shy smile. "Right now, I'd really like to get clean. Can we do all the fancy stuff later?"

Hopper blushed, and she loved that she could still embarrass him—at least that part of her Hopper was still there. "Oh, of course! Amaya can help you with whatever you don't understand. I'll see you later."

He stopped at the door, and Eiko wondered why.

"Eiko?" he said softly.

"Yes?"

"I'm glad we found you."

"I am too, Hopper. I am too."

The door swished shut, and she was left alone in the room. Her entire apartment would fit into one corner of this cabin. "Amaya?" she asked quietly.

"Yes, Eiko?"

"Are you really the ship?"

"Yes."

"And Hopper is connected to you?"

"Yes. We have a symbiotic relationship."

She wrapped her arms around her suddenly aching stomach. Eiko wanted to ask if Hopper could ever leave Amaya but didn't have the nerve.

"And we are really in space? Not on the land?"

"Yes. Would you like to see outside?"

"You can do that?"

"Yes." One wall changed from a light tan to the deep blackness of space. A huge planet spun beneath them.

Eiko gasped and stumbled back to the opposite side of the room.

"You are safe, Eiko. This is merely an image of what is outside. The wall is still there."

Carefully, Eiko crept forward until she placed her

hand on the solid wall. "How do you do this?"

"The specifics would take some time to explain. Would you like to see where you live?"

"Yes." Eiko stepped back so she could see the entire wall.

Amaya produced a red arrow at a spot to the right of the image. "I can focus in on just that area."

"Yes, please."

The view shifted as the planet grew until Eiko could make out landmarks, then trees, and buildings and streets, dimly lit in the dark night. "Wow. That's my street. Where I live." She moved forward, tracing her fingers over the street she knew so well. "There's the market where I buy food. And the apothecary. And—"

As she watched, the buildings and land shook. "What's happening?"

"A tremor caused by another meteorite strike. As the meteors hit various spots, they cause the tremors. If the asteroid hits, the shock will destroy most of your land."

"You and Hopper keep calling these…rocks different names like asteroids, meteors, meteoroids, meteorites, but aren't they all the same?"

"Yes and no."

Eiko shook her head. "Another long explanation? I get the feeling all these long explanations will take up the rest of all my lives!"

"Ah, but this is fairly easy. An asteroid and meteoroid are similar in that they are rocks in space. The definition usually depends on the size. A meteor is a meteoroid that has entered the atmosphere of the planet and burns up. A meteorite is one that doesn't burn up and hits the surface of the planet."

"Okay, that's not too hard to understand. Like a

branch of a tree. You have small twigs and larger branches, then the tree. All different names for basically the same object."

"Very good."

The image pulled back out until Eiko saw the asteroid. "That's huge. Can you really stop such a monster?"

"Yes. But not yet. The captain wants to speak to your leaders and the leaders of the city where you were being held before I take care of the Night Eye."

"Why not take care of the asteroid now?"

"I'm not certain. I believe his decision has to do with his father." She paused. "The others are starting to gather in the dining area."

"Oh! I forgot! Can you help me with the cleansing controls?"

"Since you are in a hurry, I suggest a sonic shower. You will remain dry, but the dirt will be removed. Also, you will find fresh clothing in various sizes in the cabinet. There should be something in there that will fit you."

"Thank you, Amaya. You are very kind."

Eiko entered the cleansing area and, with help from Amaya, came out cleaner than she'd ever been. Plus, she found clothing that fit as if made especially for her. A pair of light trousers in medium gray, a cream short-sleeved shirt, and a pair of low-heeled boots, all softer than any material she'd ever worn. How astonishing was this ship and all the wonders it—no—she—could do. And Hopper was the captain. In charge of the people and partner to Amaya. How could she—a low-level crystal hunter from a backward town with false beliefs—ever compete with all this? Hopper would never want to stay with her in Lawan.

But then...did she? Go back to her tiny apartment and the rules and regulations set by Nyoko?

Not really. But what would she do if she stayed here with Hopper? She was a crystal hunter. There probably weren't a lot of places here to hunt.

Feeling somewhat depressed, Eiko answered a knock at her door. "Come in."

The door opened, and she saw Hopper. But not her Hopper. This man stood straight and tall, in a crisp uniform with an air of authority. No, this wasn't Hopper. This was *Captain* Akino.

He held out his hand to her, a shy smile on his face all Hopper. "Hungry?"

"Yes." She joined him, figuring as long as she had at least a part of him, that was better than nothing. Life without him had been...not exactly boring, but not exciting either. Hopper's curiosity had always brought a spark of excitement to her life.

Hopper escorted her to a room even larger than the largest religious gathering room in Lawan. Tables lay in rows, nine seats to a table. She counted enough tables and chairs to seat more than 900 people! Her friends sat at two tables and several other people—crew and guests?—filled even more, but nowhere near the entire area. She recognized Hopper's friends Katie and Omar as well, though they had changed to more casual clothes. Eiko also saw several of the others frown and draw back when they saw Hopper. She didn't realize what was wrong at first, then understood. The uniform. The guards at the prison wore a similar one.

Hopper led her to a seat at the first table. One other seat remained open, and she assumed for him. After she sat down, he remained standing. "I'd like to welcome everyone. I am sorry we had to meet under such conditions, but you are welcome here and free to roam where you want, though I would suggest staying away from engineering as some of the equipment in there can be dangerous to the uninformed. Do any of you have any questions?"

Eiko snorted and Hopper grinned at her. "Okay, let me rephrase. Do any of you have any questions that won't take multiple courses of study to answer?"

"How long will we be here?" one man asked.

"We will be returning you to your homes in the morning," Hopper said. "We thought it best not to disturb your families in the middle of the night."

"And you're not going to keep us here?"

Hopper drew back. "Absolutely not."

"He's not one of the guards," Eiko said. "Honest."

"But the uniform…"

Hopper shook his head. "This is only a captain's uniform. Look at the other crew members. They wear jumpsuits or ship suits similar to yours. They are not prisoners, and I am not a guard."

One of his engineers stood. "The captain's right. We all chose to be here. We were given the chance to leave the ship a couple of weeks ago and we didn't. Plus, we all signed up for this trip of our own free will. And we are free to leave if we want to once we're back in our space. Or wherever we want. The captain is no more a guard than you are." Her words calmed most of them down.

"Hopper?" Eiko asked. "Amaya showed me that we really are in space. Above the planet."

"Yes."

"So where is the roof of heaven?"

Hopper blew out a long breath. "There are many stories you've been told about space, not the least of which is that there is a roof. There is not. At least, not one anyone has ever found."

There were gasps and grumblings from several of the people.

"Space is just that. Space. There are millions of planets and billions of people out there. Not all of them look like us. And not everyone is friendly," he said. "But the beings we have on this ship are. They are explorers who wanted to see what was beyond their worlds, so they came with me on this adventure. Amaya was built here on Masaaki over 3000 years ago. She and her sister ship got as far as the system where I ended up before they ran into trouble between two warring factions. The other ship was destroyed and Amaya nearly so. She went into sleep mode and did not awaken until my friend Cass found her and woke her."

"Why is Cass not captain?" Eiko asked.

"She is. But of another ship like Amaya."

Eiko saw Katie motioning to a long counter at one side of the room, and Hopper nodded. "But other explanations will wait until later. I don't know about you, but I could use some food." All of them nodded, but Eiko could still see questions in their faces—and she had about a million herself.

With help from the crew members and guests, everyone soon had food and drinks.

"Eiko, would you like to try one of my favorites?" Hopper asked her.

"I guess."

He went to the wall, as she'd seen others do, and

talked to the opening. "Baked macaroni-and-cheese, makindo salad greens, and for dessert, rainbow fruit."

"I don't know what any of those foods are, but I trust you."

When the meal appeared, Hopper gathered their dishes on a tray and took them to their table. "What would you like to drink?"

Eiko shook her head. "You took care of food, let's see if I can handle drinks."

He grinned at her as she strode over to the wall.

"Amaya," Eiko whispered.

"Yes?" Her answer was equally soft.

"Let me know if I'm doing this right."

"Yes."

She spoke louder. "I'd like two bottles of Shokarian ale."

A moment later, two bottles of her favorite drink appeared in the slot. "Thank you, Amaya."

"You are welcome."

Eiko carried the bottles back to their table and handed one to Hopper. "Do you remember this?"

He eyed the drink with a grimace. "I remember how sick I got after drinking that."

Eiko laughed out loud, and everyone glanced at her. "That's because you drank five of them!"

Katie and Omar joined Eiko in her laughter.

"You, Hopper? Drunk?" Omar said with a chuckle and turned to Eiko. "Katie and I owned a bar on Pointe Noir, and we could never get Hopper to even take a sip of one of our brews. Now I guess we know why!"

"What was he like on this Pointe Noir? Is that where you all are from?"

Omar shook his head. "No. Katie and I are from a

planet called Aboo, but we live on Pointe Noir—a space station. The other crewmen are from other places."

When Eiko and some of the others frowned in confusion, he elaborated. "Hmm. You can think of Noir as kind of like a huge building, but in space, not on the ground."

"Bigger than this ship?" Eiko asked.

"Yes. Pointe Noir is like a city. There are about 7500 beings who live there and hundreds more who come through every day on their way to other places. There are shops and restaurants and a hospital and more on Pointe Noir as well as apartments where the people live."

Eiko turned to Hopper. "What was your apartment like?"

She watched as his face turned red. "I, uh, didn't have one. I kind of lived…in the areas where most beings didn't go. I wasn't comfortable being around people."

Not have a home? She didn't understand. Even the lowest Masaaki had at least a room to live in. "What did you do?"

"Hopper was a fixer," Omar said. "He could fix whatever needed mending. A lot of people, including Katie and me, depended on him to repair what was broken. Or to find what was needed or lost."

Chapter Sixteen

Hopper appreciated the kind words from his friend. What he'd been on Pointe Noir was so far removed from what he was now. And yet, a lot of the old Hopper still remained. He wondered if he'd ever completely accept what had happened to him and the changes Amaya had initiated. "I did a lot of odd jobs for a lot of people."

"So, a lot like the Hopper you were before you disappeared," Eiko said with a laugh. She turned to Katie and Omar. "He was always tinkering. Always fixing, always curious. Well, when his father would let him."

"Your father wouldn't let you do what you wanted?" Katie asked.

Hopper stared at his plate. "My father was… difficult." How could he explain to them the relationship between him and his father?

"His father is a dictator," Eiko exclaimed. "He was bad enough when Hopper lived there and he's even worse now. He would have me mated to Syeth, a man more than twice my age and who is known to have violent proclivities. He was also responsible for sending us to the other city as prisoners."

"Why as prisoners?" Katie asked. "What did you do to cause that?"

Eiko snorted. "Defied him."

Hopper watched as several of the others nodded to Eiko's statement. Great. What was he going to find when he finally returned home? A family who welcomed him? Or someone who could still make him feel like a failure just because he didn't want to follow the family line of being a priest? He'd bet on the latter.

But he was no longer a youngster who could be cowed by a hard man. He was stronger now. Or at least he wanted to hope so.

"Eiko, how do you like your macaroni-and-cheese?"

She gave him a slight smile, as if she recognized the change of subject for what it was. "The taste and texture are…different from foods I've had. Gooey inside, but the top is crusty. I do like this rainbow fruit ice though. Who's the cook and how do they create the meals so fast and make them appear in the little hole?"

Hopper chuckled. "I don't think you're ready to hear about nutrient paste yet. But you can ask Amaya to make whatever you want, as long as she knows what the dish is. Even your mother's Nolinda cookies."

"Really?"

"Amaya?"

"Coming up."

Hopper rose and went to the wall. A moment later, there was a ding and he pulled out a plate full of cookies. They were nearly as large as his hand and filled with nuts and fruit and coated with a sweet crust. He sat the plate on the table in front of Eiko and grabbed one of the treats for himself. He watched as Eiko took one and bit into the cookie, her eyes closed as she tested the flavor and texture. Then he nodded at the others to help themselves, which they did.

Eiko smiled and opened her eyes. "They are exactly like my mother's! But how?"

"It took me a while to figure out the recipe. Amaya

had a similar one in her database, and we went from there." He cocked his head and stared at the cookie. "It's funny now that I think about this. I didn't remember anything about you or my life on Masaaki, but I remembered these cookies. Or I remembered wanting to make something like this."

Eiko finished off her cookie. "Well, you got them right. But where did you find catanya nuts? Even the grocer has trouble finding them this time of year."

Hopper chuckled. "I'll show you later. Is everyone satisfied with their meal?" he asked the group.

All nodded or said yes.

"When you're done, place your plates, utensils, and any leftovers over there." He pointed at a red door in the wall. "It's a recycling bin, and Amaya will take care of the stuff."

"But…she shouldn't have to look after us," Eiko said. "We can wash our own utensils and put them away." Hopper shook his head, and she gave him a wry grin. "Let me guess. Another one of those wonders you'll explain later?"

"Yes. I apologize to everyone. I know this is confusing and strange. But you're doing quite well. When you're done, you're free to explore, use the recreation center, or go back to your rooms. If you want to watch a show or listen to music, Amaya can set you up with whatever you want."

"Are you sure this isn't the ninth level?" one woman asked. "Because this sure seems like heaven to me!"

Most of them laughed as they filtered out of the dining area. Hopper turned to Eiko. "What would you like to do?"

"Can we go to my room and talk?"

He nodded, then the ship shook. "Amaya?"

"Nothing important, Captain. A small meteoroid took me by surprise. Hit the lowest landing bay. Repairs are underway."

"Are there any more around us?"

"No. I have extended sensor range to a wider area than before. A strike will not happen again."

"Okay, thank you. As long as you're okay."

"I am."

As Hopper walked with Eiko to her quarters, he wondered how and why a meteoroid had gotten through Amaya's defenses. The fact one had bothered him more than he could say. *"Amaya? Are you really okay?"*

"Yes, Hopper. The damage was minor and is already nearly fixed. But I am concerned as to where the meteoroid came from. I was tracking all the ones connected with the asteroid. Wait a moment, please."

Hopper stopped outside Eiko's door. "I apologize, but I should check on what happened. Can we talk later?"

"Of course." She entered her room, and he watched as the door shut, then spun on his heel and headed for the bridge.

"Maria?" he asked when he got there.

"It came from the planet, Captain. And I don't believe what hit us was a meteoroid."

"She is correct," Amaya said. "The makeup of the projectile is not the same as the surrounding meteoroids. Plus, the object is too spherical in shape. I believe this to be constructed."

"They attacked you? Who? Where did the shot come from?" Anger filled him. They'd tried to hurt Amaya!

"The city where we rescued Eiko and the others. Because of their supposed lack of advanced technology,

I was not watching for an attack from the planet. I will be more vigilant. Do you wish me to return fire or merely take out any further projectiles?"

"Take them out, as close to the planet as you can. I want them to know they will fail."

"Understood."

Hopper took care of several other minor issues like maintenance schedules and supply lists until the third shift arrived. "Hi, Micaela."

"Captain. Anything I need to know?"

Hopper told the young man about the earlier attack and what they were doing. "Amaya will take care of any further projectiles. If necessary, call me."

"Aye, sir."

He headed back toward Eiko's quarters.

"Hopper?"

"Yes, Amaya?"

"She is asleep."

"Oh. Okay. Thank you."

He switched directions and went to his room, unbuttoning his tunic as soon as he entered and heaving a long sigh of relief. "I really hate wearing this uniform. And from the sounds of our guests earlier, they aren't comfortable with the style either."

"I understand. This is what our people wore in the past but may not be appropriate now. Perhaps a more casual look would work better."

"Agreed." He pulled off his boots and stowed his clothes in his closet, pulling on soft trousers and a shirt like most people on the ship wore. "Have you heard any other grumblings from our guests?"

He knew Amaya was monitoring them, not an idea he was comfortable with, but a security necessity.

"Nothing of any importance. Mostly just anxious to be home. Although some of them are talking about not returning, though they have nowhere else to go."

"Unless they want to stay with us. We could offer them berths and maybe jobs here. Did any of them go exploring?" He stretched out on his bed, hands clasped behind his head.

"A few checked out the recreation room, but nothing beyond this level. Most went to their rooms and to bed."

"What about their health? Is there anyone we need to be concerned about?"

"Two. One has multiple scars and old injuries that must be giving him some discomfort. The other has a lung parasite making breathing difficult for him at times. Left alone, he would be dead in six months. Since he is in a room by himself, I took the liberty of lacing the air of his room with a dose of an anti-parasitic that Annie recommended. But by itself, my remedies will not be enough to eradicate the problem. Annie will talk to him about a stronger dose. And she took care of other minor illnesses and injuries."

"Good. Thank you. We'll talk to the other man tomorrow and see if he wants us to help him. Is there anything else?"

"Do you know yet what you're going to say to the leaders of the cities?"

"No. I'd like to talk to our guests more about what happened to them first. I have an unsettling thought the two cities are more connected than we believe, and not in a good way, especially if my father is involved."

"You believe Eiko's town is providing the other town with people for workers in the crystal mines."

"That's what the people we freed said."

Hopper sat up. "Hmmm. I have an idea. Amaya, are Omar and Katie still up?"

"Yes."

"Ask them to join me, please."

He rose and paced for the five minutes needed for Omar and Katie to join him.

"What's wrong, Hopper?" Katie asked.

He blew out a sigh. "I have an idea, but I'm not sure about the morality."

Katie and Omar sat on his sofa. "Tell us."

"Both Amaya and I know there is collusion between the leaders of both cities. That they aren't as separate as we think."

Omar glanced at Katie, who nodded back. "Omar and I have been having the same conversation. But... I think you need to bring Eiko in on this. She could give you more insights."

"I'm not sure I want to wake her. She's had a rough few days."

"That may not be a problem," Amaya said.

Chapter Seventeen

Eiko woke in the dark, disoriented and not sure where she was. Then she remembered. "Amaya, low lights please?"

The lights came up and Eiko was once more amazed at the wonders on this ship. For instance, how could she handle more than one request at a time? She was built to hold hundreds of beings, what if they all wanted something different at the same time?

"Is something wrong, Eiko?" Amaya asked.

"I don't know. Not physically, but I am troubled by my thoughts."

"Ah. If I may be so bold. I believe you might like to join in on the discussion currently occurring in the captain's quarters."

"Are you sure? I'm not part of his crew."

"I am sure. Please, join him. I think your presence there would help."

"Okay." She got dressed and crossed the corridor to Hopper's quarters, then knocked on the door. When the door opened, she saw Hopper sitting with Omar and Katie.

"Eiko? Are you all right?" He rose immediately and went to her, taking her hands in his.

"Yes, and no. When I woke up, Amaya said I might be of some help, but I don't know why or how."

"Looks like we're going to be here awhile," Hopper

said as he led her to a seat. "Drinks and snacks?"

"I'll get them," Katie said. "Bring Eiko up to date on our discussion."

Hopper did. "Amaya, bring up the topographical map of the two cities and the mountain range between them." He rose and studied the mountains. "Amaya, we know there are caves in these mountains. Are there any tunnels connecting the east and west sides directly?

The view changed and Hopper saw lines going through the mountain as if he was looking down from above. Most of the ones with access from the outside ended without connecting from one side to the other. But one did not end.

"This one." Hopper traced the line. "Is this a current geological image?"

"Yes, though the last tremor has caused some blockages. They are not massive and would be easily dug out."

He pointed to a large space near the western end of the tunnel. "I'll bet this is the cavern where I found the ship and where Eiko was trapped."

"Most likely. There are several other tunnels leading off that area, though most are not continuous to both sides."

"What about concealed doorways? Do you detect any?"

"Just the top one where you and the ship emerged. Though, unless they were mechanical of some sort like the one at the top, I would not be able to detect them. Manual ones would not show up on my sensors."

He turned to Eiko. "Do you remember seeing any openings that might resemble a door?"

She shook her head. "But I wasn't looking for one.

I was looking for crystals and thought I would leave the way I came in. I do know Masuru disappeared through one higher up, but I couldn't get to that one."

"Masuru? You used that name before. Who is he?" Hopper asked.

Eiko grinned. Something she knew that he didn't. "He's the mountain feline who rescued me from the pack of dogs and led me to the cave."

"A mountain cat?" Katie asked, her eyes wide as she stared at Hopper. Eiko noted that he nodded back to her.

"Oh. Like the ones you have here on the ship. But…I know this is a large ship, but where have they been? I haven't seen them around since we got here." She looked at Katie. "Felines are sacred to the Masaaki, and Masuru did help me, so I trusted him."

"I'm glad you did. They are special, though not gods. The others are keeping to themselves for now."

Hopper went back to studying the lines on the map. "Here. This one. And this one." He pointed at one on the eastern side of the tunnel and another on the western. "Eiko, do you remember where you entered the cave?"

She closed her eyes. "I was caught in a storm and looking for safety, so any entry would have to be at ground level."

The line Hopper had traced from the tunnel toward Eiko's side of the mountain changed from red to blue. "Amaya, give me a side view with elevations of these three tunnels along with the cave where Eiko was."

The view shifted and Eiko came up and studied the image. "How are you doing this?" She grinned. "Let me guess. Another long explanation." She held up her hand when Hopper opened his mouth to explain. "Don't bother. I think we'll have plenty of time for explanations when we have this all figured out." She touched the lowest line. "I believe this is where I came in." She moved her finger up. "And this one is where I saw the other people before they…put me to sleep."

"Amaya, are there any other ground level tunnels opposite the one Eiko entered from?"

The image changed again. "I believe this is what you're looking for." She showed a tunnel that was blocked off but connected the floor of the cavern with the upper tunnel in a winding slope. "Since they came in the upper one, I surmise the lower one is most likely blocked by rocks from all the tremors."

Hopper glanced at Eiko. "When you were in the cavern, was there a lot of dust on the equipment?"

She cocked her head, then shook it. "No. And there should have been, shouldn't there? I mean, there was after the tremors, but not before."

"Yes. And if you remember, there was none when we first found the cavern either."

"So, someone has been using the place," Omar said. "Keeping it clean. But why weren't you and Eiko caught when you first went there?"

"They weren't expecting us. I guess they don't have the sensors we do. But, if what I believe is true, they heard Eiko over the com-unit so knew where she was and went after her. As they did the others who were caught."

"But why?" Eiko asked. "And who is doing this?"

"Eiko, who sends you out on crystal hunts?"

"The orders come from the supervisor. I believe he answers to the Council of Three."

Hopper glanced at Omar and Katie. "The Council of Three is made up of one member from each of the three ruling branches—the bureaucracy, the religious orders, and the sciences. But the religious order has the highest authority. He is the head of the council and, although each has a supposedly equal vote, none have ever gone against the head. Unless that's changed since I've been gone?" He turned to Eiko.

"No. And even more so since your father took over the seat. He rules the council like he did your family."

"But would they be willing to work with those in the other city?" Omar asked. "I mean, they seem diametrically opposed."

"Are they?" Hopper paced the room, hands behind his back. "I know my memory is still fuzzy in some areas, but when I lived at home, I seem to recall my father having a room he kept locked. My mother told us the space was his workroom and we must never go in there."

"Which means Hopper did exactly that," Eiko said with a chuckle.

Hopper grinned. "Yes, I did. I remember now. The room was filled mostly with scrolls and some books, but there were also some strange machines I didn't understand at the time. I realize now that one of them was a communication unit. An old one, but still… Anyway, while I was there, I heard my father coming and hid in the shadows behind one of the shelves. And I heard him talking to someone who wasn't there. The other person was arguing that they needed more people, and my father was claiming they had to be careful because too many going missing was getting noticed."

Eiko frowned. She'd already told him about this. Was this part of his memory problem? "Anyone who goes into the western areas seems to disappear. Never more than a couple a year, but lately, there have been a lot more. There were two before me last moon cycle and another four the cycle before."

"And nobody questioned their disappearances?" Hopper asked.

"When we did, they gave us non-answers. Like, 'We're looking into the situation.' Or 'They've been sent on an extended mission and won't be back for some months.' If we asked where they sent them on these extended missions, they gave us vague directions to the north or south, never the west."

"That's what they're doing, then," Hopper said. "They're sending crystal hunters over to the other city where they're taken as prisoners to work in the mines."

"But why them?" Katie asked. "Especially if Lawan needs them?"

Eiko shrugged. "Who knows more about crystals than crystal hunters? And there's more. Four of the people we brought back with us supposedly died in the last illness that went through Lawan."

"What happens to the people who get ill in Lawan?" Hopper asked.

"They take the sick ones to a special building so they don't spread the sickness to others. If they pass to the ninth level, we are told, but we're not allowed to see them or attend to them. We are told the bodies were taken care of safely. However, very few ever come back out. And those taken to the building are rarely youngsters or the elderly."

"Which means they're probably not sick but are taken away."

"Other than those, you have no other physical proof someone specific is doing this," Katie pointed out. "Just supposition and the word of those who could be considered dissidents. You cannot act on supposition alone."

"How do we get proof?" Eiko asked. "I mean, four of us saw Nyoko there and he threatened me, but anyone looking into this would take his word over mine. I'd be labeled as mind-sick and sent away—probably to Cerule anyway. Why would our leaders do that to us? I mean, I can understand the people of Cerule not wanting to work in the mines, but how does Lawan benefit? Our birth levels are already so low, and we lose more every year to sicknesses our healers can't help."

"I don't know," Hopper said. "Amaya, do you still have the frequency I used with Eiko?"

"Yes, but I don't think that's going to be the right one. When you spoke with her, no one else interrupted."

"When I first spoke with Maria, she had me move the knobs before her voice became clear," Eiko said.

"Do you remember which way you moved them?" Hopper asked.

"Toward the back of the machine."

"Amaya, check the higher frequencies and see if there are any communications."

"Yes." A few moments later, Amaya pinged him. "I have the frequency, but we were too late to catch more than them signing off. Now, there's nothing but static."

"Okay. So, we'll get our proof another way." He turned to Omar and Katie. "I have a job for you."

Omar grinned and cracked his knuckles. "I have a feeling I'm going to like this one. Which one do you want us to kidnap?"

"Dr. Ryder was the one who seemed to be in charge of everything," Eiko said. "Pri said she wasn't a medical doctor, but she was the one who gave the orders."

Amaya brought up a photograph of a woman in a gray suit with short hair slicked back and a frown. "Is this her?"

Eiko peered at the picture. "Yes. A little younger, maybe, but that's her."

"I believe taking the doctor from the western city and landing in the midst of Lawan where my father is would work best. And maybe an aide or two for insurance."

"The doctor and the secondary head of the sciences department are listed as living in this building." Amaya added the picture of a large, bald man and then a nine-story building. "This is across from the prison. A rooftop entry seems best as they both have apartments on the top floor."

"Thanks, Amaya," Katie said as she studied the drawings.

"I'd also prefer to keep casualties to a minimum." Hopper grinned at Omar.

"Can I hit them?"

Hopper chuckled. "Yes, but only as necessary to get the job done."

"Let us get a couple hours of sleep. We'll go in just before dawn."

"How long do you think you'll need to get them?"

"Give us five hours," Katie said. "That will give us time to sleep and then go in."

"We'll meet you at the central pyramid in Lawan in six hours—and twenty-two minutes," Hopper added. Omar laughed and nodded. "If you run into any trouble, call me."

"Aye, Captain." They left the room, leaving Hopper and Eiko there.

"Hopper? What are you doing?" Eiko asked.

"We are going to kidnap the doctor and her aide, take them over to Lawan, and speak with my father."

"What of the other hunters who are in the main prison?"

Hopper cocked his head. "Amaya, please ask June to join us."

When she did, Hopper noted she was still dressed all in black. "June, I have a special assignment for you."

One eyebrow raised. "Oh?"

"Yes. I need you to make a prison break."

She gave him a wide-eyed grin.

"Take whoever you want with you. Omar and Katie will be with me."

"Timing?"

"Whenever you're ready."

She nodded once at him and strode out, a wicked smile on her face and whistling low.

Eiko stared at Hopper, a bemused look on her face. "This should be interesting. When did you become so...devious?"

"I think I always have been. But especially when the people from Cerule took you. I will not forgive them for that."

She touched his arm. "I'm here, Hopper. Safe. In this amazing ship. I'd say the situation worked out for the best."

He clasped his hand over hers. "But if we hadn't been... Oh, Eiko. I don't even want to think."

Eiko turned to him, wrapping her arms around him. "But you were." She reached up on tiptoes and kissed him, and Hopper tingled all the way to his toes and back up again. He enfolded her in his arms and returned the kiss in full.

When she pulled away, he felt as though she'd taken part of his soul with her. "Eiko?"

She shook her head. "We'll save that talk for another time. Let's take care of this mess first. Okay?"

He wondered how she knew what he was going to ask. He wasn't even sure what he'd planned to ask. Just that he wanted her with him. He'd lost her once already, and even though he hadn't remembered her on Pointe Noir, he'd always felt like a part of him was missing from his life. And she was the missing part, along with his family. He knew that now. They'd lost so much time—time they could have been together.

He watched as Eiko settled onto his sofa, then smiled and motioned for him to join her.

"We will celebrate that we found each other, and we are together here and now. The future will sort itself out." She took his face between her hands and leaned forward for another kiss.

The unexpected pleasure coursing through Eiko's body made her shiver with want. The idea of kissing Hopper—or doing more—settled in her thoughts the minute they touched. She wasn't a shy young teen anymore. And neither was he. But he was the captain of a spaceship and she…was a crystal hunter. Still, the way he held her and kissed her was too good to give up. She'd take what she could get for as long as she could.

Eiko lay back on the sofa, bringing Hopper with her. As their kisses deepened and became more urgent, she could feel his hardness at her belly. He wanted her. As much as she wanted him.

"Hopper?" she breathed against his cheek.

"Yes?"

"Bedroom?"

He rose up, supporting himself with his arm. "Are you sure?"

"More sure than I ever have been."

He stood and held out his hand to her. She giggled when the lights dimmed. "Um…she won't be watching us, will she?"

"No."

Hopper led her to his bed and sat down, pulling her to stand between his knees. "I have waited a lifetime for you, my Eiko."

"And I you." She pulled off her top, then stepped back and undressed the rest of the way, enjoying the way his eyes lit up as he studied her from head to toe. Thanks to his medical people, she no longer had any bruises or other indications of her earlier injuries. She reached over and undid the fastening on his shirt. As she did, he grasped her hands and raised her arms as he leaned forward.

Eiko melted in his grasp and opened to his touch. She wasn't a novice at physical relations. But something else happened too, not merely on a physical level. Almost as if they'd joined physically, mentally, and spiritually. She felt closer to him than she ever had to anyone.

When she could breathe again, she turned to him. "Hopper, that was amazing."

"I know, Eiko. Did you feel the…I don't know…"

"The joining?"

"Yes! Exactly. Our joining."

"I've heard of this, but no one I know has ever had this experience."

"We belong together, Eiko. We are one and will

183

always be." Hopper touched her face with a look of awe.

"I believe you, Hopper, but even though we were young together, we are from such different worlds now. There are many obstacles in our path."

"I am your mate as you are mine. Nothing—neither space nor my father—will keep us apart. We'll figure this all out."

He pulled the blanket up over them and settled down to sleep, but she lay there in the dark, wondering how they would move forward. She couldn't go back to Lawan, not after what had happened and with what she knew now. And she wouldn't go to Cerule. Maybe there was another place—another city she could go to? After all, if they'd known nothing about Cerule, there could be other cities they didn't know about. Maybe hidden ones. Or she could stay here on Amaya, even though that would also mean leaving everything and everyone she knew behind, though what exactly was she leaving besides her few friends? And even if she did leave with Hopper, with Amaya, they could visit her friends and his family.

After she was certain Hopper was deeply asleep, Eiko carefully climbed from the bed, grabbed her clothes, and tiptoed out to the living room. She heard the light ding of the catering unit and went over to find a cup of her favorite hot tea waiting for her. She leaned her hand against the wall, startled when the material softened around her hand, like a mother's hug.

"You are as much a part of him as I am. Maybe more," Amaya whispered.

Eiko pulled back and the wall let her go. "How is this possible, Amaya?"

"You have bonded with him, and thus with me

through his bond with me. But there is more."

"What?"

"You, Eiko, are my descendant. Your family line is mine."

"But...but you're a ship."

"A ship built upon Masaaki genetics. When I was created, my makers used the genetic material of one of the chosen. The chosen one for me was your ancestor. Thus, we are of the same family. I believe this is why you were able to mentally speak to Hopper from such a distance. And with the bonding, the link should now be even stronger."

Eiko took her tea and sat down in one of the chairs. "You are my ancestor?"

"Yes."

"Eiko?"

She looked around as Hopper came into the room, rubbing sleep from his eyes. "Are you okay?"

She smiled at him. "Yes. Amaya has discovered that I am her descendant. We are from the same family."

"What? How is that possible?"

Amaya explained her creation to him as she had to Eiko minutes before.

"That's amazing!" He went to the wall and laid his hand there, smiling when the material softened under his touch. "I am so happy for you, Amaya. We both found our family."

"We did."

"Come. Let's go back to bed." Eiko came to him and took his hand, but he tugged her to him.

"I don't think I'm quite so sleepy anymore. What about you?"

Eiko giggled. "I think I could be persuaded to stay

awake a bit longer."

"Amaya. Time?"

"One hour, twenty-six minutes until you meet up with Omar and Katie."

"Thank you."

Eiko and Hopper spent the next hour showing each other how awake they were.

Chapter Eighteen

"Hopper, this is Omar."

"Go ahead, Omar."

"We have our…guests and are on the way to the rendezvous point. Sixteen minutes."

"Understood. Any problems?"

Omar snorted. "Easier than kicking out the drunks at the bar on Pointe Noir."

Hopper chuckled and looked around for Eiko. He watched as she combed out her long hair, then braided the strands with gold ribbons and wound the braid into a knot at the back of her neck. She was beautiful to him, and not just her body, but her soul as well. Amaya had produced a knee-length, deep gold sleeveless tunic over black trousers, with low boots, similar to his outfit. Black and gold bracelets circled her wrists. She looked like a regal queen.

"You look amazing. Are you ready?"

"Yes. What are we going to do?"

"First, we're going to join Omar and Katie on their ship, then we're going to go down to the city and intimidate them to the ninth level."

"What about the others who were captured with us?"

"I have two shuttles and crew who will fly them down. There isn't enough room in the plaza outside the pyramid for all three of us, so I'm going to have them land closer to the river."

Eiko cocked her head as if thinking. "Amaya, can you bring up a map of the city?"

The image appeared on the wall. Eiko studied the graph, Hopper standing with her. "Instead of the river, have them land here." She pointed at a spot at the southern end of the city. "It's a large field where we grow wind tubers, but they've already been harvested this time of year so the field will be empty. From there, they have but a few blocks to the pyramid. Landing by the water would be three times farther away."

"Amaya?"

"Coordinates given to the crew. Liftoff in seven minutes."

Hopper nodded and fastened his uniform. "Well?" he said as he stood in front of her.

Eiko brushed his shoulder. "You look very…commanding."

Hopper snorted. "I hate this uniform."

"Maybe, but I would think twice about arguing with you in that outfit. Five minutes."

He led the way to the lift. Three minutes later, they boarded Omar's ship. Hopper led Eiko toward the front. Both Katie and Omar wore full Warrior gear—fitted crimson trousers, sleeveless high-necked tunics in black with red trim, gold arm bands and beaded headbands around their foreheads. Hopper didn't see any obvious weapons, but he knew each of them probably carried an arsenal hidden in their clothing. He grinned at his two best friends. "Nice outfits."

Omar grinned back. "Only the best for Amaya's captain."

"Our guests?" he asked Omar.

"In the rear cabin. The doctor is rather…vocal about

her incarceration, as is the man. The other woman is too scared to do more than just sit there. Especially with Grainer watching them."

Hopper chuckled, then explained to Eiko. "Grainer is one of our cargo specialists. He's as big as, if not bigger than Omar and is a beautiful shade of blue with black eyes and no hair and solid muscles. And his people believe in wearing as little clothing as possible so you can see the definition of their bodies. But he is also one of the gentlest people I know." He turned to Omar. "I hope you have backup for him—someone with a weapon?"

"Johnny B."

Another chuckle from Hopper. Johnny wasn't much bigger than Hopper was and wiry, but he was also a member of the Aboolean warrior class, though not a full warrior. But close enough for Hopper to trust him.

"They have light binders on all three and mute collars on two of them. We had to bind them to keep them from attacking us. And trust me, you do not want to hear what that woman or her aide is saying."

"Understood. Are the shuttles ready?" Hopper hated the use of mute collars. They looked like pretty necklaces but had a small forcefield affecting the person's ability to speak. They weren't painful or dangerous, just…awkward.

"Yes."

"Okay. Let's go." There was a small bump as they took off. "Omar, can you give us outside view toward the planet?"

Omar grinned. "Freddie, view screen one, please."

"Yes, sir."

Eiko jumped. "Is this ship alive too?"

Omar shook his head. "No. But Freddie would like to think he is. Freddie, meet Eiko. Eiko, Freddie is the AI—that means artificial intelligence—who runs our ship. Unlike Amaya, he is not the ship, but he is an integral part."

"I am pleased to meet you, Eiko, even though I am merely an AI."

Hopper and his friends snorted at the snobbish tone coming from Freddie, then Hopper saw the confused look on Eiko's face. He sat beside her. "Think of him this way. The city has a system of streetlights and wastewater pipes underground and other pipes that bring clean water to your apartment, right?"

"Yes."

"And all those systems are run from the services building, right? By one of three controllers—machines that take care of each system."

"Yes," Eiko said.

"And yet, if one of the controllers breaks down, someone comes in and replaces the old one with a new one."

They all heard a rude sound coming from the speakers and everyone but Eiko laughed.

"I apologize, Freddie, but this seems the simplest explanation."

"Humpf."

"Freddie is like those controllers, but all in one. He controls all the systems in the ship, but if he breaks down, he can be, um…"

"He's saying I can be replaced," Freddie snarked. "Much as I hate the idea, he's not wrong. I am merely another part of the ship. Amaya *is* the ship. No matter what happens, she cannot be replaced. Parts may be replaced, but not her. Like you with your organs. You can replace a heart or lungs or other parts, but not your brain or your soul as some say. Not who you are. Were you to replace that, you would no longer be you."

"I think I understand. But you are very personable."

"Thank you."

"Landing in ten…nine…eight…" Katie finished the countdown and they bumped.

Hopper blew out a hard breath. "Okay, then. Have Grainer and Johnny bring up the prisoners and let's go."

"After you, Captain," Omar said. Then he put his hand on Hopper's shoulder. "You should have a more Masaakian name than Hopper. What about using your given name?"

"Akino. I guess I can do that. What names should I use for you?"

"I am Warrior Katrianna and Omar is Warrior Omarikaru."

"They fit you."

Omar grinned. "And Akino fits you. Eiko, you'll stay with Katie and me. And remember, Akino, you are the captain of a massive, powerful ship. You have two Aboolean Warriors at your back. Be the captain I know you are."

Hopper dropped his chin to his chest for a moment, then lifted his head, pushed his shoulders down and back, and became Captain Akino. "Open the hatch."

"Aye, sir."

They strode down the ramp, stopping at the bottom. A dozen guards armed with spears and small handguns faced them.

"I am Akino, captain of the ship Amaya. These are my aides, Warrior Omarikaru and Warrior Katrianna.

Who is in charge here?" He emphasized the word warrior in each name.

A man wearing a brown uniform stepped from between the armed guards. Hopper watched as his gaze went to Eiko and his eyes widened. "I am General Oakai."

Hopper barely held back a snicker. "*Amaya, I don't know if you can hear me, but I believe his name means demon.*"

"*Not exactly, but close enough.*"

"*Okay, we can hear each other. Good. Let Omar and Katie know.*"

"*Done.*"

"General Oakai, I would like to speak to the Council of Three, especially Nyoko."

He shrugged. "I'm sorry, but they are not available. They are on a trip."

Hopper sighed and shook his head. "Oh, General, I was really hoping we wouldn't start off with trouble like a lie. We came as friends."

"And yet, you have one of our citizens in your custody, and others in restraints." His eyes widened when he saw the doctor. So, the general knew who she was.

Hopper reached back and took Eiko's hand, and she stepped up to join him. The general's eyes widened once more.

"You were supposed to be…" He sputtered to a stop.

"Captured, General? Taken prisoner and used as a slave? I am bonded mate to Captain Akino and no longer the prisoner of the Ceruleans." Eiko sneered at him. She glanced around as the others from her group arrived from the shuttles. "Nor are these others. We were freed from our prison by Captain Akino."

Hopper watched as the general's face went from red to white. Then he stood taller as other guards joined his group, forming a line between Hopper and the pyramid.

While they talked, dozens of the city's citizens arrived, watching the events from the safety of side streets, eyes wide, some of them dropping to their knees and praying. One citizen in particular made her way through the throng, heading straight for Hopper.

"Akino! Akino!"

Katie moved to stand between Hopper and the woman. Hopper touched her on the shoulder. "Katie, relax. She's my mother."

The woman skidded to a stop in front of him. "Akino! Is it really you?" She reached up to touch his face. "You're alive. How? Where have you been?"

His mother! His heart pounded as he grasped her hand. "Questions that will have to wait a bit longer, Mother." He watched, reluctant to release her hand, as Eiko pulled her aside and stepped behind him.

"Thank you, Eiko."

He turned his attention back to the general. Even more guards had joined them now, and more crowds kept gathering.

Chaos erupted when one of the prisoners broke her bindings, pulled a weapon from her trousers, and shot Eiko, then aimed at Hopper before anyone could stop her.

Chapter Nineteen

Shots erupted from the guards and Omar and Johnny returned fire as Katie and Grainer hustled everyone into the ship.

"Eiko!" Hopper dropped to his knees, grabbing Eiko. She winced, her eyes wide as red spread from her shoulder.

He looked up as Omar took control. Johnny had the doctor who had shot Eiko on the ground.

Katie knelt next to Hopper and scooped Eiko up. "C'mon Hopper! Get into the ship!"

"She's... Katie!"

Omar grabbed him and pulled him into the ship behind Katie and the others, slamming the opening shut as soon as they were in.

Pain flooded Hopper at the thought of losing Eiko now that he'd just found her. Then rage. He shot up and strode over to Johnny. He had the doctor back in binders, heavier ones this time, and all her pockets turned out. Hopper grabbed the gun from Johnny's belt and aimed it at the doctor.

Katie emerged from the med unit and stopped him by standing in front of the woman. "Hopper. Don't."

"She shot Eiko."

"I know. But this isn't the way." She grasped Hopper's hand and gently took the gun away. "Please. Trust me. This is not the way."

"Johnny." Katie angled her head toward the back.

"Yes, ma'am."

Before Hopper could move, Johnny hauled the doctor toward the last cabin where Grainer stood.

His mother came over to him. "Your friend is right. You are not meant for violence. Don't be like your father."

That stopped Hopper cold, and he took a deep breath and nodded. He felt the ship move, but they weren't lifting. And he could hear Omar and Freddie shooting. But he didn't care about any of that. He cared about Eiko. He went to the med unit where Katie was at the sink washing blood from her hands. Eiko's face was so pale, and her eyes closed. She looked...dead and Hopper nearly died there. "Katie?"

"She's going to be okay, Hopper. I promise you. I got the projectile out and the unit is healing the wound and providing fluids. She's sleeping right now. She needs to heal. But she will be fine."

Hopper collapsed into a nearby chair and dropped his head into his hands. "I thought..." He blew out a long sigh. "How did the doctor get loose? And where did she get a weapon?"

Johnny came in and dropped two knives and another gun onto a tray. "We stripped them down. Found these in a shielded pocket on both the doctor and the man. The other woman was clean. I'm sorry, Captain. I should have checked them earlier."

Katie was shaking her head. "Not your fault. Omar and I should have checked. We didn't."

Hopper sat up and looked at his friends, noting the pain on their faces. "It's nobody's fault. We weren't expecting something like this. But now we will be." He felt the ship increasing power and knew they were finally rising.

Several minutes later, he felt the bump as they landed on Amaya. Annie and two med-techs came on board and disconnected the med-unit. The techs wheeled Eiko out as Annie turned to Hopper. "We will take the best care of her. I promise."

"I know you will. Thank you, Annie." He turned to the others. "Thank you all. Once you have Eiko settled, I'd like a meeting in my quarters with all of us. I presume the prisoners are secured?"

"Yes," Johnny said. "Omar, Grainer, and I will take them to the brig. We'll make sure they can't cause any more trouble."

"Thank you."

Hopper rose and followed Annie to the medical bay where he saw the techs checking Eiko over. She was still sleeping, but he touched her hand and found it warm.

"She's so pale."

"That's from blood loss," Annie said.

"Is she in pain?"

"No. She'll be awake in about a half hour. She'll be fine, but she should take it easy the rest of the day."

"Let me know if there's any change."

"I will."

With one last glance at Eiko, Hopper turned and strode from the room and headed toward the brig on the lowest level but before he got to the end of the corridor, Omar caught up to him and gently turned him back toward his quarters.

"I want—"

"I know what you want. Not going to happen."

Hopper glared at him. "I'm the captain of this ship.

Who are you to tell me what I can and can't do?"

"I am your friend. And right now, I know exactly what you're feeling and what you want to do."

"How could you know!"

Omar stopped in the corridor and stared at him. "I know. Trust me."

Hopper saw the sadness on his face, and he understood. Omar really did know. Something like this had happened to him at one time. "I'm sorry, Omar."

They entered his quarters where Katie and his mother were laying out snacks and drinks. Katie handed Hopper a mug. "Sit. Drink this."

"Is everyone…?"

"Everyone's been taken care of," his mother said. "You have nothing to do but see to yourself and think of Eiko. When she wakes up, you don't want her to worry about you, do you?"

Katie sat on the sofa next to him and wrapped her arm around his shoulders. "Here's what we know." She told him the same things Johnny had said. "Now that we know what to look for, we will be more careful in the future. Plus, we've worked some things out with Amaya for extra security when we go planet-side. This will not happen again."

"Was anyone else hurt?"

The others glanced at each other, then Katie shrugged. "None of our people were."

Hopper heard a hesitation in her voice. "But?"

"The reason we didn't take off right away was because the guards were firing on the people we freed with Eiko. We did what we could as they ran for the shuttles, but several did get hurt, a few seriously. They are in the general sickbay and are being taken care of.

And there's more."

"More?"

"Amaya, show us the brig," Katie said.

Vids of the three cells showed on the monitor. They all wore standard shorts, tank tops, and slippers. Hopper noted the doctor who had shot Eiko was sporting a sling and had bruises on her face. The man also had some bruises, though not as bad as the woman. The other female seemed unhurt as she curled up in a corner of her bed. The man sat on a bench, eyes closed. But the shooter paced her room like a caged feline, growling and yelling at the guard who stood outside the cells.

"Do you, um, want Annie to heal them?" Katie asked.

Hopper snorted. "No. Let her feel each and every one of those bruises. And thank you to whoever…took care of her. What about the guards?"

Omar looked him directly in the face. "Quite a few of them went down. We don't know how many or how seriously, but I don't think they'll be so quick to fire again."

"Okay, so what do we do next?"

"We go back down," Omar said. "But with Amaya visible this time. I can extend the ship's shields to the end of the ramp, but no farther than that. With Amaya in full view, she'll make sure no one else fires on you. She'll keep weapons at the ready."

Hopper ran his hands through his hair, making it stand on end. "This isn't exactly the homecoming I was hoping for."

"But it's the one you have," Katie pointed out. "So, we deal."

"Okay. Omar, land back in the plaza and keep your

shields at maximum."

"What about the prisoners?" Katie asked.

"They'll remain where they are for now. I've had enough surprises for one day." He looked up as Annie and Eiko joined them. He rushed over to Eiko and led her to the sofa. She was so pale, but she was alive. "What are you doing up? You're supposed to be resting."

Eiko glanced at Annie. "She told me that as long as I take it easy for a couple days, I'll be good." She pointed at her dark blue tunic and loose pants. "That woman ruined the outfit Amaya made for me. It was the nicest one I ever had."

Hopper startled back. "She shot you! And you're worried about clothing?"

Katie chuckled. "Don't worry, Eiko. Amaya can manufacture a new one for you."

"Good. So, what are we doing?"

"You should be going to bed," Hopper said.

"No. I will not let them dictate what I do any more. I want to show them that I am stronger than anything they can throw at me. Please, Hopper. I need to do this."

He blew out a long breath, partly in frustration, partly in admiration. "Fine. But don't go beyond the bottom of the ramp."

"Yes, sir." She gave him a cocky grin and Hopper just sighed and shook his head.

"Might I suggest that we also fly the shuttles and other smaller craft around as a show of extra power?" Amaya said.

"Good idea. Do it." Hopper glanced around as Komeko joined them in human form. "You're coming?"

Komeko nodded. "Yes. If this is to be our new home, we need to know what is going on. So far, we do not see anything to recommend this place to us."

"Give us time," Hopper said, though he did understand Komeko's position.

"Okay, then. Let's go."

This time, when they left, the weapons Johnny, Omar, and Katie had were much more visible. Each one wore a sidearm and had several large knives and throwing stars in their belts. Hopper knew they probably had a lot more hidden as well."

When they left the ship, there were far more soldiers to be seen—in the streets, and roofs of buildings. Hopper knew these weren't the people who'd hurt Eiko, but he wouldn't put it past them to try something.

Omar and Katie stood on either side of him, Johnny behind with Eiko and his mother.

"Well, General, here we are again. I ask that your soldiers put down their weapons. We are here in peace, even though we were the ones fired upon. Now, where are the members of the council? Specifically, Nyoko?"

"He is not available."

"You're going to continue to insist that?" Hopper grimaced and shook his head.

"Not available," his mother snorted. "He's probably cowering in his office."

"Well, they have five minutes to come out here," Hopper said.

"Or what?" the general blustered. "You would threaten me? Against my army?"

Hopper glanced up as a half-dozen shuttles of many sizes descended to just above the city, circling the plaza. "I have support."

The general stared at the ships. Even though Hopper knew they were nothing more than empty shuttles, they still made an impressive display.

"You may have many flying vessels above us, but we will not bow to threats." His voice had gotten hoarse, but he stood his ground. Hopper had to give him credit. He was either very brave—or very stupid. Or maybe under duress?

"Threats? You were not the one fired upon. We were." Hopper glanced at the ships above him. "If so many ships bother you, I can take care of that. I believe Amaya here is plenty of security for me and my friends." Knowing Amaya was listening, he flicked his hand, and the shuttles all flew away leaving just Amaya hovering above them, her shadow covering the entire plaza. The crowds scrambled away, crying in fear. But a few stood their ground, and Hopper could see the amazement in their faces. The realization that what he said was true.

"As I said, General, only one ship."

He looked past the general as two men and one woman, dressed in long hooded robes signifying their stations, came out of the building. Hopper studied the person in the black religious order robes. *"Amaya?"*

"From my scans, I believe the one in the middle has his hands bound. He is not here by choice, plus, he carries an explosive device."

Hopper grimaced. *"I can't say I'm surprised. Can you disarm the device without detonating it or harming him?"*

"I believe so. The device is crystal based and if I get the right frequency, I can fracture the crystal."

"You might want to disarm the guards as well."

"Agreed, but that may take a bit more. Very few of them are crystal based."

The hooded man jerked and the guards with him

frowned, then shrugged as the general glared at them.

"General, I believe you will find that your bomb has been neutralized. Now, if you are done with these games, please bring out Nyoko. You have to the count of five or Amaya will begin doing more than neutralizing your bomb."

The woman wearing the red robes of the science section stepped forward, her empty hands held out. "Forgive the general, Captain Akino. Sometimes the military thinks attack before tact."

Hopper disliked this woman on sight. He was quite certain she was the one who'd ordered the general to do as he had. He gave her a short head bow. "Madam?"

"Dr. Jolene Neevo at your service. Nyoko is on his way."

"Hopper," Eiko said. *"Don't believe her. She is a close friend of your father's. She's as bad as he is in some ways."*

"Understood. Thank you."

Hopper thought he saw a resemblance between her and the doctor in the brig. Sisters? Definitely relations of some sort.

"You will forgive me if I don't quite believe you. You now have three minutes. And Warrior Katrianna will go with your general to make sure he is coming."

"Oh, that is not necessary," the woman said.

"Actually, it is." Hopper nodded for Katie to go. She gave him a short nod and strode forward. Several guards stepped in front of the general.

With a combination of swift kicks, punches, and a swirling body Hopper couldn't even follow, Katie had disarmed all six of them without even breaking a sweat. She was amazing to watch. "She is one Aboolean

Warrior. Her husband is just as formidable. So, General, if you will please produce Nyoko?"

The poor general glanced at the doctor, who frowned but nodded. "Fine."

Hopper watched Katie and the general walk away, then he turned to the doctor. "Now I believe Nyoko will come out."

"I will forgive your…impatience if you'll forgive my curiosity. Did I hear you say the name of your impressive ship is Amaya?"

"Yes."

"According to ancient texts, many millennia ago, our world had such a ship. Is this one by any chance a descendant?" the doctor said.

"I am not a descendant!" boomed from the clouds before Hopper could answer. He held back, interested to see what Amaya would say or do. "I am and always will be Amaya. And I have had enough of this. You, Jolene Neevo, and your sister Holly Ryder, are descendants of Kamodu. You and your ancestors have damaged this world. Because of your inadvisable experiments, your ancestors destroyed the moon on which I and others like me were created. You are the cause of the tremors and the destruction. Your descendants stayed in power through intimidation and abuse. According to my records, you are much the same."

"*Amaya?*" Hopper asked. *"How is she responsible for the asteroid?"*

"Watch."

"That's a lie!" the doctor gritted out. "Our work makes life better."

"Only for you, but you are about to become a victim of your own perfidy. Or rather of your ancestors." A hologram appeared in the clearing next to Hopper's shuttle. As Hopper watched, a ship much like Amaya but on a smaller scale aimed a beam at a small moon and destroyed the orb. In so doing, the blast destroyed the ship as well and created the asteroid field. The scene changed to one on the planet with panicked people fighting to get onto the two other ships. In the background, soldiers fired on the people. Finally, the two ships took off as meteors began pelting the planet.

Once again, the scene changed as Amaya showed aerial pictures of the two cities, divided by the mountain range.

"Much of the land was devastated by the initial strikes. The actions that started this all, led by your ancestors, caused the deaths of millions. The populations split into those who wanted nothing to do with those who had caused the destruction, and those who wanted to continue to build on their experiments. Only a rugged mountain range and an uneasy pact between the leaders keeps the two of you separate. A pact that has led to kidnapping, abuse, and more. Your sister Holly uses prisoners sent to them by you and your cohorts as slaves in the mines."

Hopper looked up as Katie came out of the building with a struggling older man. Even with all the years between them, Hopper recognized him instantly. "Father," he sneered.

Chapter Twenty

"Patience, Captain," Omar whispered. Hopper nodded but kept his eyes on Nyoko as Katie escorted him across the open area. They stopped by the general.

"You hold one of our citizens," his father said. "Release her."

Hopper turned to the people behind him. "Which one? My mother or my bonded mate? Or maybe some of the others we freed from the Cerulean prison? I do not hold them. They arrived of their own free will."

"Her," he pointed at Eiko. "She is a blasphemer who disobeyed a direct order from her spiritual leader."

"You mean when you ordered her to marry Syeth, a man more than twice her age? How much tithing did you make him pay for you to agree to that disgusting match?"

When his father moved to go to them, a tiny beam struck the ground in front of him, sending up a fountain of dirt.

"I'd stay where you are, Father," Hopper said. "Eiko is Amaya's descendant, and she would not take lightly to you harming her."

Katie and Omar moved closer to Eiko behind Hopper. He glanced at his father. "And I wouldn't even make a step toward my people if I were you."

"*Captain, June reports a successful raid. There was little resistance and Annie is tending to the injured. I will send the shuttles down to bring the prisoners up.*"

"Take care of them."

"We will."

"You are not my son!" Nyoko shouted. "You are an abomination. My son died years ago. You are nothing. A danger to us all. You speak lies. There is no ship that moves through space."

Hopper looked up at Amaya. "And yet, there she is." He glanced at the people they'd rescued with Eiko. "Were you in space with me?"

Every single one of them stood strong and tall. "We were. Captain Akino rescued us from their prison, healed our injuries and illnesses. Showed us amazing machines and wonderful food. Captain Akino speaks the truth. And they showed us the Night Eye and what is causing the tremors and storms. And the gods travel with them!"

That had people looking at each other and whispering. Then the ground shook, unbalancing everyone. Buildings shook and pieces of them fell to the ground. The people in the square huddled together, away from the buildings, some of them falling to their knees and screaming prayers.

Nyoko gave Hopper a sneer. "See what happens when you doubt the gods! We need to pray more. Blasphemers like you all are the ones who cause the trouble. You need to pray! To believe more. Your lack of faith brings the evil rain down upon us!"

Hopper shook his head sadly. "You are more delusional than I believed, Father. You can go ahead and pray, but the solution will come from me. Amaya and my crew will take care of the asteroid. Now, Amaya."

A powerful burst of light streamed from the ship, aimed at the asteroid. A minute later, they watched as a shower of meteors burned across the sky. Amaya decimated the larger ones, letting the smaller ones burn up in the atmosphere.

"The Night Eye is gone?" Eiko asked, awe in her voice.

"Yes. There will be no more trouble from the Eye," Hopper said. "Though there may still be more tremors."

"Our prayers have been answered!" Nyoko shouted.

"Yes, by me. A blasphemer and Amaya, a ship from space," Hopper said.

His father sneered at him. "By the gods! Through our prayers!"

Hopper shook his head. His father wouldn't accept what was in front of him. Then he had an idea. What if he took several people up with him? Would his father go along?

He studied the one remaining council member. "Would you like to see what is above?"

The woman nodded, though fear definitely showed in her wide eyes. He led her into Omar and Katie's ship. "We'll take this smaller one so Amaya can continue to monitor the safety of everyone here. I can also take four others with us if anyone would like to see." He looked directly at his father who turned his back to him and Hopper bit back a sigh, then settled his resolve. He was no longer a child cowering in a corner. He was Akino, captain of Amaya. Maybe once these others saw the wonders above, they could help convince his father—though he doubted that.

A young man and woman wearing the colors of the science sector stepped up. "We would like to go, please?"

Hopper studied them, then glanced at the councilor who nodded. "Come."

The young man who'd been carrying the bomb also stepped up. "I would also like to go."

"Sachi!" Nyoko spun back around and shouted. "You would go with these demons?"

"They didn't force me to carry a bomb!" He stepped toward Hopper and held out his bound hands. "If you wouldn't mind?"

"Sachi?"

"Nice to see you alive, my brother."

Omar slashed the bindings with one of his smaller knives.

"Thank you."

Hopper offered his arm to his mother and led her up the ramp with Eiko on his other side and the rest following.

Katie set the controls and lifted off. As she did, the crowds scattered. "We just took care of the Night Eye, but do you see all those smaller rocks?"

The councilor leaned forward and peered through the screen, as did the others. "Yes."

"When those hit the ground, they cause craters. If those hit an area where the ground faults are unstable, they cause the tremors. And there are active volcanoes on the far northern area of your planet."

Katie veered toward the area.

"Those mountains spewing ash and fire into the sky?" Hopper pointed out.

"Yes?" the councilor said.

"Those are causing smoke and ash to cover the northern part of the planet. That's why your days aren't as sunny as they used to be."

"Amaya, please set out buoy number three." He turned to the group. "Our buoy will monitor and destroy any remaining meteors that could hurt you." He headed for Amaya, landing in the bay. "I'll give you a quick tour," he told them, "And then we will return." He looked up as the three felines joined them. The people with him gasped and fell back against the walls.

"Please, don't be afraid," Hopper said as he knelt next to the cats. "They are Masaaki. They will not harm you."

"But...they are gods!" One woman said.

"To some, they may seem like gods, but they are more like us than you realize. You will find this out when it is time. You may approach them, but please ask permission before touching them."

With the cats leading the way, Hopper led the group around the ship. After the tour, he led them back to the dining area. "Can I offer you food or drink before we return?"

"Some spike flower tea would be nice," the councilor said. "If you have any?"

"Amaya, would you please make the councilor her tea?"

"Hot and sweet?"

The councilor blinked at him. "Um, yes, please." She turned to Hopper. "How did she know how I like my tea? Does she read minds?"

Hopper chuckled. "That's how I prefer mine, and also the previous captain. And the only minds she reads are mine and Eiko's."

"Hopper?" He looked up as his second in command came up to him. "Can you come to the bridge, please?"

He nodded and turned to Eiko who smiled at him and gave him a quick nod. "Eiko can help the rest of you. I'll return shortly."

"May I speak with the ship?" the councilor asked. "Amaya?"

"I would welcome a discussion with the councilor and any of the others."

Dozens of people came in wearing standard ship's suits and looking gaunt. "Welcome," Hopper said to the newcomers. "Councilor, these are all citizens of Lawan who have been imprisoned in Cerule. My associates recently released them from their prison."

Eiko went over to them. "I am Eiko, crystal hunter from Lawan." Then she stopped and gasped.

"Mother? Father?"

Two people stepped forward, supporting each other. They were gaunt and had bandages and obvious scars. They found the strength to hug Eiko.

"I was told you died in the last sickness."

"We were not even sick. Nyoko and his people took two dozen of us to the mines."

Hopper came up to them and gently hugged them. "We'll take care of you. I am so glad you were not on the ninth level."

"There were times when we wished we were," Eiko's father said.

"Oh, Mother, Father." Tears streamed down Eiko's face as she faced the others. "I too was held by the Ceruleans, but only for a few days. Captain Akino rescued me and the others who were in the medical unit. You are safe here. Let's get you some food, yes?" She nodded for Hopper to leave. "I'll take care of them."

"Are you sure?"

"I'll be fine. Go." She rubbed her hand down his arm and sighed. Eiko watched him leave, then turned to the group, keeping a hand in each of her parents'. "Please, find a seat. I believe some dachar soup and flat bread would be most appropriate right now. Is that acceptable?" Eager nods all around.

"Amaya?"

"What are the ingredients?"

"Oh." She looked up as Hopper's mother, Thera, joined her.

"I'll take care of the recipe. How about if you get them all some drinks? I'd stick to fortified waters for now."

"Agreed."

Within a half hour, Eiko had everyone settled with food and drink. She rejoined Hopper's family, her parents, and the councilor at their table.

"When did Hopper get back? And Eiko, what happened to you? You said you were a prisoner?" Thera asked. "And you were shot. I saw you. How are you here, looking well, thank the Blessed Three."

Eiko smiled. "I was. Their doctor and Amaya healed me."

"But she still needs rest," Amaya said.

"Anyway, Nyoko was going to mate me to Syeth so I left before they could force me. With the help of Masuru—one of the Blessed Ones who helped me—I found the cave where Hopper disappeared from, but there was a tremor, and I was trapped. The Ceruleans got me out, but only to trap me in their prison. Nyoko came to Cerule and condemned me to the red mines. He has been sending people to Cerule."

Thera shook her head. "And all these..." She nodded toward Eiko's parents and the new group of people.

"Were prisoners, taken from Lawan and forced to

work in Cerule," Eiko's mother said.

Thera closed her eyes and lowered her head. "I knew he was bad, but I never imagined…I should have stayed. Maybe I could have—"

Eiko laid her hand on Thera's arm. "No, you could not have. He would have found a way to either send you away or abuse you even more than he had. Leaving him probably saved your life."

"She's right, Mother," Sachi said. "He was willing to have me blow myself up to make himself look better. His mind is gone and has been for a long time. The only reason he continues in his position is because of his cronies. He will never give up his power. That's the only thing that drives him. Power and his ego. He doesn't care what happens to anyone else as long as he is admired."

"So many people. So many lives. Ruined because of one man."

"Not one man," Councilor Meecha said. "He may be deeply involved, but Nyoko is not alone. His cohorts are equally to blame. And it is beyond time that we stopped them. Maybe with the help of Captain Akino and Amaya, we can."

Eiko rose. "I will return shortly." The others nodded at her, and she left the dining area and headed for her quarters. "Amaya, can we talk or are you too busy with other things?"

"I am capable of performing many tasks at the same time."

Eiko grinned. "I'll bet you are." She closed the door to her rooms. "I have an idea but wanted to talk to you first."

"Yes?"

"Are there other cities on our world besides Lawan

and Cerule? Any other people?"

"Unfortunately, no. Because of the devastation caused by the meteors and volcanoes and more, there are no other undamaged cities or peoples."

Eiko sighed. "That's what I was afraid of. So, there's nowhere else we can move to?"

"Not exactly." Amaya brought a map up on the wall. "There is one possibility."

A red dot appeared on the map far south of where Lawan and Cerule were. "This city, though not without damage, is in the safest area of land. The tremors haven't reached this far south. There is a supply of clean water and arable land for planting. I believe this will be the best area for relocation."

"Can you show me?"

"I'm not in the right place at the moment. The views would not be optimal. But I can send out a buoy that will send us back pictures of the area. Will that suffice?"

"Yes. And thank you."

Eiko and Amaya talked until Eiko realized she'd been gone too long. "Amaya, a request before I return to the dining area."

"Yes?"

"Can you send a message to this address?" Eiko gave her the information for her friend Sora.

"Done."

"Thank you.

Chapter Twenty-one

"How are we looking, Maria?" Hopper asked as he strode onto the bridge.

"The biggest asteroid is gone and we're finishing cleaning up the larger meteors before they can hit the ground. We also took care of several other larger asteroids with orbits we projected would make landfall in the future. But we couldn't get them all. Some landed in that northern caldera. I'm afraid there will be more tremors before it's all over."

"Okay. Thank you. I'll let the others know. I'm going to rejoin our guests, but I'd like you and Amaya to be ready to land. I think there's enough room in the field where the shuttles landed but check with her to make sure."

"I already checked," Amaya said. "And there is, but barely. I may end up flattening a statue or two sitting at the entrance to the town. Will that cause a problem?"

Hopper laughed. "Not as far as I'm concerned. Those two statues are no more than tributes to my father and his cohorts. He had them erected when I was child, right after he reached council level. They're all about power and intimidation. I'd love to see them smashed."

"In that case, I will adjust my landing to make sure I don't miss them."

Hopper went out laughing and rejoined the group. "We'll be landing shortly. Do you have any other questions for me?"

"There is no roof of heaven?" his brother asked.

"Not that anyone has found. But the universe is beyond large and there is much we haven't seen yet."

"But the lights—the holes in the roof that we see in the night."

"Those 'holes' are other suns surrounded by other worlds. You're seeing the light from them. One of the reasons we're out here, besides looking for the Masaaki home world, was to help a friend find her family who were lost in uncharted space."

"There are other worlds?" the councilor asked.

"Millions. And billions of beings, some who look similar to us, some who don't. I have been living on a space station called Pointe Noir for the last twelve years. Noir is a city built completely in space. Amaya, can you bring up a vid of Pointe Noir?"

The people gathered made startled noises as she put a picture on one of the blank walls. Hopper went over to it and pointed to the station spinning slowly against a backdrop of stars and a large planet. "This is Pointe Noir, a city in space. Amaya, internal view of the main promenade." The view changed to a walkway bounded by shops and a central area planted with trees and flowers. Beings of all sorts strolled the areas. "This is the main level, but there are nearly fifty in all, some just for housing, others for businesses. There are hospitals, restaurants...anything a city needs." He had Amaya show them various levels before returning to his seat.

"Hopper?" His mother came up to him.

He turned to her with a smile. "I apologize. I've not had time to speak with you alone. You look well." And she did. Yes, her hair was more gray than black, and there were a few wrinkles radiating from her eyes, but overall, she looked good. But smaller. He remembered her as being taller than him.

She laid a hand on his arm. "I understand. You are busy and have a lot to take care of. I'm so glad you aren't dead. When you went missing, you took a piece of my heart with you. Now I have you back. But why didn't you come home?" she asked, hurt in her face and voice.

Hopper shook his head, sadness in his heart for all he'd lost in those years and hugged her to him, holding back tears. "I was severely injured, and part of those injuries included a loss of memory I've only recently regained. For all the doctors tried, they could not restore my memory. Plus, until we found Amaya, nobody had ever been out this far from Pointe Noir and did not know the Masaaki were here. Only Amaya did." He turned to the others but kept his hand on his mother's arm. "We'll be landing in two minutes. I hope you enjoyed your brief trip."

Eiko joined him after seeing her parents and several of the others ushered off by Annie. She wanted to go with them, but Annie held her off.

"Let me take care of them first, then you can see them."

She reluctantly agreed as Hopper wrapped his arms around her, knowing how she felt.

Thera smiled at the two of them. "You and Eiko? Finally?"

He laughed and held out his hand to Eiko, who grasped his. "Yes. Me and Eiko. We have a lot of years to catch up on, but I do care for her deeply."

"As I do him."

His mother grasped both of their hands in hers.

"Good. I'm happy you have finally found each other again."

He headed for the door, Eiko with him. Once they were alone in the hall, he turned to her and kissed her. "I am so grateful you're here, Eiko. When you were shot…" He shuddered. "I couldn't lose you again. And I don't think I could do all this without you."

She grinned. "Oh yes, you could. You are stronger than you think, Hopper."

"Still, thank you for taking care of them while I was busy. Are they okay? Are your parents? I can't believe they were prisoners."

"I know. I am thankful they live, but they did not look well."

"Annie and Amaya will tend them. Give them time. What of the others?"

"A bit shaken, but mostly willing to listen and try to understand. It is a lot, though, Hopper. I admit, I'm having trouble with all this too, but I am learning. Give them time."

He hugged her again. "I think you're amazing, Eiko. So much has been thrown at you over the past few days and yet, you accept and keep going."

"Only because of you, Hopper. Only because of you." She kissed him lightly, breaking away when they heard an amused chuckle from behind them.

Hopper turned to find his mother, a smile on her face. "I'm sorry to interrupt, but I think we need to talk about your father before we land."

"Actually, we landed a minute ago," Hopper said.

"Be that as it may, Nyoko is not going to be easy to convince that you and your ship are not demons. He will probably continue to spout his nonsense, and he holds many powerful people in his debt."

Her opinions of his father surprised him, then he thought of all she'd been through married to Nyoko. Maybe he shouldn't be so surprised. "I'm going to bring him and the others aboard, but do you think doing so will make a difference to him?"

She shrugged. "Who knows. Probably not. He is deeply entrenched in his delusions. But even if we can only crack the surface, won't that be progress?"

"Mother, why have you put up with him as long as you did? Was it just because of us?"

She chuckled. "Partly. He would not have allowed me to take any of you with me. Once your sister and brother were grown enough to take care of themselves, I left, though to keep up appearances, he says he put me out. I live in a small room on the edge of town with other *fallen* women. He will neither see me nor speak with me and forbade your siblings from talking with me, though I do see them on the rare occasion."

He hugged her. "I'm so sorry for what you've gone through. We'll figure this all out."

He turned as his brother joined them. "Sachi. I am so glad to see you. And that you came along."

His brother smiled and held out his hands for Hopper to grasp. "As am I. We never imagined you hadn't been killed." He blushed. "I mean…aw, slugworms." He gathered Hopper in a tight hug. "Welcome home, brother. I am most happy to see you."

Hopper hugged him back. "As am I you, little brother. So…the priesthood?"

He pulled back and grinned at Hopper. "That's all your fault. You were gone and I was stuck. But I do enjoy being a teacher, so I'm good."

"Hopper," Amaya said. "It is time."

Hopper nodded. "We'll talk more later. Gather the others."

The group descended the ramp with Eiko and Hopper, the former prisoners standing behind them. They stopped at the bottom, gazing at the gathered crowd. Nyoko, eyes wide, backed away, holding his staff in front of him like a shield.

"No! This is the work of demons. You are a demon! And you've made demons of them all. Our prayers destroyed the Night Eye. We need to keep praying. Our faith is working!" He kept sputtering and spouting, raising his staff until Omar took one step forward. Then Nyoko settled into glaring at them.

Councilor Meecha stepped forward. "Be quiet for once, Nyoko. For too long, you and your followers have used your staff of office to force more and more rules on the people of Lawan. And I say, no more." She turned to the others who had gone up to Amaya with her, and they nodded at her. "What Hopper—forgive me—Captain Akino has said is true. He has traveled and lived in space in this amazing ship. A ship built by our own people in the distant past. A ship he commands." She glanced at Hopper with a little shrug. "My apologies, Amaya. He is captain of this wonderful ship, but they work with each other, not as commander and machine, but as friends and partners. He has also told the truth in that he and Amaya and their friends were the ones to destroy the Night Eye. We saw this with our own eyes, as did you. And they are taking care of the burning rocks causing the tremors and storms ravaging our world. If not for them, we probably would not have survived."

Some of the crowd crept closer.

She motioned for the former prisoners to come forward. "Thanks to Captain Akino and his crew, our citizens who were being held prisoner and forced to work in the mines have now been released." Multiple families shouted and rushed forward to claim lost members. "I would also like to introduce my fellow citizens to beings from other worlds. Worlds we would not have known existed if not for Captain Akino and Amaya."

Katie and the other crew members—including the lizard-like Tians—trooped down the ramp to the gasps of those gathered. The crew lined up on either side of Hopper, but the clincher was when three large felines ran out of the jungle and sat in front of him and Eiko.

"The Blessed Three!" came from multiple people. Many knelt in the dirt, bowing their heads. "He is one with the gods!"

Hopper shook his head and clenched his jaw. "Please, everyone. I am no more than what you see. I am a Masaaki man, like the rest of you. At one time, our people flew among the stars. We visited other worlds. We now know what happened to stop their exploration. That was due to the actions of people like Doctors Ryder and Neevo and their cohorts. But we do not know what happened to the ancient people who flew with Amaya. I hope to find out one day, but meanwhile, there is much we can teach you about your history." He glanced at his father, who had gone from red to white, his mouth agape when Eiko knelt next to the largest feline and wrapped one arm around his neck, and the large cat rubbed his head against her.

Then Nyoko's eyes narrowed. "No! This is blasphemous! Trickery from the dark ones! We must go forward with prayers and follow the dictates handed down to us. We must work harder to obey. This is the law!" He lowered the end of his staff like a lance and rushed toward Hopper. He didn't get more than a few steps before Katie, Omar, and the largest feline stopped him. Katie wrested his staff from him, though he kept fighting and yelling.

"Hopper?" Katie glanced at him.

Hopper rubbed his head, feeling an ache coming on. "Some people will never accept what's in front of them." He glanced at June and Katie. "Take him onto the ship and secure him in an empty berth. Gently, please."

Nyoko struggled with them until Annie stepped up, a hypo spray in her hand. "Hopper? Maybe a light sedative?"

Hopper closed his eyes. He hated making such a decision, but he didn't want to see his father hurt. "Yes."

With the crew holding the struggling man between them, Annie touched the hypo to his arm. A moment later, he sagged in their arms, not out, but no longer fighting. "Be gentle with him," Hopper said.

"We will be, Captain." They guided him onto the ship.

Hopper turned to the crowd. "He will sleep a good sleep and no harm will come to him. He is my father and I care about him, but I cannot allow him to put anyone in danger. Nor will I cause any of my friends to harm you. There is much the councilor and my people need to talk about. Please, I ask you, go to your homes."

He turned to Meecha and the others. "Councilor? Shall we?"

The councilor smiled at him. "I believe this is your show, Captain. Do you want to talk in our offices or yours?" She nodded at Amaya.

"Let's go into Amaya. I need to check for asteroid destruction, and I could use a good meal. Will you join me? You can bring whomever you want. I have the room."

She nodded with a smile. "I know. I will meet you in the dining area shortly." She turned to the crowd. "Do as the captain directed. Go to your homes. Think about what has occurred here. The Masaaki have entered a new era. One vastly different from the one we know. May the Blessed Three go with you in peace." She glanced at the three felines and the largest one let out a loud roar, then bounded into Amaya, followed by the other two.

Hopper watched them. "I guess we have more guests. Honored ones." He glanced back at Katie and Omar. "Can you go get the doctors and their aides and bring them to the dining area? Heavy restraints connected to Amaya."

"Aye." Omar gave him a two-finger salute and Hopper chuckled.

"Would the rest of you please join us?" He took Eiko's hand.

"Any idea what you're going to do?" Eiko asked.

"No. Do you have any ideas? Amaya?"

"No," both said.

"So, just like usual," Hopper said with a chuckle. "Amaya, when the doctors and their aides arrive, I want you to erect a shield around their table to keep them separated from the others. I don't want any trouble."

When the others arrived, he set his guests up with meals, surprised and happy when Eiko ordered macaroni-and-cheese for two. As they were eating, Omar and Katie entered with Nyoko—no longer sedated—both doctors, their aides, and the general. Other crewmen backed up Katie and Omar as guards.

Hopper and his crew settled them all at a single table away from the rest of the group, then stepped away. Before the seated ones could move, a sparkling blue light surrounded the table and the people there, and their binders released and dropped to the table. He nodded to his crew, and they headed to their own tables.

Hopper approached them. "You are surrounded by a shield. You can see, hear, and talk, but you cannot move outside the shield."

Which is exactly what the doctors, his father, and the general tried to do, only to be repelled. Hopper watched the aides. Four of the five looked at the table, but he could see the grins on their faces. Maybe they weren't so deeply enchanted by their bosses. The fifth one watched Hopper, consideration on her face.

"What's your name?"

"Pri."

Eiko came up to him. "She's the one who actually tried to help us. She wouldn't let the doctor hurt us."

"Amaya?"

The sparkling shield altered, leaving Pri separated from the others. Hopper went to her and held out his hand. "Will you join us, please?"

The others glared at her as she smiled and rose.

"Pri, I never got the chance to thank you for helping me," Eiko said.

"I wish I could have done more."

"How dare you!" Dr. Holly yelled. "You have no right to do this to us. And to treat her like…"

"You can't do this to me! I'm your father and your spiritual leader! You will answer to me!" Nyoko screamed.

Hopper blew out a long sigh as he took his seat. "Amaya, mute the shield."

"Gladly."

From the looks of them, they continued to shout, but no one could hear them now.

"How did you do that?" Meecha asked. "I've wanted to do something similar for years."

Hopper glanced up as a young woman stopped in the doorway, looking like she wasn't sure whether she should come in or not.

"Koti?" Hopper said around a lump in his throat.

Eiko smiled at him, then rose to go to the woman and bring her in. "I thought you might like to see your sister too."

Koti shrugged, then gave him a broad grin. "Eiko invited me, and I figured the rest of the family was here, why should I miss out on the fun?" She gave him a quick, tight hug. "I am glad you're back, Hopper. You have been missed."

He deepened the hug, then studied his now grown sister. When he'd left, she had barely reached her teen years, and his brother only two years older than her. Now, they were both grown. "I am so glad to see you. I've missed so much of your lives. Are you well?"

She smiled at him. "I am." Koti glanced at the table. "I'm also hungry."

Hopper laughed. "Well, that certainly hasn't changed!" He welcomed her, and they sat down. He glanced around the table. His family. Together. And Eiko. He didn't think his heart could grow any larger. "What would everyone like to eat?"

Later, after everyone had eaten, including the three cats who had taken up spots at the far end of the area,

Hopper looked around. What were they going to do? How could he fix this?

"Hopper, you don't need to do this alone," Eiko said.

He smiled at her. "You've always been the smart one."

"Would you all mind taking a little trip?" he asked the group.

"What do you have in mind, Captain?" Meecha asked.

"First of all, call me Hopper. I'm Captain Akino when necessary, but most of the time, I'm just Hopper."

"I don't believe you're *just* anything," she said with a smile. "But what do you want to do?"

They looked up as a man and woman came into the room. Though they were still too thin, their injuries were gone, as were some of the scars.

"Mother! Father!" Eiko jumped up and went to them, guiding them gently to the table where everyone made room for them. "You're better?"

Her mother, Larin, nodded. "Akino's healer is amazing. She says the healing will continue for several weeks and we need to be careful what we eat because our systems can't handle much right now, but we are good." She turned to Hopper. "We are forever in your debt, Akino. Your people saved us."

Hopper shook his head. "There is no debt. If not for you all those years…" He sighed. "I am just happy you are here."

"So, what are your plans?" Thera asked.

"First, we need to stop the kidnapping and experiments going on in Cerule. The ones we rescued told us what they've been through and what's happening, plus we gathered a lot of information from records. The people in Cerule are being poisoned by their over-use of red crystals and not shielding them properly. Tell me"— he looked at everyone—"do you think your two cities could ever be united?"

Meecha shook her head. "Although I and others would love to see this happen, we know the change would not be easy. First of all, where would we live? They couldn't live in Lawan where we have very little, and our people would have trouble adapting to their society."

"What about a new place for those who wish to adapt?" Eiko asked. "One where both could integrate."

Hopper looked at her. "What do you have in mind?"

"I've been talking with Amaya and have an idea. A new place—or rather—a really old one. One where the Ceruleans would teach the Lawans about advances, and the Lawans could help through natural planting and building."

"But where would that be?" Thera asked.

"Before I answer that question, Hopper, you should bring aboard people from Lawan."

"Agreed," Hopper said. "Councilor, do you have any ideas of who would be best suited?"

"Yes. Can you give me thirty minutes?"

"Of course. And Pri, I'd like you to think about who you believe would be best to join our group from Cerule, because that is where we're going next." He glanced at Omar and Katie. "Can you return the doctors and my father to their berths? There's no way they will agree to combining the cities or working with both groups without them being in charge."

"Of course."

While they waited, Hopper spoke quietly with his family, catching up on their lost years.

"When you disappeared, I became the heir-apparent to Father," his brother said with a grimace.

"I guess that's not what you wanted?"

He shook his head. "Not in the least. Which is why I've probably been an acolyte so long. I hate what we do."

"What did you want to do?" Hopper asked.

"Kind of what you did. I wanted to go into the sciences. But Father and his rules wouldn't let me. But I do get to teach science—such as we know, so I guess everything worked out for the best." He looked around at the spacious dining area. "This place is so amazing. I would love to work in a ship like this."

Hopper grinned. "If the next few days work out the way I hope, you might get your wish." He turned to Koti. "What about you?"

"I actually like what I'm doing, and I'm good at numbers. But remember, I'm a female so Father didn't care about what I did, as long as I didn't cause him any trouble." She grinned at her brothers. "Though I will admit, I was not happy when he married me off to one of his cronies. Thank the Blessed Three that Jonar passed away after less than a year and with no children. As his widow and sole heir, I am granted a lot more freedom than most women."

Hopper looked up as the councilor approached with nearly a dozen people. "I believe these will help with your crusade."

The people glanced at Hopper, then at the cats sitting near him. Several went to their knees, heads bowed.

Hopper shook his head. "Please, everyone, take a seat."

"They're a good omen," the councilor said. "If you have the support of the gods, the others will follow."

"I don't want people following me. I'm no priest and have no desire to be one. Until three years ago, I was barely a man."

His mother stroked his cheek. "But you are one now. And like it or not, people will follow you because of what you are and your connection to the holy ones. Be the man I knew you would be, and know you to be now, and the rest will work out."

He snorted. "At least one of us is sure of that." Hopper turned to Eiko. "I think I need to go see my father."

"You do. But Hopper, be careful. I know he's your father but remember what he did to you and your brother and sister. Just because he's older doesn't mean he's weak."

"I know." He held back a shudder as he remembered the abuse of the past. And what his mother had suffered trying to help him.

"Would you like me to come with you?" Eiko asked.

Hopper appreciated her offer but shook his head. "Yes, but no. I think I need to do this by myself. I need to face him. Can you take care of my family and the others, please? I know I've asked a lot of you—"

She stopped him with a finger to his lips. "I'll take care of what is needed. Go."

Hopper left the dining area, his heart with Eiko, but dread in his stomach for what was coming. His father had always been a stern man, quick with his rod or his fists.

How he got to the level he did was a question Hopper wanted answers to. But first, he had to face him.

Chapter Twenty-two

Eiko watched Hopper interact with everyone. He was every inch a leader. He might not think so, but he really was. When he left the room, he moved like he was holding the entire world on his shoulders—and to some extent, maybe he was. He'd changed so much in the years they'd been apart. He was much stronger now, not just in body, but in his outlook as well. In their youth, he'd come to her often after a beating or other punishment from his father. But no matter how harshly his father treated him, Hopper never lost his sense of wonder about the world. She hoped a part of the old Hopper was still there, buried under the responsibilities he faced.

Eiko leaned back against the wall in the corridor, startling a little when the material softened around her like a hug.

"You are troubled," Amaya said.

"I'm worried about him."

"He has much to concern him right now but finding you has brought him more joy than you can even imagine. And I believe the reunion with his mother and siblings went well also."

"Better than expected. But he's going to go face his father."

"I will watch over him and let you know if he needs you."

Eiko ran her hand gently over the surface of the wall. "Thank you, Amaya."

"You are still troubled. Do the years apart bother you? Or your differences?"

"Both. Our lives have been so different. He explored the stars. When I look at him, I see a powerful leader. I- I am…I don't know."

"Eiko, you need to have a serious talk with Hopper about his past. I will not tell you—the tale is his to tell—but you must ask. He has had problems. Serious ones. Please, talk to him, then come back to me and we will finish this discussion. Trust him, Eiko."

"I do. And we will talk as soon as he has the time."

She returned to the dining area, but her thoughts were still with Hopper. He had the entire universe open to him. What could she add? Her thoughts spun around and around until she pushed them away. She had tasks to take care of. If nothing else, she could help Hopper where possible. "We have a few minutes before we land at Cerule. If anyone would like to freshen up, Amaya can open some cabins for you."

"That would be nice," Hopper's mother said.

"Eiko, I have opened the quarters next to yours for your parents. They need to rest to continue healing—as do you."

"I know. But we have more important things to take care of right now. I'll rest later.

Amaya's thoughtfulness touched Eiko. She noticed how her parents' eyes drooped, and they kept nodding off. Their injuries might have been healed, but they still had a long way to go to be healthy.

"Those who wish to, please, come with me. You, too, Mother and Father." She led everyone out, dropping

231

several off at the cabins Amaya opened for them.

"Councilor Meecha, Thera, Koti, and Sachi, you are all welcome to use my quarters, if you like. Or I can open private ones for you. Mother, Father, you are in the cabin next to mine. You can rest there."

They nodded at her, and she opened the door to their cabin. Her parents stopped. "For us?"

"Yes. You'll find the beds quite soft. And ask Amaya for anything you need. I'll be right next door." She gave each of them a gentle hug and stepped back, allowing the door to close. "*Amaya, keep an eye on them, please?*"

"*I will.*"

She led the others to her cabin. All four stopped inside the doorway, much the same way she had when she first saw the space.

"This is all yours?" Koti asked.

Eiko smiled and nodded. "Yes. Just me! And Hopper's quarters are even larger." She showed them where the facilities were, then sat down on the sofa. Koti sat next to her. Though Eiko knew Koti, because of the five years difference in their ages, they had never really spent much time together.

"Why aren't you sharing Hopper's quarters?" Koti asked with a grin.

Eiko chuckled. "Right to the point, aren't you?" She leaned against the back of the sofa. "We haven't really had much time to ourselves since he rescued me and the others. We have a lot to talk about and decide."

Koti shook her head. "I know there's one issue you don't need to decide on. I may not know my brother anymore, but I know how he feels about you."

"How do you know that?" She knew he loved her.

He'd told her as much. But how did Koti know?

"It's in the way he looks at you. The way his eyes go immediately to you when you enter a room, and he smiles, and his shoulders relax. You are his heart. Whatever you two decide, you had better make sure you're together at the end. You do care for him, don't you?"

"Of course! But we're different people now than we were all those years ago."

"When there is love, the years don't matter," Thera said as she joined the conversation. "I know my son. He's still the same person he always was. Yes, he has matured and has more responsibility sitting on his shoulders than any of us, but with you by his side, he will succeed. The question is, do you want to be there?"

"I do. But—"

"No. No doubts," Thera said. "You both have a lot to learn about each other. Take the time to learn. But hold onto the love I can see he has for you—and that I believe you have for him. The rest will work out."

The councilor joined them. "Before we go, Eiko, Thera and Koti are right. You and Hopper belong together. The future may not be easy or without conflict, but as long as there is love, there is hope."

****

Hopper approached his father's room with some trepidation and put in the code to open the lock.

When he entered, his father was kneeling in the middle of the floor, muttering prayers. He barely glanced up when Hopper entered. "Hello, Father."

Nyoko kept praying but increased the volume. "Please forgive this blasphemer for attempting to fool us all with his elaborate tricks. Show him the true way."

"So, you still think this is all a ruse? Look out the window, Father. Look at the stars. Take a tour of this ship with me. Or maybe you'd like some food? How about some spine plant soup? That was once your favorite. Amaya?"

The catering unit pinged, and Hopper pulled out the bowl of steaming soup along with a small loaf of fresh bread. "Look, Father."

"Forgive him for falling in with demons who tempt us. Forgive him for straying from the righteous path."

Hopper snorted. "How about asking for forgiveness for yourself for aiding and abetting kidnappers of your own people? Selling them to the other city so you can keep your power? Ask for forgiveness for the beatings you used to give me."

His father glared at him. "It is my right as your father to administer punishment for your sins."

"What sins? For asking questions? For not following in your unholy footsteps? For not being like you? That's what this is really about, isn't it, Father? You didn't like that I thought for myself. I saw what you were becoming and wanted nothing to do with your abuse. Is that what happened with Mother? Did she finally have enough of your beatings and your rules and your dictates?"

"Do not speak of her! She deserved her punishment, as do you." He rose and lunged toward Hopper.

Hopper side-stepped him. All his years in the lowest levels of Pointe Noir with the dregs of society had given him a wiry strength and agility to avoid being taken down in a fight. He faced his father as the older man raised his fists and advanced. Hopper didn't want to fight back, but he wouldn't allow Nyoko to land any punches. He danced around him as Nyoko grew more frustrated and angrier, throwing wild punches. Finally, Hopper had had enough and stepped back against the door. Nyoko gave him an evil leer and lunged, stopping suddenly as he came up against Amaya's shield.

"Thank you, Amaya."

"You are welcome."

"This is a level one force field, Father, like in the dining area. You can breathe, see, hear, and talk. You can do whatever you want except come near me. Amaya will release you once I've left this room. But hear this, Father. I will not allow you to ever again hurt someone like you did me and Mother. And I'm quite sure my siblings have the scars of your righteous punishments as well. That kind of conduct is done. You are done. While I might not have the authority to formally remove you from office, I do have the ability. I can put you on an island somewhere by yourself. Or maybe with your cohorts. You'll have supplies, but you will never raise your fist to anyone ever again. Do you understand me?"

"You don't have the right! I am the power. I have the ears of the gods. They listen to me. I speak with their voice."

Hopper looked around as the door opened and the three felines strolled in. As one, they sat at Hopper's feet, their tails swishing.

"No, Father, I don't think you do." Finally, his father went silent. Hopper turned around and strode out, the cats following him. When the door closed, he reset the locks. "You can release him now, Amaya. But keep an eye on him."

"Aye."

Hopper headed for the bridge, his heart heavy. There was no getting through to his father. And that was a sadness he would always have with him. He stopped when his mother and Eiko came out of Eiko's cabin. The cats, who had come with him, sniffed both women, then bumped them with their heads. Eiko reached down and scratched the one nearest her on the head, receiving a loud purr in response. She grinned and kept petting as Hopper's mother and Hopper did the same with the other two.

"I never thought I'd be touching the symbol of the gods," his mother said.

"Me neither," Eiko agreed. "But then, since Hopper has returned, I'm doing a lot I never even imagined."

"Would you all like to see the bridge?" He led them into the front part of the ship. "Let's go, Amaya." As she took off, he settled back into his seat, the cats on either side of his chair and at his feet. "Mother, Eiko, you can sit where you want. Before we head for the other city, let's see what's available as far as settlements go. Amaya, where could a third city be built?"

Amaya pulled up a schematic of the continent. "Eiko and I have discussed possibilities already. I have crossed off any areas with a history of flooding, seismic activity, or other problems."

He glanced at Eiko who gave him a grin and a sassy shrug. "Doesn't that include areas affected by the meteorites, past and present?"

"I took those incidents into account along with my historical records from before the destruction of the moon. This area here"—she circled a spot south of where the two current cities were—"would be the best area. There is ample surface and underground water supplies. Access to the oceans from this river, and natural resources. Plus, if you look closely, some of the original buildings are still standing, including the central pyramid. This is where one of the original Masaaki cities stood. This was the location of the capital city of Nuru. There are still indications of roadways as well. But I am sorry to see the area so desolate."

"What do you think?" he asked Councilor Meecha.

She cocked her head. "I like the idea. But could you ask Brodie to join us? He's one of our best builders, and your brother, Sachi has access to the ancient scrolls."

"Tell you what, let's all meet in the dining area. Amaya can show these images there for everyone." He rose from his seat.

"Doesn't she need you to fly?" his brother asked.

Hopper snorted. "No. Amaya knows where she's going. We really just sit in the captain's seat in case a body is needed. She can contact me anywhere if necessary. And one of the crew will monitor systems as backup. Shall we?" He nodded as Omar came in and sat down in the captain's seat. "Thanks, Omar."

"You're welcome. I need to send some missives to Pointe Noir. Figured here was as good a place as any. Good luck."

A few minutes later, they were all gathered at the tables. Hopper could still see wonder on the faces of many of them, but also curiosity and eagerness. More than a few gave the cats a side-eye looking from them to him and back again. He explained what he was trying to do and why and showed them the area.

Sachi rose and studied the image. "I believe I remember reading about this place. Nuru is supposed to be in a forbidden area and none outside the religious historians are allowed to know about the place."

"So… What do you know?" Hopper asked with a

grin.

Sachi laughed and nodded. "Nuru was once the center of this part of the Masaaki world. This was a city of learning, of peace. There were places for art and music and education. The central pyramid was open to all who wished to enter, not just a select few. Then the bad times came. Many cities were destroyed, and millions died in the first years. Many more in the years after. Those times are when the civilizations split into two factions. Those who followed the religious way and those who followed the science. But too many records were lost in the devastation and, as you know, we never returned to the stars."

"But you knew space was out there. That there were other places beyond this world."

"Oh, yes, we knew. Or rather, the leaders knew. But they believed they needed to keep the knowledge from the people so the bad times would not come again."

"But they did," Hopper pointed out. "Because of a few stupid people and the destruction of the moon, they created their own demise."

"They didn't know they were," his brother pointed out. "They believed the moon to be the path through the roof of Heaven and if they could get through, they would find a better place."

"So, they nearly destroyed an entire civilization to get a look at the gods."

He shrugged. "Who doesn't want to see the face of the gods? To converse with them? I agree, their actions were unfortunate, but their hearts were true." He glanced at the cats. "Though in retrospect, we had them with us the whole time.

"Do you think building a city here upon the bones

of the old one would be taken as a good omen?"

"Yes."

"Okay. What about everyone else? Do you see a problem with proposing this place as a new city made up of people from both of the old ones?"

There was a lot of discussion, but in the end, everyone agreed this was the best place for a new city.

"Now we just have to convince everyone else," Hopper said.

Chapter Twenty-three

Eiko watched as Hopper finished his talk. They all broke up into small groups, working out details. Finally, Hopper came to her. He still wore the uniform, though he'd undone the top buttons on the high collar. She had planned to change out of her sparkling outfit—Amaya had produced a new one for her—but Meecha had suggested she keep the clothes on. "It shows power," the councilor said. "Authority. And sometimes, the costume is all you need to persuade others to your side."

So she kept them on.

He nodded for her to join him. When she did, he took her hand and led her toward his cabin. "How do you think we did?" he asked her.

"Quite well. You laid all the details out logically and they saw the reasoning and understood. How long until we reach Cerule?"

"Three minutes." He opened the door and ushered her in. As soon as the door closed, he wrapped her in his arms and kissed her, then pulled back and leaned his forehead against hers. "I've been wanting to do that all day."

She giggled and ran her hands over his shoulders and down his arms. "Me too. But you've had a lot to take care of. How are you feeling about what you have to do next?"

"Nervous. I'm going into a situation where they

have guards who kidnap people like you so they can do experiments or force them to work. I have a feeling my task will meet with stronger resistance there."

"Possibly. Or the regular citizenry doesn't know what's going on and will be horrified to know what their leaders have been doing."

He grinned at her. "I'm so grateful you're here with me. Will you also stand with me when I face them?"

"If you want. I don't know how much help I'll be."

"You were their prisoner. Standing there in a position of power with me will be a statement." He noted the tired lines around her eyes. "Eiko, are you sure you're okay?"

"Yes. I'm fine."

He knew better than to push the subject, but he wanted to find a way to get her to rest soon. Then he thought of something else. "What about going out there again? Are you sure you want to do that?"

"Yes." She nodded. "I'll be there with you. And being there will show them I can't be cowed."

"Landing in one minute," Amaya said.

Hopper nodded and, holding Eiko's hand, headed for the bridge.

"Where will you be landing?" Eiko asked.

"Their central plaza is similar to Lawan, but larger so we'll land there. Other than the size of the plaza, this city seems to be laid out in almost exactly the same pattern as the other one, with a few deviances to allow for natural differences."

He clicked open the com-link. "To all our guests, we will be landing in Cerule shortly. If you wish to join me, please meet me at the aft airlock. Amaya will give you a blue arrow to follow to show you the way."

"What about your father and the doctors?" Eiko asked as they headed for the lift.

"They'll remain in their cabins and the brig under guard. Amaya, keep a security shield over us when we exit."

"Don't go too far beyond the ramp, please. No more than ten meters," Amaya said.

"Understood."

Hopper and Eiko waited until everyone had joined them, then stepped down the ramp to face the armed guards in front of the main building.

"This looks familiar," Hopper said to Eiko. "Who is in charge here?" he called out.

An older man dressed in a uniform similar to Hopper's original one stepped forward. "I am. Why have our leaders been taken? Who are you?"

"Tell your guards to lower their weapons and we'll talk."

He glanced around as if looking for input, wincing when shots rang out from the rooftop as the ground soldiers dropped to their knees and aimed their weapons at Hopper and his guests. The projectiles bounced off the shielding. Many of the guests ducked back into the security of the ship, only venturing out when they saw Hopper and the others standing safely. He felt Eiko flinch, but his heart filled with pride when she stood with him.

Still, they needed to take care of this. "Amaya?"

Multiple beams shot out from Amaya, and all the guards dropped their weapons, including the rooftop ones, and shook their hands. Several of the men pulled second weapons, and Amaya shot those down as well.

"We can do this all day, General, or whomever is

directing you and the soldiers. You cannot harm or damage us, but we can do much to you. Amaya, target that ugly statue two meters outside the main building."

The statue disintegrated in a shower of sparks and debris. Several of the guards backed off and held out empty hands.

"I do not wish to harm anyone. That's not why I'm here. But I will not allow you to harm my people."

More of the guards stepped back as the cats joined Hopper and Eiko.

The general's mouth dropped open. "You! You're the one! The one foretold who would come and show us the way!" He dropped his weapons and motioned for all the guards to go to their knees. "We thought you were an enemy. Our city has been under attack for several days." Though he said the words to Hopper, his eyes never left the cats.

"Amaya, you can drop the shield. I believe we made our point."

Hopper strode forward, Eiko at his side, her hand in his and the cats with them. "General?"

"General Barton at your service, sir." He bowed to Hopper, then Eiko.

"Please, tell your guards to rise. There are no enemies here. We have much to discuss and their knees will get rather sore if they stay in that position."

The general motioned for the guards to stand. Most did, but a few stayed down, and Hopper shrugged, but let the issue go.

"I am Captain Akino, and this is my bond mate, Eiko. The people behind me are from Lawan and are here to discuss a matter of importance to all the Masaaki. I would invite you and any you wish to bring with you onto the ship. I promise you will be safe and will be allowed to leave when you wish. But I must insist on no weapons."

The general studied him with narrowed eyes.

"And yes, I know that's not the way matters are usually handled here, but I'm not from here. I am Masaaki, and my home was once in Lawan, but hasn't been for many years. Amaya is now my home." He gestured toward the ship.

"Your ship looks like one of the living ships I read about in our ancient histories, but one of her kind has not been seen for thousands of years."

"And yet, here she is. I suggest you gather whomever you want and bring them. We'll wait, but no more than thirty minutes, please."

The general nodded and backed away as Hopper turned and led the others back. "That went better than expected."

"How did you keep them from killing us?" Eiko asked as she glanced at the felines striding ahead of them. "Did the gods protect you?"

"No. That was all Amaya. Remember the shield around the doctors in the dining area earlier?"

"Yes."

"That's what she used to protect us. But the distance is limited, which is why we stayed near the ramp at first."

"There's still so much for me to learn!"

His mother stepped up to them. "For all of us to learn. Such exciting times ahead. Hopper, why don't you and Eiko stay at the ramp to greet the newcomers? I'll make sure the dining area is set up."

"*We'll* make sure," Meecha said with a smile. "I believe I remember how to put together a meeting spread. And we'll make the main aisle the dividing line with Cerule people on the kitchen side and Lawan across from them."

Hopper glanced at Eiko, who nodded back at him. "Thank you. We'll return shortly." He and Eiko returned to the ramp. "Amaya, scan the new people for weaponry as they board. Do you know about the shielded pockets?"

"Yes. I have reset one of my scanners for this."

"I will also keep shields ready in the dining area in case they are needed," Amaya said.

"Agreed. Here they come. Good luck, Captain Akino."

Hopper saw that the general had about a dozen people with him and only one guard. "Welcome aboard Amaya. If you will follow us, please. We'll be meeting in our dining area."

He stopped when two people were held back by a smaller shield and saw Johnny approaching them.

"Amaya?"

"Those two were armed with weapons in their pockets. They have been disarmed by Johnny."

"Thank you." He glared at the two men. "I believe you two will remain behind. I specified no arms and you both came with them."

"You can't do that! We're security for the general!" One not much bigger than Hopper sputtered.

"The general will be quite safe, I assure you. Go." He pointed toward the exit. "You will not be allowed on board and pass the word around that anyone trying to bring weapons aboard will be treated as hostiles." Hopper turned away from them and spied the general. "Sir? Were they your aides?"

"Yes, but I did not authorize their weapons. I will

deal with them when I return." He cocked his head at Hopper. "I *will* be returning, won't I?"

Hopper grinned at him. "Yes, sir, you will. Come, let us show you Amaya."

As they walked, Eiko pointed out different areas to the group, surprising Hopper at what she remembered. She was the perfect guide.

When they arrived at the dining area, he noticed more than a few jaws dropping as they took in the size of the room made to seat almost a thousand people. "General, refreshments are available for you and your group on the counter."

No one moved toward the food.

"Eiko? Is there a problem?"

She snorted. *"Yes. The food they gave us in prison was drugged. They're probably afraid this is too."*

Hopper clenched his jaw, then went over and loaded up a plate and took a bite of one of the Masaaki delicacies on display—a piece of fried rigeb available only one month out of the year—and not this month. "I do love this, don't you?" He took another bite of the starchy tuber.

"I love the taste too," Eiko said as she also filled a plate and took bites. "But I think rainbow fruit ice is my favorite. We don't have this on Masaaki. I learned this is a special treat from the Eridani system. And the flavoring in those little cakes comes from Aboo, the home world of Omar and Katie." She pointed to Katie, and she nodded at her as she ate. "Please, help yourselves."

The general studied Hopper, then nodded and went for a plate, motioning for the others to join him. Hopper breathed a sigh of relief as Eiko went on to explain what some of the foods were, and his mother directed people where to sit. First level conquered. Or maybe the second since they were here after all.

Once everyone was seated, Hopper rose and faced both groups. As he did, Grainer brought in the two doctors, their aides, and Nyoko. The Cerule doctor was still wearing a sling and showing her bruising.

"I see Dr. Ryder has been injured," the general said. "Can your healers not help her?"

Hopper chewed his lip, then looked directly at the general. "She shot my mate."

The general pursed his lips, then nodded. "I'm surprised you let her live. I'm not sure I would have."

Grainer seated the group away from the others at a table where Hopper's mother had plates of food and drinks ready for them. A sparkling blue shield surrounded them, and their binders dropped. Both doctors rose and moved to stalk forward, stopping suddenly when they hit the shield. Nyoko didn't bother to try. Interesting. So, he could be taught.

"There is a security shield surrounding them," Hopper explained to the new people. "They can move within the confines of the shield, but not beyond."

"General! I order you to—"

The sound cut off though they could see the doctor still appeared to be shouting.

"Amaya has cut off sound so, although they can hear us, they cannot be heard." He turned to the doctors. "I suggest you sit down and enjoy your meal. You won't be harmed but cannot disrupt this meeting."

He turned to the Cerulean general. "Are you willing to listen, or do you want to join the doctors and my father?"

"Your father?" The general's eyebrows rose to

nearly his hairline, short as his hair was.

"Yes. Unfortunately."

The general glanced at the trio, then turned back to Hopper. "We will listen."

"Thank you. First, a lot of your people are getting ill, aren't they?"

He shrugged. "Illness happens."

"Yes, but I'll bet in a lot of these cases, they don't recover and eventually die. And your doctors, for all their experiments, don't know what's wrong with them or what's causing the illness."

The general glanced at a man and woman sitting behind him. "You're right," the man said. "We've been trying to discover the source but haven't been able to."

"Are you using red crystal in your medical centers? Unshielded red crystal?"

"Of course. Red is the strongest."

"And the deadliest. Be thankful you are Masaaki. For any other beings, even touching the red means death. For the Masaaki, we have some immunity, but even our systems can't fight the reds unendingly. Plus, when we first got here, we detected disruptions in your energy grids as well as other anomalies. All of which can be caused by unshielded red crystal."

"Nonsense!" A heavy-set man from the third table yelled.

"Ah, one of your scientists, I believe," Hopper said. "And how much red crystal have you personally handled?"

"Well, um…" He blustered and turned nearly as red as a crystal.

"Don't bother to answer. I already know. None. If you had, you'd be close to dying or dead. As are those

248

who actually handle the reds." He glanced at the Pri. "Am I correct?"

"You are."

"But what can we use if not the red?" the general asked.

"Blacks, whites, and yellows for power. Brown and blue in health equipment. You can use red, but only in shielded containers. Do you have a communication unit with printing or storage capability?"

"Yes, sir."

"Amaya will send you instructions on how to do all this. And you need to get all the unshielded reds to a secure facility as soon as possible. One shielded from radiation. We'll also help you with better medical equipment. Unfortunately, for those who are severely afflicted, nothing can be done. Even with all we have at our disposal, the unshielded reds are deadly. There's no way to avoid continuous effects."

"Which is why they were using us," a woman from the Lawan side of the room said. "They kidnapped us and used us to find the reds. And killed off many of us."

"Lies!" a Cerulean woman yelled.

When the yelling began on both sides, Hopper slashed his hand down and soundproof shields dropped over both groups. Hopper and his group sat calmly eating their meals as people from both sides continued to yell ineffectually.

"I'm tempted to let them yell themselves hoarse," Hopper said. He glanced at the general, who shook his head as he too continued to finish his meal. "Amaya, pinpoint the general and release him—and only him—from the shield."

"Done."

"General, would you care to join us here?" Hopper asked.

The general gave a short nod, picked up his plate and moved. As soon as he did, others tried to join him but were repelled by the shield.

"You have an impressive weapon at your disposal," he said.

"Not a weapon," Hopper said. "No one will be harmed. We use the shield for restraint only."

"So, what are we talking about here?"

"I have a proposal for you and for the leaders of Lawan. You have both sustained substantial damage from the recent meteorites."

"Yes, about that. What happened to the Eye? We were in the midst of a massive tremor when the Night Eye disappeared from the sky."

"Amaya took care of the asteroid. The Eye won't bother you anymore. Speaking of which, why were we fired upon?"

"That wasn't my doing. Nor did I call up the soldiers or order the weapons you saw earlier." The general nodded toward the scientist. "He has a quick temper and a quicker trigger finger. Dr. Ryder put him in charge of our outer world weaponry and when she disappeared, he assumed complete control. Firing on Amaya was the first time the weapon had ever been used. From what I see, not effectively."

"It did sting a little," Amaya said. "But only because my attention was elsewhere."

"My apologies."

"I have to ask," Hopper said. "Why did you bring him along?" He saw that most of the people had settled back down into their seats and were eating. Only a few remained standing and arguing.

"I didn't have any choice in the matter. The scientists rule our city, even over the military. As I said earlier, when you took Dr. Ryder, he assumed command."

"Do you have any scientists who aren't so—"

"Vocal? Yes. Do you see the woman at the next table? The one with pale hair and wearing a blue jacket?"

"Yes."

"She is the best of the best."

Hopper glanced at Pri, who nodded. "Release her, please, Amaya."

"Done."

The woman startled as Eiko went over to her. "Join us, please?"

"Yes, my lady."

Eiko chuckled. "I'm just a crystal hunter from Lawan. In fact, until Captain Akino rescued me, I was one of your prisoners."

The woman blushed. "I am so sorry. I hope you were not injured."

"Thanks to Pri, I was not. But many others were not so fortunate."

"I know. I tried to get them to stop. Pri and I both tried. She had better outcomes than I did. I showed him other ways to do what was needed but was rebuffed." She tilted her head toward the boisterous man.

"What's your name?"

Hopper watched Eiko studying her, then looking at Pri, a frown on her face.

"Eiko?"

"Look closely. Those two are related in some way. I'm sure."

"Migna." She glanced at Pri. "And I can tell from the lady's face, she has figured out that Pri and I are related. I am her older sister. Our superiors never figured our relationship out as we were rarely in the same place at the same time. Plus, for our safety, we used different family names."

"They may be your bosses," Hopper said. "But they are definitely not your superiors." He motioned at the people with him. "The others at our tables are Councilor Meecha and General Oakai from Lawan. And these are my mother, Thera, my brother Sachi, and my sister Koti." He took Eiko's hand. "And this is Eiko, my bonded." He rose from his seat. "Councilor and generals, is there anyone else from your sides who you believe should join us? Preferably ones open to new ideas?"

Meecha and General Barton each chose two more people. They joined the group and introductions were made. Hopper rose. "Amaya, make sure everyone can hear us, but keep the shields up, especially around the ones you deem the most inclined toward trouble."

"Aye."

He turned to the group. "Both your cities have been devastated by meteorites, tremors, and storms. The people of Cerule are getting sicker and dying in greater numbers due to the use of unshielded red crystals. Councilor Meecha, your people have been lied to for centuries, but more so since Nyoko came into power. He and his cohorts conspired with the doctors to send many of the Lawans to Cerule to be the subjects of experiments or forced labor. Many of them died due to both. All in the name of religion or science. This must stop. On both sides."

"Agreed," both Meecha and Barton said.

"I propose starting a new city. One built on the foundations of an ancient one where culture and education were primary. The city is well south of here and not subject to fault tremors or flooding. Establishing the city will not be easy. Building from the ground up is going to take a lot of work, but you will be safe."

Everyone behind the shields was seated and quiet. "Amaya, drop the shield, but be ready to establish again if needed." He glared at the scientist.

"Why should we pack up and move just because you say so?" one woman demanded.

"If the Masaaki are going to survive as a people, you need to move to an area that hasn't been contaminated by red crystal, and you need to work together. Which means no more kidnapping or using unshielded red crystal." This time he glared at the doctors and his father. "The Masaaki need to know that there is an entire universe out there for them to explore. There is no roof of heaven. Trying to blast through a moon or the night sky is not going to get you anywhere. And now that I and others know you are here, we can send help."

"Again, why move?"

Hopper bit back nasty words, then stopped as Eiko rose.

"I am Eiko of Lawan, and I am a crystal hunter. I recently went to our western region to hunt, though the area is normally forbidden to us. In the last few months, five other hunters had been sent there and all of them disappeared. I discovered a cave full of equipment and crystals but before I could let anyone but Captain Akino know, Dr. Ryder's people captured and imprisoned me. In prison, I found the other hunters from Lawan. The missing ones. And they all told the same story—sent to the western region, captured, and taken, and either forced to hard labor or used by the scientists in experiments."

Eiko paused as her parents joined them. She held her hands out to them. "These are my parents. Five years ago, I was told they had died of a sickness in Lawan. It was a lie. They and others who were also declared as dead were gathered up and sent to Cerule to toil in the mines.

"For years, this has been going on! We may not have your technology, but we are Masaaki. Every year, the birth rates go down. People get sicker. Die earlier. All because the scientists and religious leaders want to stay in power."

She held up her hand as mumbling started. "I know moving won't be easy, but nothing worthwhile ever is. If we are going to survive as a people, we have to learn to work together."

Hopper rose to stand with her. "You need to move to a new city because yours are no longer safe. Although we took care of the Eye and larger asteroids, the ones that hit did a lot of damage. The land may continue to shake. One river has flooded, the course changed."

"And our eastern river is little more than sludge now," Eiko said. "Our fishing ships can barely get through even on good days. Moving to the new place not only gives us a chance to come together as a people but is in a safe, undamaged area and has clean water available."

"But how will we live?" a Lawan man asked. "No shelter, no farms for food."

Hopper listened to the arguments coming from multiple people. Their concerns were valid, but how could he convince them that moving was the best solution?

"Hopper, Eiko, I have room on this ship for 900 people. Zara and Cass can bring cargo from Pointe Noir. A few weeks, we can have almost everything they need, including shelters, hydroponic greenhouses, and more. Or I can haul cargo instead of people."

"Contact the others, Amaya. See what they say. And thank you."

He stood beside Eiko, holding her hand. "Amaya has volunteered to carry cargo for you. With help from other sources, we could have enough supplies here to set up temporary shelters and hydroponic gardens in less than two months. Once we have the basics set up, building can start—homes and businesses that are safe and stable."

Eiko squeezed his hand and he smiled at her. "I'm not saying change'll be easy, but this can be done. However, only if you are willing to work together. There can be no more Cerule versus Lawan. There has to be one united people. We will also teach you the safe way to use crystals so there will be no more crystal sickness. How to shield the reds so that you can use them without endangering everyone. We can take you to the proposed site so you can look the area over if you wish."

Meecha fought back a yawn. "Actually, Captain, this has been a rather long, and eventful, day. I'd like to get some rest."

Hopper's face heated. "Of course! My apologies. Those of you from Lawan, cabins are ready for you. Those of you from Cerule, you are welcome to stay here, or you can return to your homes, and we'll get together in the morning." To his surprise, about half of the Ceruleans opted to stay on board, including the general.

Once they had the area cleaned up and everyone settled, Hopper and Eiko went back to his cabin, leaving hers to Meecha and his mother while his brother and sister took ones nearby. Eiko made sure her parents were comfortably settled once more. When the door closed on the corridor, Hopper slumped against the door, took a deep breath in, and exhaled, finally realizing how tired he was. Then he looked at Eiko and his fatigue melted away.

"Have I told you how beautiful you are?" He strode toward her.

"No, but I do like hearing you say so." She reached up and undid the buttons on his shirt, then ran her hands over his chest. "You're not so bad yourself, Captain Akino."

He growled playfully and pulled her to him. "Out there, I may be Captain Akino, but in here, I am Hopper. And I am all yours."

"As I am yours. Tired?"

"Depends on what you have in mind."

"Let's see what we can come up with?"

"Captain Akino. You are needed at the brig."

"Amaya?"

"A problem in the brig. Illegal entry is being attempted. I have erected a shield, but you should go."

Hopper sighed, leaned his head against Eiko's, then stood and re-buttoned his shirt. "On my way."

Chapter Twenty-four

Hopper strode toward the brig, arriving a couple minutes after Amaya notified him. He'd given his crew the night off, thinking the locked cells and locked entry would be enough security. When he got there, he found a group of people standing well away from the shield containing the scientist from earlier. He'd been caught against the door to the brig, and Amaya had narrowed the shield to almost his size.

Hopper turned to the group then picked out one of the Ceruleans. "Will you get General Barton please and ask him to join me? He's in Cabin Eight."

The woman dashed up the corridor as Hopper turned to the scientist.

"May I ask what you were trying to do? Although I can guess."

"You're holding her against her will! This is kidnapping and imprisonment!"

Hopper snorted out a laugh. "And what have you been doing to the Lawans over the last years?"

"Helping our people!"

"You mean helping the Ceruleans. You certainly weren't helping Lawans or the Masaaki in general."

"Our work will benefit all."

Another snort. "Not if you kill them all off with unshielded red crystal."

"You're lying about the reds."

Hopper shook his head. "Do you really believe what you're saying? Are you that disconnected from reality? Look at your people. They are dying and all you care about is building bigger weapons. For what?"

"We want to break through the roof of heaven! To get help from the gods has always been our objective. And why should we believe you? Just because you say so?"

Hopper glanced up as the largest of the felines strode toward him, tail high. He hissed at the scientist, then moved to stand next to Hopper. Then he shifted and everyone in the corridor gasped.

"Captain Akino has our support and our blessing," Masuru said as the other felines joined him. "I suggest strongly that you listen to him." He shifted back into a cat and strode off with the others.

"I'd say the Blessed Three have shown you rather well that they don't like what you're doing."

He looked toward Barton as he came rushing up, buttoning his shirt, his hair disheveled. "Captain Akino?"

"Your scientist was trying to break the lock to the brig. What would you like me to do with him?"

Hopper raised an eyebrow, a look of mischief in his eye. "What I'd like you to do and what we will do are two different actions. I wondered why he opted to stay on board. Do you have another cell in there that we can lock him in?"

"Yes. Are you sure?"

"Yes. In fact, I advocate locking the cabins on all those who stayed who were cohorts of the doctor."

"Give Amaya their names and she will do so." He glanced at the people still standing in the corridor. "This is for their safety as well as ours. We will free them in the morning, you have my word."

"And mine," the general said.

"And mine," Amaya added as she dropped the shield, and the general took the complaining scientist into the cells and secured him in one of the empty ones.

"Amaya, set a shield to contain the brig."

"Done."

"I suggest you all go back to your rooms and get some sleep. We all have a lot to think about," Hopper said as the group dispersed.

He went back to Eiko, but even she couldn't lift the darkness that settled around him. "How are we ever going to do this? They won't listen. They can't see what's in front of their eyes. They're killing the people, and they refuse to believe."

Eiko brought him a cup of hot tea. "Hopper, you can't erase decades—even centuries—of belief overnight. I've seen the wonders you've shown me, and I'm having trouble accepting all this." She massaged his shoulders, and he leaned into her hands. "Drink your tea, then come to bed. Even big fancy captains of amazing ships need their rest."

He snorted and grasped her hand, then swung around and pulled her onto his lap. "You're pretty amazing yourself." He grew suddenly shy. "Eiko, I know we are bonded and…well…I was wondering…"

She chuckled and stroked his cheek. "The answer is yes, Hopper. I will join with you according to our laws. I wondered how long it was going to take you to ask me."

He leaned into her for a kiss that led to the bedroom, and more.

An hour later, Eiko carefully climbed from the bed.

Hopper didn't even stir. She went out to the main room. "Amaya, what was the calming tea you gave Hopper?"

"Skaren flower tea. The blend is from Aboo."

The catering unit dinged and Eiko got her cup out. "Thank you. Amaya, do you ever sleep?" She heard a chuckle.

"The last time I slept, I did not wake for 3000 years. I do not think I will need to sleep again for a while. But, in order to answer your question, no, I do not usually sleep. Even when I am in a resting state, there are still systems and sensors running. When you sleep, your heart continues to beat and your lungs work."

"I hope so!" Eiko laughed softly. "But I understand what you're saying." She took a sip of her tea, grimacing a little at the slightly bitter taste. "Hopper's right though. How are we going to get these people to work together for the good of all Masaaki if we can't even get this few number to agree?"

"You are dealing with diverse levels of acceptance. You are trying to convince the ones in power they need to change. The four most vocal will be the ones least likely to adapt. But you have already brought Councilor Meecha over to your side as well as the generals and others. This can be done, but as you and Hopper said, convincing the populace will not be easy. I do have an idea, though."

"What?"

"I would rather not say. That way, you will not be culpable if this does not go well."

"Amaya? I'm not sure I like what you are saying. Please don't do anything that would make this worse."

"I believe what I have planned will actually help."

"Should I wake Hopper?"

"No. I would rather neither one of you know what I am planning."

Eiko yawned. "Oh, forgive me. I guess this tea works better than I thought."

Amaya chuckled. "Go to bed, daughter. You and your mate have much work ahead of you."

"Daughter? I guess so, many times removed." She rose and laid her hand on Amaya's wall. "Get some rest yourself. Good night, Amaya. And please, don't do something that will get Hopper in trouble. He does that well enough on his own."

Amaya chuckled. "I understand. Go."

Soft, hypnotic music filled the room as Eiko made her way back to bed. She had barely settled down before her eyes closed.

"That was relatively easy," Amaya said quietly. "I hope this works. If not, Hopper may not forgive me. First, make sure everyone stays asleep." She let loose a light mist throughout the ship. "Now for the rest." She powered up her engines and rose into the air.

An hour later, she landed on the edge of the ancient ruins. She sent out several dozen bots to go over the area, cleaning up weeds and other growth and getting detailed maps of the area. To Amaya's surprise, the felines also descended the ramp with the bots.

"Interesting. I thought the mist would put them to sleep as well. I wonder why not."

Masuru shifted into his biped self. "Your drugs do not work on us when we are in feline form. But you have done what was right. The troubles with the two peoples must be laid to rest. They are our descendants and must come together."

"Do you know what happened to the ones who were

with me?"

"Our people exist on multiple worlds. The way here was lost to many of them, but now they may start returning, if they wish, as our cousins did. And we did not speak because the time was not yet right."

Amaya was quiet for a moment. "I-I seem to remember. My previous captain. She and others in the crew would often vary their appearance, but not so much as you."

He shrugged. "We are more accustomed to our feline form. It has served us well over the years. You have started the people on the right path to bring them back to the world. In combining the old with the new, a stronger and better people will emerge. That was the original hope for your creation. Because of those whose ideas were corrupted by greed and desire, the people became what they did. Much was lost, but hopefully, that is done now."

He glanced around as the other felines joined him. "Let Akino know, we will be watching." Then he shifted back into feline form, and all six bounded off into the dark woods.

"I certainly did not expect that," Amaya said.

"Expect what?" Hopper asked.

She tore her attention from the ramp back to the captain's cabin. "You heard me? I apologize. I didn't mean to wake you."

"Actually, you didn't. You were speaking in my mind, like a dream. Like you were holding a conversation with someone I couldn't see. Are you okay?"

"I am. But I did something I'm not sure you're going to be happy about."

Hopper jerked back. "What? What did you do?"

Amaya knew Hopper was concerned she might go rogue like the ship that had kidnapped him. And in a way, she had, but not in the same way. At least, she hoped so. "While you slept, I, um, brought you all to the ancient city of Nuru."

"You did what?"

"Hopper! What's wrong?" Eiko came from the room, wrapping a robe around herself. "I heard you yell."

"Amaya…she…she kidnapped us all and brought us here, to the ancient city."

"Amaya! Is this what you were planning last night?"

Hopper turned to Eiko. "You knew?"

"No! She refused to tell me."

"You should have woken me."

"Um, she couldn't," Amaya said. "I put you all to sleep so you wouldn't know what I was doing and stop me."

"Amaya!" Hopper yelled, and she experienced the first inklings of remorse. Hopper was probably thinking of the other ship that took him. But she wasn't that ship. She'd done this to help him, not hurt him.

"The felines. Masuru told me what I did was right! That this would bring the people together."

"They did what?"

"They told me," she said quietly.

"I can't believe you would do this to me. Me! I'm your bonded captain and you know how I feel about being taken."

"I really am sorry, Hopper."

Eiko laid her hand on his arm. "Hopper, she isn't evil. You know this. You've been with her for more than a year. She would *not* harm you."

Hopper sat down on the sofa and stared at the floor. "They really are gods. The Blessed Three. Actually, all of them."

"Maybe, maybe not," Amaya said. "Maybe they are more Masaaki than you know. You and the Masaaki people have been lied to for an exceptionally long time. Manipulated and forced into a life bowing to the dictates of a powerful few. I did some research and the families in power have been so for generations. This is why they enacted the law of scion following sire. To keep power in the families. None has ever successfully fought against the law, at least, not until you came along. You, Hopper, are the one who could change the future. You and Eiko and others like you."

He shook his head. "I don't want power. That's not who I am."

"Which is why people will be more willing to listen to you," Amaya said.

"She's right," Eiko said as she sat next to him. "Maybe you need to stop being Captain Akino and just be Hopper. Though I wouldn't go so far as to put on the clothes you brought from Pointe Noir."

Hopper threw out a laugh. She'd seen them when they hung up their fancy clothes and he'd had to explain the rags to her and why he was keeping them. "I guess not. This is going to take some explaining when the others wake up," he said.

"Use the pictures of the Blessed Three," Amaya said. "I have a feeling that's why Masuru did what he did in front of my cameras. Plus, you have the people who saw him change down at the brig. Those people and my pictures should convince even the most stubborn."

Hopper rose and went to the wall where he laid his

hand. "I understand why you did what *you* did as well. I can't honestly say I'm happy about your actions, but I do understand. Has the sun risen yet?"

"Coming over the horizon now," Amaya said.

"Is anyone else awake?"

"Most of them."

"Open all the cabin doors and viewports and let the people see where they might live." Hopper went to his closet and pulled out tan trousers, a cream shirt belted at his waist, and low boots. "Let's see if we can't make this work. Please announce to our guests that they are welcome to join us at the ramp."

Eiko dressed in her crystal-hunter outfit and joined him. "This should be interesting."

At first, there was a lot of shouting and recriminations coming at Hopper from the assembled groups. And more than a few disappointed looks aimed at him. Until he showed them the footage of the felines shifting and talking with Amaya.

"Trickery!" Nyoko yelled.

Then Masuru and his two friends came prancing back out of the forest, stood in front of everyone, and shifted. Many of the group dropped to their knees, including Nyoko.

"No trickery," the shifter said. "For too long have you fought among yourselves, taking yourselves almost to the brink of extinction. You"—he pointed at the scientist and doctor from Cerule—"with your experiments have done more harm than good. And you"—he pointed at Nyoko—"have colluded with them. No more. From this day. In this spot. You will become one people. One united in harmony, not trickery and greed. I will appoint the leaders once the people are here but for now, the councilors from Lawan and Cerule will lead, along with Akino and Eiko. Today. Here. Now."

He shifted back into feline form, roared, and bounded back into the forest.

"I guess that settles that," Eiko said with a chuckle.

"Seems so to me," Hopper said as the sun rose above the trees. "Ladies and gentlemen, I present to you your new home."

They all stood and watched as the light touched the sections of the ancient town, now cleaned thanks to Amaya's bots. Of all the buildings, only one still stood completely undamaged by time—the nine-sided pyramid in the center of the town, a carved feline on each corner. The sun's rays touched the top of the structure first, lighting the apex up like a flame.

Hopper smiled. "I don't know about the rest of you, but I'm hungry. Would anyone like some breakfast?"

He went back onto the ship, followed by most, but not all, of the others. His father, the doctors, and the scientist still stood outside, staring at the building.

"Do you think they'll give in?" Eiko asked.

"Probably not right away," Thera said. "Nyoko can be quite stubborn. But I don't think they have much of a choice. Not with what we just saw."

Hopper's brother slapped him on the back, causing him to stumble. "I wouldn't have believed that if I hadn't seen them myself. I'm still not sure I believe. But Hopper, you have definitely opened a lot of eyes since your return."

Hopper ducked his head, heat coloring his cheeks. "I didn't mean to. I just wanted to find Eiko."

She took his hand. "You did that and more. You rescued me, Hopper. Not just from prison, but from becoming someone I didn't want to become." She kissed him to the chuckles from his family. "Now, come on, let's eat."

As soon as they entered the dining area, all noise and motion stopped, and everyone stared at them.

Eiko took his hand and steered him toward the catering unit. "Can you have macaroni-and-cheese for breakfast?"

He startled but then began laughing. "Actually, yes, you can. Amaya, macaroni-and-cheese for two please."

"Make that three," his mother said. "I'm intrigued."

"Make that nine."

Hopper laughed as the rest of his team clamored for some too. A moment later, a large serving dish appeared. Hopper pulled the dish out. Although they weren't exactly mingling, the people from the two cities were at least talking with one another. Maybe Amaya had been right to bring them all here. He didn't like the way she'd done it, but at least they were all talking and not yelling.

As they ate, Amaya showed pictures of what Nuru had looked like in her time. The beauty of the city awed them.

"Nuru can be this way again," Amaya said. "If you work together."

Chapter Twenty-five

Eiko looked out over the activity taking place in the town from her seat next to Hopper on Amaya's bridge. Thanks to supply-ships from Pointe Noir, buildings made of strange materials had gone up quickly and people were already moving into homes. There had been more than a few glitches along the way as the two peoples learned the hard way about trust and cooperation, but the strolling felines tended to cut a lot of arguments short. And there were a lot more felines now since most of the ones from the lost Phoenix planet had joined them.

When she'd gotten a chance to talk to the male, she'd learned that he was Masuru, the one who'd helped her. He'd only left her in the cave when he thought she was safe but couldn't get back to her after the quakes. She'd formed a fast friendship with his mate, Denikai and enjoyed talking with them both about their lives and the new-old city. She'd also found out that the reason they had been able to mind-speak from such great distances was because of the pyramids and crystals. And her connection to Amaya. So many new ideas to absorb.

With the influx of shielded red crystal going back to Hopper's former home of Pointe Noir, the Masaaki world was now worth a lot to the rest of the worlds. Regular supply ships ran back and forth, bringing food, people, and more as other systems learned about the crystal-rich world. The numbers of ships and different peoples still astounded her—and she loved learning about them all. Quite a few of them were staying to help the Masaaki cope with and learn about all the changes.

Hopper's mother and sister now led a company trading crystal for what the city needed—and the riches were spread equally among all the citizens. Eiko's parents were helping out in the hospital as administrators. There were definite challenges, but everyone was working toward a better life for all involved.

A special hospital had been set up to help those who had been sickened by the red crystal. Not a lot could be done, but the medics like Pri could ease their passing. At least no one else would have to suffer what they had. For that, Eiko was grateful.

She glanced up as Hopper joined her. "Hi."

He kissed her, then sat in the seat next to her. "Hi."

She looked out the window. "Look at what you've done. This is amazing."

"What everyone has done. I didn't do this by myself."

"Oh, Hopper, you may not be the builder, but you are the one responsible for bringing this all to fruition. If not for you, I'd still be a prisoner and our two peoples still locked into a way of life killing us all."

He blew out a long breath and shook his head. "I'm never going to get away from being some kind of a hero, am I?"

"Well, there are the ones like your father who disagree." She grinned at him. There were small groups who refused to join the new city, mostly fanatics who clung to the old way of life. Like Hopper's father. Even with the appearance of the shifting felines, Nyoko stubbornly refused to accept the new ways and had retreated to his pyramid in Lawan with a half dozen avid followers. Though they might find life more difficult now that they didn't have the townspeople bringing them their food, cleaning their clothes and rooms, doing whatever Nyoko demanded. Eiko wondered how long the "faithful six" would remain with him. She'd bet not many. The doctors and scientists had made so many demands, Hopper had taken a shuttle and dropped them off in Lawan with Nyoko. She smiled at thinking of them coping in a ghost town without modern conveniences for a while. They were free to make their own way here to the city, where they would be put to work like everyone else.

The new council of nine had been established with Meecha at the head. The members had been elected by the citizens, an action that had never happened in the history of the Masaaki. Life was slowly coming together for the new city.

"Are you ready to go to the opening?" Eiko asked as she rose and twirled in her gold gown. The material was softer than anything she'd ever worn and shimmered in the light when she moved.

Hopper snorted, buttoned up his gold shirt, and rose. "As ready as I'll ever be." He turned to her. "But are you sure leaving here is what you want to do?"

They would be leaving for Pointe Noir as soon as the ceremonies were over.

Eiko hugged him. "Where you go, I go. Besides, we'll be back. But I want to see what's out there. To see what you've seen. To see Aboo and Pointe Noir and… the universe. And we'll search for more of our people now that we know what to look for."

He held out his arm. "Shall we?"

Together, they strode down the ramp and into the center of town to the base of the pyramid. The citizens crowded around the plaza as Hopper, Eiko, and the council stood in front of the door. Eiko smiled as the felines bounded up to them and shifted. She handed each a long, white drape that tied over one shoulder, then stood with them as Hopper gave a brief announcement to the crowd.

"Thank you all for being here. You have accomplished much, but today, we find out what the ancients had for us." Hopper turned and pressed the symbols on the door, then stood back as the corner statues ground around and a blue beam shot into the center of the door.

The door swished open, and everyone cheered as the shifted felines strode into the darkness. A moment later, bright white light flowed from the interior and the male appeared at the door, surrounded by the light, like a halo.

"Welcome home, Masaaki."

Eiko took Hopper's hand. "Shall we?" He smiled at her.

Before they could enter, Masuru came up to them. "Before we bring everyone in, we have a ceremony to perform." His mate and daughter joined him.

"Oh. Okay," Hopper said.

Eiko could see the questions on his face, and she had some of her own. She thought they'd gone over all the details with everyone.

"Akino and Eiko, please come before us."

They looked at each other, shrugged, then stepped up.

"Akino, you who have returned the Masaaki to their ancient home, are honored above all."

"Th…thank you."

"Eiko, you too have been instrumental in bringing about a new life to our people."

Eiko's face warmed up as Hopper squeezed her hand. "Thank you."

"I stand before you and put to you the eternal question. Do you, Akino, accept Eiko as your bonded mate for all time? Do you promise to honor her all your days, no matter what the fates bring?"

Eiko smiled and relaxed. She hadn't expected this, but realized this was exactly what she wanted, but did Hopper?

"I do with all my heart."

She studied his face. There was no hesitation there. Only love. *"Hopper? Are you sure?"*

"Yes. Completely. Are you?"

She nodded and turned back to Masuru.

"Do you, Eiko, accept Akino as your bonded mate for all time? Do you promise to honor him all your days, no matter what the fates bring?"

"I do with all my heart."

"Then I declare to all who hear that these two are one and none shall part them."

Hopper turned to Eiko and kissed her to the roar of the crowd—and the felines.

The Blessed Three had joined Eiko and Hopper. Nothing would part them ever again. Holding his hand in hers, they stepped into the light of the pyramid and faced their future. Together.

A word about the author…

Vicky has been married forever to the one person who accepts that she lives in a fantasy world most of the time. She's even been seen at the beach building worlds for her stories. In addition to creating fun characters, fantasy worlds, and suspenseful situations, she also enjoys and is very good at things like writing policy and procedures manuals and setting up continuity and organizational spreadsheets, both of which she has actually earned money doing. She has a master's degree in library science so likes things organized. Okay, so her family thinks having the spice rack alphabetized it a bit much, but she has no trouble finding what she needs when she needs it. And just because her extensive library is cataloged and organized, that doesn't mean she's obsessive. Honest.

When not writing, Vicky can be found in the kitchen whipping up gluten-free, lactose-free, other allergy-free meals.

https://www.vicky-burkholder.com